ANGEL OF DEATH

ANGEL OF DEATH

Jack Higgins

MICHAEL JOSEPH
LONDON

MICHAEL JOSEPH
Published by the Penguin Group
27 Wrights Lane, London w8 5TZ
Viking Penguin Inc., 375 Hudson Street, New York, New York 10014, USA
Penguin Books Australia Ltd, Ringwood, Victoria, Australia
Penguin Books Canada Ltd, 10 Alcorn Avenue, Toronto, Ontario, Canada M4V 3B2
Penguin Books (NZ) Ltd, 182–190 Wairau Road, Auckland 10, New Zealand

Penguin Books Ltd, Registered Offices: Harmondsworth, Middlesex, England

First published in Great Britain 1995

Copyright © Jack Higgins 1995

Typeset by Datix International Limited, Bungay, Suffolk
Printed in England by Clays Ltd, St Ives plc
Set in 12/14½ pt Monotype Bembo

A CIP catalogue record for this book is available from the British Library

ISBN 0 7181 3902 X

The moral right of the author has been asserted

Between two groups of men that want to make inconsistent kinds of worlds I see no remedy except – force . . . it seems to me that every society rests on the death of men.

OLIVER WENDELL HOLMES

Belfast
London

1994

ONE

A COLD WIND BLEW in from Belfast Lough, driving rain across the city. Sean Dillon moved along a narrow street between tall warehouses, relics of the Victorian era, mostly boarded up now. He stood on the corner, a small man, no more than five feet five, wearing a trenchcoat and an old rain hat.

He was on the waterfront now. There were ships out there at anchor, their riding lights moving up and down for there was a heavy swell driving into the docks. There was a sound of gunfire in the distance. He glanced in the general direction, lit a cigarette in cupped hands and moved on.

There was an air of desolation to the whole area. Examples of the devastation caused by twenty-five years of war everywhere and his feet crunched over broken glass. He found what he was looking for five minutes later, a warehouse with a peeling sign on the wall that said *Murphy & Son − Import & Export*. There were large double doors with a small Judas gate for easy access. It opened with a slight creak and he stepped inside.

It was a place of shadows, empty except for an old Ford van and a jumble of packing cases. There was an office at the far end with glass walls, one or two panes broken, and a dim light shone there. Dillon removed his rain hat and ran a hand nervously over his hair which he'd dyed black. The dark moustache which he'd gummed into place on his upper lip completed the transformation.

He waited, still clutching the rain hat. It had to be the van – the only reason for it being there – so he wasn't surprised when the rear door opened and a rather large man, a Colt automatic in one hand, emerged.

'Slow and easy, my grand wee man,' he said in the distinctive Belfast accent.

'I say, old chap.' Dillon showed every sign of alarm and raised his hands. 'No problem, I trust? I'm here in good faith.'

'Aren't we all, Mr Friar,' a voice called and Dillon saw Daley appear in the doorway of the office. 'Is he clean, Jack?'

The big man ran his hands over Dillon and felt between his legs. 'All clear here, Curtis.'

'Bring him in.'

When Dillon entered the office, Daley was sitting in a chair behind the desk, a young man of twenty-five or so with an intense white face.

'Curtis Daley, Mr Friar, and this is Jack Mullin. We have to be careful, you understand?'

'Oh, perfectly, old chap.' Dillon rolled his rain hat and slipped it into his raincoat pocket. 'May I smoke?'

Daley tossed a packet of Gallaghers across. 'Try an Irish cigarette. I'm surprised to find you're English. Jobert & Company; now, that's a French arms dealer. That's why we chose him.'

Dillon lit a cigarette. 'The arms business, especially at the level you wish to deal, isn't exactly thriving in London these days. I've been in it for years ever since getting out of the Royal Artillery. I've worked as an agent for Monsieur Jobert all over the world.'

'That's good.'

'Monsieur Jobert told me I'd be meeting your leader, Mr Quinn?'

'Daniel? Why should he expect that? Any special reason?'

4

'Not really,' Dillon said hurriedly. 'I did a tour with the Royal Artillery in Londonderry, nineteen eighty-two. Mr Quinn was quite famous.'

'Notorious, you mean,' Daley said. 'Everyone after him. The police, the Army and the bloody IRA.'

'Yes, that does rather sum it up,' Dillon said.

'Loyal to the Crown, that's what we Protestants are, Mr Friar,' Daley said, genuine anger in his voice. 'And what does it get us? A boot up the arse, interference from America and a British Government that prefers to sell us out to damn Fenians like Gerry Adams.'

'I can appreciate your point of view.' Dillon managed to sound slightly alarmed.

'That's why we call our group Sons of Ulster. We stand here or die here, no other route, and the sooner the British Government and the IRA realize that the better. Now, what can Jobert offer?'

'Naturally I've put nothing on paper,' Dillon said, 'but in view of the kind of money we're talking about a first consignment could be two hundred AK47s in prime condition, fifty AKMs, a dozen general-purpose machine guns. Brownings. Not new, but in good order.'

'Ammunition?'

'No problem.'

'Anything else?'

'We had a consignment of Stinger missiles delivered to our Marseilles warehouse recently. Jobert says he could manage six, but that, of course, would be extra.'

Daley sat there frowning, and tapping the desk with his fingers. Finally he said, 'You're at the Europa?'

'Where else in Belfast, old chap?'

'Right. I'll be in touch.'

'Will I be meeting Mr Quinn?'

'I can't say. I'll let you know.' He turned to Mullin. 'Send him on his way, Jack.'

5

Mullin took Dillon back to the entrance and as he opened the Judas gate there was a hollow booming sound in the distance.

'What was that?' Dillon said nervously.

'Only a bomb, nothing to get alarmed about, my wee man. Did you wet your pants, then?'

He laughed as Dillon stepped outside, was still laughing as he closed the door. Dillon paused on the corner. The first thing he did was peel away the moustache above his lip, then he removed the rain hat from his pocket, unrolled it and took out a short-barrelled Smith & Wesson revolver which he slipped into his waistband against the small of his back.

He put the hat on as the rain increased. 'Amateurs,' he said softly. 'What can you do with them?' and he walked rapidly away.

At that moment Daley was ringing a Dublin number. A woman answered. 'Scott's Hotel.'

'Mr Brown.'

A moment later Daniel Quinn came on the line. 'Yes?'

'Curtis here. I'm glad I caught you. I thought you might be on the way to Amsterdam tonight.'

'How did it go?'

'Jobert sent a man called Friar. English. Ex-army officer. He offered to meet all requirements, including some Stingers if you want them.'

'That's good. What was he like, this Friar?'

'Second-rate English public school type. Black hair and moustache. Frightened to death. Said he thought he was meeting you.'

'Why should he think that?'

'Jobert told him he would. Apparently he did a tour with the Royal Artillery in Londonderry in eighty-two. Said you were quite famous.'

6

There was a moment's pause, then Quinn said, 'Take him out, Curtis. I smell stinking fish here.'

'But why?'

'Sure, I was in Londonderry in eighty-two, only not as Daniel Quinn. I used the name Frank Kelly.'

'Jesus!' Daley said.

'Take him out, Curtis, that's an order. I'll call you from Beirut.'

Dillon was staying at the Europa Hotel in Great Victoria Street by the railway station, the most bombed hotel in Belfast if not the world. He was still wearing the rain hat when he entered the suite.

The woman who sat reading a magazine was thirty years of age, wore a black trouser suit and horn-rimmed glasses. She had short red hair. Her name was Hannah Bernstein and she was a Detective Chief Inspector in the Special Branch at Scotland Yard.

She jumped up. 'Everything work out?'

'So far. Have you heard from Ferguson?'

'Not yet. When do you make your move?'

'Daley said he'd get back to me.' He took off his hat. 'I need a shower. I want to get rid of this hair dye.'

She made a face. 'Yes, it's just not you, Dillon.'

He took off his coat and jacket and made for the bathroom. At that moment the phone rang. He raised a hand – 'Leave it to me,' – and picked the phone up.

'Barry Friar,' he said, putting on the public school accent.

'Daley. Mr Quinn will see you tomorrow night at six.'

'Same place?' Dillon asked.

'No, drive from the Europa to Garth Dock. It's close to where you were tonight. I know you have a hire car, so use that – and make sure you come alone. You'll be picked up. Mr Quinn will be there.'

The phone went dead. Hannah Bernstein said, 'Now what?'

'Daley. The next meeting is tomorrow evening at six to meet Quinn. I'm to drive there alone.'

'It worked,' she said. 'You were right.'

'I usually am.'

'Where's the meeting?'

'Oh, no,' he said. 'I tell you, you'll tell Ferguson and he'll have some SAS hit squad on my case. No go, Hannah.' He smiled. 'I'll be all right, girl dear. Go and do your bit with Ferguson and I'll have a shower.'

'Damn you, Dillon!' But she knew better than to waste her breath in argument. She left the room, closing the door quietly behind her.

He stripped and went into the bathroom, whistling cheerfully as he turned on the shower, stood under it and watched the black dye run from his hair.

In most places in the world by the early seventies, terrorism was a growing problem, especially in Britain because of the IRA and in spite of the activities of the Security Services and Scotland Yard. The Prime Minister of the day had decided drastic measures were needed and had set up an elite intelligence unit responsible to him alone and no one else.

Brigadier Charles Ferguson had headed the unit since its inception. He had served every Prime Minister in office and had no personal political allegiance. He usually operated from an office on the third floor of the Ministry of Defence, overlooking Horse Guards Avenue, but when Hannah Bernstein rang him on the red phone, she was patched through to his flat in Cavendish Square.

'Bernstein, Brigadier. Dillon made contact.'

'With Quinn?'

'No, Curtis Daley. Dillon has a meeting tomorrow night at six. He won't tell me where. Says he doesn't want you sending the heavy brigade in. He has to drive there alone.'

'Awkward sod,' Ferguson said. 'Will Quinn be there?'

'So it seems, sir.'

Ferguson nodded. 'Catching him is the name of the game, Chief Inspector. Some of these Loyalist groups are now as big a threat as the IRA. Quinn is certainly the most dangerous leader to be found amongst their rather numerous factions. Sons of Ulster.' He grunted. 'I mean, my mother was Irish, but why do they have to be so damned theatrical?'

'Dillon always says it's the rain.'

'He would, wouldn't he? Everything's a joke.'

'So what do you want me to do, sir?'

'You do nothing, Chief Inspector. Dillon wants to do things his own way as usual, get close enough to Quinn to put a bullet between his eyes. Let him get on with it, but I won't have you in the line of fire. You provide back-up at the Europa only. If he pulls this thing off tomorrow night, get him straight to Aldergrove airport. I'll have the Lear jet waiting to fly you to Gatwick.'

'Very well, sir.'

'I'll have to go. I've got my weekly meeting with the Prime Minister at Downing Street in an hour.'

Hannah Bernstein checked her make-up and hair, then left her room and took the lift downstairs. She went into the bar, but there was no sign of Dillon so she sat at a corner table. He came in a few minutes later wearing a roll-neck sweater, Donegal tweed jacket and dark slacks, his hair, washed clean of the black dye now, so fair as to be almost white.

'Half a bottle of Krug,' he called to the barman and joined her, taking out an old silver case and lighting a cigarette.

'Still determined to take a few years off your life,' she said.

'You never give up, do you, sweetheart.' His voice was Humphrey Bogart to perfection. 'Of all the gin joints in all the towns in all the world she walks into mine.'

'Damn you!' she laughed as the waiter brought the Krug and opened it.

'You could have a Guinness instead. After all, you're in Ireland.'

'No, I'll force a little champagne down.'

'Good for you. Did you speak to Ferguson?'

'Oh, yes. I brought him right up to date.'

'And?'

'You can go to hell in your own way. If it works, the Lear will be waiting at Aldergrove and I get you straight out.'

'Good.' He raised his glass. 'Here's to us. Are you free for dinner?'

'I can't think of anything else to do.'

At that moment he noticed a poster by the bar. 'Good God, Grace Browning.' He went over to inspect it and turned to the barman. 'Is it still playing?' he asked, reverting to his English accent.

'Last night tomorrow, sir.'

'Could you get me a couple of tickets for tonight's performance?'

'I think so, but you'll have to be sharp. Curtain up in forty minutes. Mind you, the Lyric isn't too far.'

'Good man. Ring the box office for me.'

'I will, Mr Friar.'

Dillon went back to Hannah. 'There you go, girl dear, Grace Browning's one-woman show. *Shakespeare's Heroines.* She's brilliant.'

'I know. I've seen her at the National Theatre. Tell me, Dillon, don't you ever get confused? One minute sounding like you've been to Eton, the next Belfast-Irish?'

'Ah, you're forgetting my true vocation was the theatre. I went to the Royal Academy of Dramatic Art before Grace Browning did. In fact, I played the National Theatre before she did. Lyngstrand in *Lady from the Sea*. Ibsen, that was.'

'You've mentioned it several times since I've known you, Dillon.' She stood up. 'Let's get moving before that monumental ego of yours surfaces again.'

Ferguson's Daimler was admitted through the security gates at the end of Downing Street and the front door of the most famous address in the world was opened to him instantly. An aide took his coat and led the way up the stairs, knocking on a door and ushering him into the study.

John Major, the British Prime Minister, looked up and smiled. 'Ah, there you are, Brigadier. The week seems to have gone quickly. I've asked Simon Carter, Deputy Director of the Security Services, to join us, and Rupert Lang. You know him, I take it? As an Under-Secretary of State at the Northern Ireland Office I thought he might have a useful contribution to make to our weekly consultation. He serves on a number of Government committees.'

'I have met Mr Lang, Prime Minister. Like myself, Grenadier Guards until he transferred to the Parachute Regiment.'

'Yes, fine record. I know you don't care for Simon Carter, and the Security Services don't care for you. You know what they call you? The Prime Minister's private army.'

'So I believe.'

'Try and get along, if only for my sake.' There was a knock at the door and two men entered. 'Ah, come in, gentlemen,' the Prime Minister said. 'I believe you all know each other.'

'Hello, Ferguson,' Carter said frostily. He was a small man in his fifties with snow white hair.

Rupert Lang was tall and elegant in a navy-blue striped suit and Guards tie, hair rather long, an intelligent, aquiline face, a restless air to him.

'Nice to see you again, Brigadier.'

'And you.'

'Good. Sit down and let's get started,' the Prime Minister said.

They worked their way through a variety of intelligence matters for some forty minutes with particular reference to

11

terrorist groups of various kinds and the new menace of Arab fundamentalism in London.

The Prime Minister said, 'I'm sure everyone tries, but look at this group January 30. How many have they killed in the last few years, Mr Carter?'

'Ten that we know of, Prime Minister, but there's a particular difficulty. Other groups have specific aims and targets. January 30 kill everybody. KGB, a CIA man, IRA both here and in Belfast. Even a notorious East End gangster.'

'All with the same weapon,' Ferguson put in.

'Could that indicate just one individual?'

'It could, but I doubt it,' Carter said. 'And the name is no help. January 30 was the date of Bloody Sunday, but they kill, amongst others, members of the IRA.'

'A puzzle,' the Prime Minister said, 'which brings me to the Downing Street Declaration.' He spoke about the Government's discussions with Sinn Fein and the efforts, so far unsuccessful, to achieve a ceasefire.

It was Rupert Lang who said, 'I'm afraid we're going to have as many problems with the Protestant factions from now on, Prime Minister.'

'True,' Carter said. 'They're killing just as many as the IRA.'

'Can we do anything about that?' the Prime Minister queried. He turned to Ferguson. 'Brigadier?'

Ferguson shrugged. 'Yes, I'm conscious of the Protestant Loyalist problem.'

'Yes, but are your people doing anything about it?' Carter said with some malice.

Ferguson was nettled. 'Actually I've got Dillon taking care of something rather special in that direction at this precise moment in time.'

'So we're back to that little IRA swine?' Carter said.

Rupert Lang frowned. 'Dillon? Who's he?'

Ferguson hesitated. 'Go on, tell him,' the Prime Minister said, 'but this is top secret, Rupert.'

'Of course, Prime Minister.'

'Sean Dillon was born in Belfast and went to school in London when his father came to work here,' Ferguson said. 'He had a remarkable talent for acting and a flair for languages. He went to the Royal Academy of Dramatic Art for a year and then joined the National Theatre.'

'I've never heard of him,' Lang said.

'You wouldn't. Dillon's father went back to Belfast on a visit and got caught in the middle of a firefight. He was shot dead by paratroops. Dillon joined the IRA and never looked back. He became the most feared enforcer they had.'

'Then what?'

'He became disenchanted with the glorious cause and switched to the international scene. Worked for everybody. Not only the PLO, but the Israelis.'

'For money, I presume?'

'Oh yes. He was behind the mortar attack on Downing Street during the Gulf War. That was for the Iraqis.'

'Good God!'

Carter broke in. 'And he employs this man.'

'He also flew drugs into Bosnia, medical supplies for children. The Serbs held him under death sentence. I did a deal with them and him. He came to me, slate wiped clean.'

'Good heavens,' Lang said faintly.

'Set a thief to catch a thief,' the Prime Minister said. 'He's been more than useful, Rupert. Saved the Royal Family from a dreadful scandal involving the Duke of Windsor's involvement with the Nazis. Then there was a rather tricky business involving Hong Kong, but never mind that. What's he up to now, Brigadier?'

Ferguson hesitated. 'Actually he's in Belfast.'

'Doing what?' Ferguson hesitated again and the Prime

Minister said impatiently, 'Come on, man, if you can tell anyone, you can tell us.'

'All right,' Ferguson said. 'The Deputy Director wanted to know what we're doing about Protestant terrorism. As you know there are numerous factions. One of the worst call themselves the Sons of Ulster. Their leader is undoubtedly the most dangerous man on the Loyalist side of things. Daniel Quinn. He's killed many times, soldiers as well as IRA.'

'And dares to use the word Loyalist,' Carter said. 'Yes, I know about Quinn.'

'The trouble is that he isn't just another thug,' Ferguson replied. 'He's astute, cunning and a first-class organizer. Dillon has been staying at the Europa under the name of Barry Friar with my assistant, Detective Chief Inspector Hannah Bernstein. He posed as an arms dealer for a Paris outfit and met with Quinn's right-hand man, Curtis Daley, tonight.'

'I know that name too,' Carter said.

'What's the point of all this?' the Prime Minister asked.

'To draw Quinn into the open and deal with him,' Ferguson said.

'You mean shoot him?'

'That is correct, Prime Minister. Dillon has a meeting with Quinn tomorrow at six. All he would tell Chief Inspector Bernstein was that he was to drive there alone. Wouldn't say where because he knew she'd tell me and thought I might send in the heavy brigade.'

'Arrogant bastard,' Carter commented.

'Perhaps.' The Prime Minister nodded. 'But he does seem to get results.' He closed the file in front of him. 'You'll keep me informed, Brigadier.' He stood up. 'Good night, gentlemen.'

As Ferguson went to his Daimler outside Number Ten, Carter paused on his way to his own car. 'He'll get you into trouble one of these days, Ferguson.'

'Very probably,' Ferguson said and turned to Lang. 'Have you got a car or would you like a lift?'

'No thanks, I feel like the exercise. I'll walk.'

Lang went out through the security gates and walked along Whitehall. He stopped at the first phone box and made a call. After a while the phone was picked up at the other end.

'Belov.'

'Oh, good, Yuri. Glad I caught you at home. Rupert here. Something's come up. I'll be straight round.'

He put the phone down and hailed the first cab that came along.

TWO

Twenty minutes later he was ringing the bell of the small cottage in a mews off the Bayswater Road. The door was opened within moments and Belov stood there, dressed in a navy-blue pullover and slacks. A small, dark-haired man with a humorous mouth, he was in his late fifties. He motioned Lang inside.

'Good to see you, Rupert.'

He led the way into a small sitting room, where a gas fire was burning cheerfully in the hearth.

'This is nice,' Lang said, 'on a night like this.'

'A Scotch would make it even better, yes?'

'I should say so.'

Lang watched him get the drinks. Belov was Senior Cultural Attaché at the Russian Embassy just up the road, a job which masked his true vocation as Colonel in Charge of the London Station of the GRU, Russian Military Intelligence, the KGB's great rivals. He handed Lang a glass.

'Cheers, Rupert.'

'How are you? Still having trouble with the KGB?'

'They keep changing their name these days.' Belov smiled. 'Anyway, what was so important?'

'I've just had one of my regular meetings with the Prime Minister, Simon Carter and Brigadier Charles Ferguson. Tell me, does the name Sean Dillon mean anything to you?'

'Oh, yes,' Belov said. 'Quite a character. He was very big

in the IRA, then moved on to the international scene. I've the best of reasons for thinking he was behind the attack on Downing Street in ninety-one, then Brigadier Charles Ferguson got his hands on him.' Belov smiled again. 'You British really are devious bastards, Rupert. What's it all about?'

So Lang told him, and when he was finished, Belov said, 'I know all about Daniel Quinn. Believe me, my friend, if the Anglo-Irish Agreement and the Downing Street Declaration really do bring Sinn Fein and the IRA to the peace table, you are going to have serious problems with the Protestant factions.'

'Well, that seems to be the general opinion and that's why Dillon hopes to meet Quinn and eliminate him tomorrow night.'

'Only one problem,' Belov said. 'My man at our Embassy in Dublin told me yesterday that Quinn is in Dublin en route for Beirut under the alias of Brown. An associate of his named Francis Callaghan went to Beirut last week.'

'Do you know why?'

'There is a KGB involvement, but I believe it's a rather nefarious one. Some connection with gangsters from Moscow. What you call the Russian Mafia. I understand an Arab faction, the Party of God, are also involved. They make Hezbollah look like a primary school outing.'

'But what could it be? Arms?'

'Plenty of ways of getting arms these days. Something big, that's all I know.'

'All right,' Lang said. 'Let's look at this thing. This man Daley has arranged a meeting for Dillon tomorrow to meet Quinn, only we know Quinn won't be there. What does that tell you?'

'That Dillon's cover is blown. They intend to kill him, my friend.'

'Is that what you think will happen?'

17

'Dillon's reputation goes before him. He's the original survivor. In fact I would imagine he knows what he's doing.'

'Which means you think he'll survive this meeting?'

'Possibly, but more than that. Dillon is extremely astute. What he wants is Quinn. Now, if he expects skulduggery he will also expect not only to survive it but to come out of it knowing Quinn's whereabouts.'

'Beirut?'

'Which is where Charles Ferguson will send him.' Belov got up, reached for the bottle of Scotch and replenished the glasses. 'And that would suit me. We of the GRU and the KGB don't hit it off too well these days. They have a disturbing tendency to associate with the wrong people, the Moscow Mafia for example, which doesn't sit well with me. I'd like to know what they're up to with Quinn in Beirut; I'd like to know very much.'

'Which means it would suit you to have Dillon on their case.'

'Unquestionably.'

'Then you'd better pray he survives this meeting tomorrow night.'

'Exactly.' Belov nodded. 'A great inconvenience if he didn't, but I get the impression you have thoughts on this?'

Lang countered, 'You have your associates in Belfast who could provide back-up when necessary, equipment and so on?'

'Of course. Why do you ask?'

'Tom Curry is in Belfast at the moment, doing his monthly two or three days as a visiting professor at Queen's University. By coincidence, Grace Browning has been there doing her one-woman show at the Lyric Theatre.'

'How convenient.'

'Isn't it. Dillon could have an invisible support system, a phantom minder watching his back.'

'My dear Rupert, what a splendid idea.'

'Only one thing. If he's to be followed from the hotel, they need to know what he looks like.'

'No problem. I have his file at the Embassy. I can fax Tom Curry at his office at Queen's tonight. He only needs to know it's on its way.'

'And I'll take care of that.' Rupert Lang raised his glass. 'Cheers, old sport.'

Half an hour later Tom Curry, at his office at Queen's University and working his way through a mass of papers, cursed as his phone went.

'Curry here,' he said angrily.

'Rupert. Are you alone?'

'Well, I would be, old lad, considering it's ten o'clock at night. I've been hacking my way through exam papers, but what brings you on? I'll be with you on Sunday evening.'

'I know, but this is important, Tom. Very important, so listen well.'

About half an hour later Dillon and Hannah Bernstein returned to the Europa. They got their keys at the desk and she turned to him. 'I really enjoyed that, Dillon, she was wonderful, but I'm tired. I think I'll go straight up.'

'Sleep well.' He kissed her on the cheek. 'I think I'll have a nightcap.'

He went into the Library Bar, which was reasonably busy, and ordered a Bushmills. A moment later Grace Browning walked in with a man in an open-necked shirt, tweed jacket and slacks. He looked in his forties, had brown hair and a pleasant, rather amiable face. They sat down at a corner table and were immediately approached by a woman who'd been to the show. Dillon recognized the programme. Grace Browning signed it with a pleasant smile which she managed to retain even when a number of other people did the same thing.

Finally, the intrusion stopped and the waiter took a half bottle of champagne over and uncorked it. Dillon swallowed his Bushmills, crossed the room and paused.

'Not only a great actress, but a woman of taste and discernment, I see – Krug non-vintage, the best champagne in the world.'

She laughed. 'Really?'

'It's the grape mix.'

She hesitated, then said, 'This is my friend, Professor Tom Curry and you are . . .?'

'God save us, that doesn't matter one damn bit. Our only connection is that like you I went to RADA and did the odd thing for the National.' He laughed. 'About a thousand years ago. I just wanted to say thank you. You were magnificent tonight.'

He walked out.

She said, 'What a charmer.'

'He's that all right,' Curry said. 'Just have a look at the colour fax Belov sent me.'

He opened an envelope, took out a sheet and passed it across. Her eyes widened as she examined it. 'Good God.'

'Yes, staying here under the name of Friar, but in actuality Sean Dillon, a thoroughly dangerous man. Let me tell you about him, and more to the point, what we're going to do.'

The following evening just after half-five Dillon stood at the window of his suite, drinking tea and looking out across the city. Rain was driving in and it was already dusk, lights gleaming out there. There was a knock on the door and he went and opened it.

Hannah Bernstein entered.

'How are you?'

'Fine. The grand cup of tea they give you here.'

'Can't you ever take anything seriously?'

'I could never see the point, girl dear.' He opened a

20

drawer, took out a 9mm Browning pistol with a silencer on the muzzle and slammed in a twenty-round magazine.

'Dear God, Dillon, you really are going to war.'

'Exactly.'

He slipped the Browning into the waistband of his slacks at the rear, pulled on a tweed jacket and his rain hat, took another twenty-round clip from the drawer and put it in his pocket. He smiled and put his hands on her shoulders.

'We who are about to die salute you. A fella called Suetonius wrote that about two thousand years ago.'

'You're forgetting I went to Cambridge, Dillon. I could give you the quote in Latin.' She kissed him on the cheek. 'Try and come back in one piece.'

'Jesus,' he said. 'You mean you care? There's still hope for me?'

She punched him in the chest. 'Get out of here.'

He walked to the door, opened it and went out.

The rush hour traffic was already in place as he turned out of the Europa car park and moved along Victoria Avenue. He expected to be followed although monitored would be a better description. It was difficult, of course, with all those cars, but he'd seen the motorcyclist in the black helmet and leathers turn out of the car park quite close behind him, then noticed the same machine keeping well back. It was only when he turned down towards the waterfront through deserted streets of warehouses that he realized he was on his own. Ah, well, perhaps he'd been mistaken.

'You sometimes are, old son,' he said, and as he spoke a Rover saloon turned out of a side turning and followed him.

'Here we go, then,' Dillon said softly.

At that moment, a Toyota saloon emerged from a lane in front of him and blocked the way. Dillon braked to a halt. The man at the wheel of the Rover stayed where he was. The two men in the Toyota jumped out carrying Armalites.

'Out, Friar, out!' one of them shouted.

Dillon's hand slipped under his coat and found the butt of the Browning. 'Isn't that you, Martin McGurk?' he said, getting out of the car. 'Jesus, and haven't you got the wrong man? Remember me from Derry in the old days?' He pulled off the rain hat to reveal his blond hair. 'Dillon – Sean Dillon.'

McGurk looked stunned. 'It can't be.'

'Oh, yes it can, old son,' Dillon told him, brought up the Browning and fired through the open door, knocking McGurk on his back, then swinging and shooting the man beside him through the head.

The man at the wheel of the Rover pulled forward, drew a pistol and fired through the open passenger window, then put his head down and took off. Dillon fired twice at him, shattering the rear window, but the Rover turned the corner and was gone.

There was quiet, except for the steady splashing of the rain. Dillon walked round to the two men he had shot and examined them. They were both dead. There was a burst of Armalite fire from somewhere above. As he ducked, an engine roared and the motorcycle he had noticed earlier passed him, sliding sideways on the cobbles.

As it came to a halt, he saw the black-suited rider raise some sort of weapon. He recognized the distinctive muted crack of a silenced AK47. A man fell from a platform high up in a warehouse on the other side of the street and bounced on the pavement. The rider raised an arm in a kind of salute and rode off.

Dillon stood there for only a moment, then got in behind the wheel of his car and drove away, leaving the carnage behind him.

★

He parked near the warehouse with the sign *Murphy & Son* where he had first met Daley. As he turned the corner, he saw the Rover at the kerb. The big man, Jack Mullin, was standing by the Judas gate, peering inside. As Dillon watched, Mullin went into the warehouse.

Dillon followed, opening the gate cautiously, the Browning ready. He could hear Jack Mullin's agitated voice. 'He's dead, Curtis, shot twice in the back.'

Dillon moved quickly towards the office, the door of which stood open. He was almost there when Mullin turned and saw him. 'It's Friar,' he said and reached inside his coat.

Dillon shot him, knocking him back against the desk. He slumped to the floor and Daley got to his feet, panic written all over his face.

'No Daniel Quinn,' Dillon told him. 'Naughty, that, and you made another mistake. It's not Barry Friar, it's Sean Dillon.'

'Dear God!' said Daley.

'So let's get down to business. Quinn – where is he?'

'I can't tell you that. It's more than my life is worth.'

'I see.' Dillon nodded. 'All right, I want you to watch something.' He reached and pulled Mullin up a little. The big man moaned. 'Are you watching?' Dillon asked, then shot him through the heart.

'No, for God's sake, no!' The panic was in Daley's voice now.

'You want to live, then? You'll tell me where Quinn is?'

'He's on his way to Beirut,' Daley gabbled. 'Francis Callaghan's been there for a while setting up a deal. Some Arab group called Party of God and the KGB are going to start supplying us.'

'With arms?'

Daley shook his head. 'Plutonium. Daniel says we'll be able to cause the biggest bang Ireland's ever seen. Really show those Fenian bastards we mean business.'

'I see. And where does all this take place?'

'I don't know.' Dillon raised the Browning and Daley screamed. 'It's the truth, I swear it. Daniel said he'd be in touch. All I know is Callaghan is staying at a hotel called Al Bustan.'

He was obviously telling the truth. Dillon said, 'There, that wasn't too hard, old son, was it?'

He aimed the Browning very quickly and shot Daley between the eyes, tumbling him back out of the chair, then he turned and walked away.

No more than a mile away from Garth Dock, where the shootings had taken place, the motorcycle turned into a narrow side street and entered a yard, driving straight into an open garage. Tom Curry closed and barred the gate to the street, then went into the garage. The black–clad rider pushed the motorcycle up on its stand, then turned and took off the helmet.

Grace Browning smiled, pale and excited. 'Quite a night. A good job I was there.'

She unzipped her leather jacket and took out the AK47, butt folded.

'What happened?' Curry asked.

'They'd set him up. Quite a man, our Mr Dillon. He killed two and shot up the second car. They had an extra man up on a platform with an Armalite. He tried to shoot Dillon; I shot him. End of story, so I cleared off.'

She was taking off the leathers as she spoke, revealing jeans and a jumper. She draped the leathers over the motorcycle.

'Just leave everything' Curry told her. 'Belov's people will clear up.'

'You've got my bag?'

'Sure.' He handed her a holdall and she opened it and took out a light raincoat.

'The car's parked not too far away in the main road,' he told her.

He opened the side gate and they left the yard.

'Do we claim credit for January 30 on this?' Curry asked.

'Well, we're entitled to one, so why not the lot? Somehow I don't think Dillon and the Prime Minister's private army would be happy to go public.'

'Right. I'll phone the news desk at the *Belfast Telegraph*.'

'Good.' She checked her watch. 'Just after seven. We'll have to hurry. Curtain up at eight.'

The Lear jet with two RAF pilots at the controls climbed steadily after lifting from Aldergrove, levelling off at thirty thousand feet. Hannah Bernstein sat on one side of the aisle, facing Dillon, who sat the other. He found the drawer containing the bar box and the thermos of hot water. He made coffee for her and tea for himself, then took a miniature of Scotch from the selection of drinks provided and poured it into his tea. He drank it slowly and lit a cigarette.

All this had been done in silence. Now he spoke. 'You haven't said much.'

'It's a lot to take in. Plutonium? Do they mean it?'

'It's been available on the black market in Russia for a while now. It was always only a matter of time before some terrorist group or other had a go.'

'God help us all.' She sighed. 'Anyway, how about you? Are you all right?'

'Fine.'

'Who do you think it was on the motorcycle?'

'I haven't the slightest idea, but they saved my bacon as we used to say in County Down.'

'I wonder what gave you away?'

'Oh, that was me. I told Daley I'd known of Quinn when he was on the run in Londonderry, but Quinn used an alias there. Frank Kelly. I wanted to draw their fire.'

She shook her head. 'You're quite mad. And what about this man, Mullin, and Curtis Daley? Did you have to kill them?'

'It's the business we're in, girl dear. Twenty-five years of war.'

'And for many of those years you fought for the IRA yourself.'

'True. I wasn't much more than a boy when my father was killed by British soldiers. Joining made sense to me then, but the years go by, Hannah, long weary years of slaughter, and to what end? That was then and this is now. Something clicked in my head one day. Put it any way you want.' He found himself another miniature of Scotch. 'As for Daley, three months ago he and Quinn stopped a truckload of Catholic roadworkers at Glasshill. Lined them up on the edge of a ditch, all twelve of them, and machine-gunned them.'

'So it's an eye for an eye?'

He smiled gently. 'Straight out of the Old Testament. I'd have thought a nice Jewish girl like you would have approved.' He reached for the phone. 'And now I'd better report in on the secure line. Ferguson always likes to hear bad news as soon as possible.'

It was no more than an hour and a half later that Ferguson was ushered into the Prime Minister's study at Downing Street. Simon Carter and Rupert Lang were already seated.

'You used words like urgent and gravest national importance, Brigadier, so what have you got for us?' John Major demanded.

Ferguson brought them up to date, in finest detail. When he was finished there was silence. It was Rupert Lang who spoke first.

'How extraordinary that January 30 have claimed responsibility.'

'Terrorist groups habitually claim credit for someone else's hit,' Ferguson said. 'And there is the business of the gunman on the motorcycle.'

'Yes, strange, that,' Carter said. 'And yet you had no back-up whatsoever, did you?'

'Absolutely not,' Ferguson told him.

'None of which is relevant now,' the Prime Minister said. 'The really important thing that Dillon has come up with is this possibility of the Sons of Ulster getting their hands on plutonium.'

'With the greatest respect, Prime Minister,' Simon Carter said, 'having plutonium is one thing, producing some sort of nuclear device from it is quite another.'

'Perhaps, but if you have the money and the right kind of connections anything is possible.' Ferguson shrugged. 'You know as well as I that terrorist groups on the international circuit help each other out, and since the breakdown of things in Russia there's plenty of the right kind of technical assistance available on the world market.'

There was another silence, broken only by the Prime Minister drumming on the desk with his fingers. Finally he said, 'The Anglo-Irish Agreement and the Downing Street Declaration are achieving results and President Clinton is behind us fully. Twenty-five years of bloodshed, gentlemen. It's time to stop.'

'If I may be a devil's advocate,' Rupert Lang suggested, 'that's all very well for Sinn Fein and the IRA, but the Protestant Loyalist factions will feel they've been sold out.'

'I know that, but they'll have to make some sort of accommodation like everyone else.'

'They'll continue the fight, Prime Minister,' Carter said gravely.

'I accept that. We'll just have to do our best to handle it. Machine guns by night are one thing, even the Semtex bomb, but not plutonium. That would add a totally new dimension.'

'I'm afraid you're right,' Carter said.

The Prime Minister turned to Ferguson. 'So it would appear to be Beirut next stop for Dillon, Brigadier.'

'So it would.'

'If I recall the details on his file, Arabic is one of the numerous languages he speaks. He should feel quite at home there.' He stood up. 'That's all for now, gentlemen. Keep me posted, Brigadier.'

When Ferguson reached his Cavendish Square flat the door was opened by his manservant Kim, an ex-Ghurka corporal who had been with him for years.

'Mr Dillon and the Chief Inspector have just arrived, Brigadier.'

Ferguson went into the elegant drawing room and found Hannah Bernstein sitting by the fire, drinking coffee. Dillon was helping himself to a Bushmills from the drinks tray on the sideboard.

'Feel free with my whiskey by all means,' Ferguson told him.

'Oh I will, Brigadier, and me knowing you to be the decent old stick that you are.'

'Drop the stage Irishman act, boy, we've got work to do. Now, let's go over everything in detail again.'

'I suppose the strangest thing was the mystery motorcyclist,' Dillon said as he finished.

'No mystery there,' Ferguson told him. 'January 30 have claimed responsibility for the whole thing. Someone phoned the *Belfast Telegraph*. It's already on all the TV news programmes.'

'The dogs,' Dillon said. 'But how would they have known about the meet?'

'Never mind that now, we've more important things to consider. It's Beirut for you, my lad, and you, Chief Inspector.'

'Not the easiest of places to operate in,' Dillon said.

'As I recall, you managed it with perfect ease during the more unsavoury part of your career.'

'True. I also sank some PLO boats in the harbour for the Israelis and the PLO have long memories. Anyway, what would our excuse be for being there?'

'The United Nations Humanitarian Division will do nicely. Irish and English delegates. You'll have to use aliases, naturally.'

'And where will we stay?' Hannah asked.

'Me darling, there is only one decent hotel to stay these days in Beirut,' Dillon told her. 'Especially if you're a foreigner and want a drink at the bar. It's the place Daley told me Francis Callaghan was staying. The Al Bustan. It overlooks the city near Deirelkalaa and the Roman ruins. You'll find it very cultural.'

'Do you think Quinn will be there, too?' she asked

'Very convenient if he is.' He turned to Ferguson. 'You'll be able to arrange hardware for me?'

'No problem. I've got an excellent contact. Man called Walid Khasan.'

'Arab, I presume, not Christian.' Dillon turned to Hannah Bernstein. 'Lots of Christians in Beirut.'

'Yes, Walid Khasan is a Muslim. His mother was French. The kind of man I like to deal with, Dillon. He's only interested in the money.'

'Aren't we all, Brigadier, aren't we all.' Dillon smiled. 'So let's get down to it and work out how we're going to handle this thing.'

It was just after eleven at the Europa Hotel when Grace Browning and Tom Curry finished their late supper in the dining room and went into the bar. It was quite deserted and the barman, watching television, came round to serve them.

'What can I get you, Miss Browning?'

29

'Brandy, I think, two brandies.'

He went away and Tom Curry said, 'You were splendid tonight.'

She took out a cigarette and he lit it for her. 'To which performance are you alluding?'

He shook his head. 'That's all it is to you, isn't it? Another performance.' He nodded. 'I've never really seen it before, but I think I do now. On stage or before the camera, it's fantasy, but roaring up to Garth Dock on that bike – that was real.'

'And in those few moments of action, I live more, feel more and with an intensity that just can't be imagined.'

'You really are an extraordinary person,' he said.

The barman, pouring the drinks, called across, 'I've just seen the late-night news flash. A real bloodbath. Three men shot dead at Garth Dock and three more not far away at some warehouse. January 30 has claimed. That's Bloody Sunday, so the dead men must be Loyalists. The Prods will want to retaliate for that.'

Grace murmured, 'Dillon certainly doesn't take prisoners.'

'You can say that again.'

The barman brought the brandies and served them with a flourish. 'There you go.' He shook his head. 'Terrible, all this killing. I mean, what kind of people want to do that kind of thing?' and he walked away.

Grace Browning turned to Curry, a slight smile on her face, and toasted him. 'Well?' she said.

London
Belfast
Devon

1972–1992

THREE

IF IT BEGAN ANYWHERE, it began with Tom Curry, Professor of Political Philosophy at London University, a Fellow of Trinity College, Cambridge and who had in his time been a visiting professor at both Yale and Harvard. He was also a major in the GRU, Russian Military Intelligence.

Born in 1949 in Dublin into a Protestant Anglo-Irish family, his father, a surgeon, had died of cancer when Curry was five, leaving the boy and his mother in comfortable circumstances. A fierce, proud, arrogant woman whose father had fought under Michael Collins in the original Irish Troubles, she had been raised to blame everyone for the mess Ireland had been left in after the English had partitioned the country and left. She blamed the Free State Government as much as the IRA.

Like many wealthy young women of intellect at that period, she saw Communism as the only answer, and as part of her brilliant son's education taught him that there was only one true faith, the doctrine according to Karl Marx.

In 1966 at seventeen Curry went to Trinity College, Cambridge to study Political Philosophy, where he met Rupert Lang, an apparently effete aristocrat who never took anything seriously, except Tom Curry, for the bond was instant and they enjoyed a homosexual relationship which lasted throughout their period at university.

They went their separate ways, of course – Lang to

Sandhurst and the Army following the family tradition, and Curry to the University of Moscow to research for a PhD on aspects of modern politics, where he was promptly recruited by the GRU.

They gave him the usual training in weaponry, how to handle himself in the field and so on, but told him that he would be regarded as a sleeper once back in England, someone to be called on when needed, no more than that.

On 30 January 1972, Rupert Lang, having transferred from the Grenadier Guards, was serving as a lieutenant in the Parachute Regiment in Londonderry in Northern Ireland, a day that would be long remembered as Bloody Sunday. By the time the paratroopers had stopped firing, thirteen people lay dead and there were many wounded, including Rupert Lang, who took a bullet in the arm, whether from his own side or the IRA he could never be sure. On sick leave in London he had lunch at the Oxford and Cambridge Club and was totally delighted when he went into the bar to find his old friend sitting in a window seat, enjoying a quiet drink.

'You old bastard, how marvellous,' Lang said. 'I thought you were in Russia?'

'Oh. I'm back now at Trinity, putting the thesis together.' Curry nodded at Lang's arm. 'Why the sling?'

Lang had always been aware of his friend's politics and now he shrugged. 'I don't expect you'll want to speak to me. Bloody Sunday. I stopped a bullet.'

'You were there?' Curry called to the barman for two Bushmills. 'How bad was it?'

'Terrible. Not soldiering, not the way I thought it would be.' Lang accepted his whiskey from the barman and raised his glass. 'Anyway, to you, old sport. I can't tell you how good it is to see you.'

'That goes double.' Curry toasted him back. 'What are you going to do?'

Lang smiled. 'You could always read me like a book. Yes, I'm finished with the Army as a career. Not straight away, though. My captaincy's coming up and I want to keep the old man happy.'

'I see he's a Minister at the Home Office now.'

'Yes, but his health isn't good. I think he'll stand down at the next election, which will leave a vacancy for one of the safest Conservative seats in the country.'

Curry said, 'You're going to go into Parliament?'

'Why not? I've all the money in the world, so I don't need to work, and I'll walk into the seat if the old man steps down. What do you think?'

'Bloody marvellous.' Curry stood up. 'Let's have a bite to eat and you can tell me all about Bloody Sunday and your Irish exploits.'

'Terrible business,' Lang said as they walked through to the dining room. 'All hell's going on at Army Intelligence HQ at Lisburn. I heard the Prime Minister is going through the roof.'

'How interesting,' Curry said as they sat down. 'Tell me more.'

Curry's control was a 35-year-old GRU major named Yuri Belov, who was supposed to be a cultural attaché at the Soviet Embassy. Curry met him in a booth at a pub opposite Kensington Palace Gardens and the Soviet Embassy. Belov enjoyed London and had no great urge to be posted back to Moscow, which meant that he liked to look good to his superiors back there. Curry's version of Bloody Sunday and his account of the sensory deprivation methods used to break IRA prisonera at Army headquarters at Lisburn was just the sort of stuff Belov wanted to hear.

'Excellent, Tom,' he said when Curry was finished. 'Of course your friend has no idea you've been pumping him dry?'

'Absolutely not,' Curry said. 'He knew what my politics were when we were at Cambridge, but he's an English aristocrat. Couldn't care less.' Curry lit a cigarette. 'And he's my best friend, Yuri, let's get that clear.'

'Of course, Tom, I understand. However, anything further you can learn from him would always be useful.'

'He intends to leave the Army soon,' Curry said. 'His father's a Minister of the Home Office. I think Rupert will step in when the old man leaves.'

'Really?' Yuri Belov smiled. 'A Member of Parliament. Now that *is* interesting.'

'Yes, well, while we're discussing what's interesting,' Curry said, 'what about me? This is the first time we've spoken in nine months and I'm the one who's come to you. I'd like to see a little action.'

'Patience,' Belov said. 'That's what being a sleeper is. It's about waiting, sometimes for many years until the time comes when you are needed.'

'A bloody boring prospect.'

'Yes, well, spying usually is, most of the time, and after all, you've got your work.' Belov stood up. 'Hope to see you again soon, Tom.'

But he didn't and it was to be fourteen years before they met again. Belov was transferred back home, and Tom Curry went to America – Harvard for five years, Yale for four – before returning to Cambridge where he became a Fellow of Trinity College.

Rupert Lang's father died in office and Lang promptly left the Army and put himself forward for the seat in Parliament, winning with a record majority. He and Curry were as close as ever. Lang often spent vacations with him during the American period and Curry always stayed, when in London, at Lang's beautiful town house in Dean Court, close to Westminster Abbey and within walking distance of the Houses of Parliament.

In 1985 Curry became a Professor of Political Philosophy at London University and visiting Professor at Queen's University, Belfast. His mother had been dead for some time, but he had his friendship with Lang, his work and the fact that due to his academic standing, he had been invited to sit on a number of important government committees. The arrangement made with Yuri Belov was so long ago that it might never have happened. Then one day, out of the blue, he received a telephone call at his office at the university.

Belov had put on a little weight and there was a scar on his left cheek. Otherwise he had changed little: the same sort of Savile Row suit, the same genial smile. They sat in a booth in the pub opposite Kensington Palace Gardens and shared half a bottle of Sancerre.

The Russian toasted Curry. 'Good to see you, Tom.'

'And you. What about the scar?'

'Afghanistan. A dreadful place. You know, those tribesmen skinned our men when they caught them.'

'But you're back now?'

'Yes, Senior Cultural Attaché at the Embassy, but you must treat me with respect.' He grinned. 'I am now a full colonel in the GRU and Head of Station here in London. You, by the way, have been promoted to major.'

'But I haven't done anything,' Curry said. 'Except sit on my arse for years.'

'You will, Tom, you will. With all these government posts you hold, particularly on the Northern Ireland Committee, and your friend, Lang. He's doing well. A Government Whip? That's very important, isn't it, and I hear Mrs Thatcher likes him.'

'Don't set too much store by that. Rupert doesn't take life too seriously.'

'He still isn't aware of your connection with us?'

'Not a hint,' Curry told him. 'I prefer it that way. Now, what do you want?'

'From now on, full and intimate details of all those committee meetings, especially Irish affairs and anything to do with the activities of our Arab friends and their fundamentalist groups. They're all over London these days. The English are far too liberal in letting them in.'

'Anything else?'

'Not for the moment.' Belov stood up. 'You're too valuable to waste on small things, Tom. Your day will come, believe me. Just be patient.' He took out his wallet and passed over a slip of paper. 'Emergency numbers if you need me, Embassy and home. I've a cottage in a mews just up the road. I'll be in touch.'

He smiled and went out, leaving Curry more excited than he'd been in years.

It was perhaps a year later on a wet October evening that Curry received a phone call at the Dean Court town house. Lang was at the Commons, making sure in his capacity as a Whip that as many Conservative MPs as possible were available to vote on a bill crucial to the Government.

'Belov here,' the Colonel said. 'I must see you at once. Most urgent. I'll pick you up at the entrance to Dean Square.'

Curry didn't argue. He'd seen Belov only twice in the previous year although in that time he had passed on a continuous stream of information.

It was raining hard outside so he found an old Burberry trenchcoat, a trilby hat and black umbrella and let himself out of the front door. He stood by the entrance to the garden in Dean Square and within ten minutes a small Renault car coasted in to the kerb and Belov leaned out.

'Over here, Tom.'

Curry climbed in beside him. 'What's so important?'

38

Belov pulled out from the kerb. 'I'm supposed to meet an Arab tonight in about thirty minutes from now at a place on the river in Wapping.'

'Who is this Arab?'

'A man called Ali Hamid, who has apparently fallen out with a fundamentalist group called Wind of Allah. They gave us a lot of trouble in Afghanistan. This man is offering full documentation on their European operation. The meeting place is called Butler's Wharf. You'll be at the river end at seven. You give him that briefcase on the rear seat, fifty thousand dollars. He'll give you a briefcase in return.'

'Can you be sure all this is kosher?' Curry asked.

'The tip came from a colleague, Colonel Boris Ashimov of the KGB, Head of Station here in London.'

'Why doesn't he handle this himself? Why this gift to you?'

'Strictly speaking, it's none of their business. Division of labour. The Arabs are a GRU matter and I can't go myself for the simplest of reasons. I'm hosting an Embassy Cultural evening at the Savoy. I'm due there in thirty minutes. Notice the black tie.'

'Very capitalistic,' Curry told him. 'Shame on you. All right, I'll do it.'

He reached for the briefcase and Belov pulled in at the kerb. 'You can get a cab from here. I'll be in touch.'

Curry got out and watched the Renault drive away, then he put up his umbrella and moved along the pavement.

It was no more than thirty minutes later that a cab dropped him in Wapping. The rain was very heavy now, and there was no one about. He found Butler's Wharf with no difficulty, walked to the end and stood by an old-fashioned streetlamp, the umbrella up against the rain, which poured down relentlessly. There was the faintest of footfalls behind him

The Arab wore a black reefer coat of the kind used by

seamen and a tweed cap. His brown face was gaunt, his eyes pinpricks as if he was on something. Curry felt a certain alarm.

'Ali Hamid?'

'Who are you?' the man asked in a hoarse voice.

'Colonel Belov sent me.'

'But he was to come himself.' Hamid laughed in a strange way. 'It was all arranged. It was Belov I was paid to kill, but instead you are here.' He laughed again and there was a kind of foam on his mouth. 'Unfortunate.'

His hand came out of his right pocket, holding a silenced Beretta automatic pistol and Curry swung the briefcase, knocking the Arab's arm to one side and closing with him. He grabbed the man's wrist, the gun between them, was aware of it going off, a kind of punch in his left arm. Strangely, it gave him even more strength and he struggled harder, aware of the Beretta discharging twice, Hamid dropping it and falling back, clutching his stomach. He lay there, under the lamp, legs kicking, then went very still.

Curry crouched and felt for a pulse, but Hamid was dead, eyes staring. Curry stood and examined his arm. There was a scorched hole in the Burberry and blood was seeping through. There wasn't too much pain although he suspected that would come later. He eased off the Burberry, tied a handkerchief awkwardly around the arm over his jacket sleeve then pulled the raincoat on again. He picked up the Beretta, opened the briefcase and slipped it inside.

He retrieved his umbrella and stood looking down at Hamid. There was a lot to be explained, but no time for that now. He had to get moving. Surprising how calm he felt as he hurried along the wharf. Hardly sensible to take a taxi. It was going to be a long walk to the town house in Dean Close and how in hell was he going to explain this to Rupert? He turned into Wapping High Street and hurried along the pavement, aware of the pain now in his arm.

★

Rupert Lang, having returned from Parliament only fifteen minutes before, was pouring a large Scotch in the drawing room when the front doorbell sounded. He swallowed some of the whisky, put down his glass and went into the hall. When he opened the door, Curry, almost out on his feet, fell into his arms.

'Tom, what is it?'

'Quite simple, old lad, I've been shot. Get me into the kitchen before I bleed all over your best carpet.'

Lang got an arm round him, helped him into the kitchen and eased him into a chair. Curry tried to get his Burberry off and Lang went to his assistance.

'Dear God, Tom, your sleeve's soaked in blood.'

'Yes, well, it would be.'

Lang reached for a towel and wrapped it around Curry's arm. 'I'll call an ambulance.'

'No you won't, old lad. I've just killed a man.'

Lang, on his way to the door, stopped and turned. 'You've what?'

'Arab terrorist called Ali Hamid tried to kill me, that's when I stopped the bullet. Took a couple himself in the struggle. I left him on Butler's Wharf in the rain. It's all right. No one saw me and I didn't get a cab on the way back. Long bloody walk, I can tell you.' Curry managed a smile. 'A large whisky and a cigarette would help.'

Lang went out and returned with a glass and a bottle of Scotch. He poured, handed the glass over and found a packet of cigarettes. As he gave Curry a light he said, 'I think you'd better tell me what's going on.'

'We've been friends a long time,' Tom said.

'Best of friends,' Rupert Lang said.

'No one's known me better than you, old lad, and I've always been honest. You know my politics.'

'Of course I do,' Lang said. 'Come the revolution you'll take me out and have me shot, with great regret, of course.'

'Just one thing I never told you.'

'And what's that?'

Curry swallowed the Scotch and held out the glass for another. 'Let's see, you were a captain in 1 Para when you retired?'

'That's right.' Lang poured more whisky.

'Well, the thing is, old lad, I outrank you. I'm a major in Russian Military Intelligence, the GRU.'

Lang stopped pouring, then carefully replaced the cap on the bottle. 'You old bastard.' He was smiling, suddenly excited. 'How long has this been going on?'

'Ever since Moscow. That's when they recruited me.'

'Shades of Philby, Burgess and Maclean.'

Lang put the bottle down and lit a cigarette himself. He paced around the kitchen, full of energy. 'Tell me everything, Tom, not only what happened tonight. Everything.'

When Curry finished talking, he tried to stand up. 'So you see, much better if I get out of here.'

Lang pushed him down. 'Don't play silly bastards with me, although I must say you have done. My God, all that stuff from the Northern Ireland Office going to our Russian friends. Dammit Tom, I sat on one of those committees with you.'

'I know, isn't it terrible?' Curry said.

'You say Belov's at the Savoy?'

'That's right.'

'Good. I'm going to ring him up. He can sort this mess out for you. After all, it's his kind of business.'

He reached for the kitchen phone, but Curry said, 'For God's sake, old lad, you can't afford to get involved. Just let me go. I shouldn't have come back here. Only a guest, after all.' It was as if he was losing consciousness. 'Not your affair.'

'Oh, yes it is.' Rupert Lang wasn't smiling now. He ran a hand over Curry's head. 'Rest easy, Tom, I'll handle it.'

He rang through to the Savoy and asked that Colonel Yuri Belov come to the phone urgently.

Rose House Nursing Home was a discreet establishment in Holland Park. It had once been the town mansion of some turn-of-the-century millionaire and stood discreetly in two acres of gardens behind high walls. In a lounge area on the second floor, Belov and Rupert Lang drank coffee and waited. Finally a door opened and a small cheerful Indian walked in, clad in green surgical robes.

'This is Dr Joel Gupta, the principal of this establishment,' Belov said to Lang. 'How is he, Joel?'

'Very lucky. The Beretta fires 9-millimetre Parabellum. At close quarters, it's enough to take a man's arm off. This time it only chipped the bone and passed through flesh. He'll be fine, but I want him in for a week.'

'When can we see him?' Belov asked.

'He's woozy right now. Give him half an hour, then five minutes only. I'll see you later.'

Gupta went out. Lang said. 'He seems to be on your side.'

'I knew him in Afghanistan,' Belov said. 'Helped him come to England. Don't get the wrong impression. He helps me out on the odd occasion, but most of the time he specializes in drug addiction. He does fine work.'

'So what went wrong tonight?' Lang asked.

'My dear man, do you really want to get into this any more than you have to?'

'I'm already up to my ears,' Lang said. 'And Tom Curry is the best friend I have in the world.'

'But you're in the Government.'

'So?'

'And Curry, like me, is a committed Communist. We believe that we are right and you are wrong.'

'But I often am,' Lang told him. 'I'm sure you'll lead me to the guillotine when the moment arrives, but I take

43

friendship seriously, so what about Tom? What went wrong?'

'Colonel Boris Ashimov went wrong. He's Head of Station at the London Embassy for the KGB. As you know, GRU is Military Intelligence and we have our differences. I hadn't realized how deep they were until tonight.'

'He set you up?'

'So it would appear. If it hadn't been for the Savoy affair I'd have gone personally.'

'But instead, poor old Tom takes the bullet.' Rupert Lang wasn't smiling. His eyes glittered, and there was a wolfish look to his face. 'I took a bullet myself once. Not nice.'

'Of course,' Belov said. '1 Para. Bloody Sunday. You were a lieutenant then.'

Just then a nurse appeared. 'He's surfaced. You can go in now if you like.'

Curry managed a weak smile. 'Still here, am I?'

'For a long time yet,' Rupert Lang told him.

Curry turned to Belov. 'What went wrong, Yuri?'

'It would appear Ashimov set me up. Ali Hamid was supposed to knock me off. Unfortunately I sent you — unfortunate for you, that is, not for me. However, we must cover the trail as much as possible, give an explanation for Hamid's death. He's a known terrorist. Both Scotland Yard and MI5 will find that out soon enough.'

'What would you suggest?' Lang asked.

'Someone should claim credit for his death,' Belov nodded. 'That would take care of things nicely.'

'Like the Provisional IRA?' Curry demanded.

'No, something new, something to confuse them all.'

'You mean an entirely new terrorist group?' Lang asked.

'Why not?' Belov smiled. 'Bloody Sunday, wasn't that 30 January 1973? What if I put a call through to *The Times* claiming credit for Hamid's killing on behalf of January 30?

That would certainly give the anti-terrorist units at every level something to chew on.'

'Rather like that Greek group we read about,' Lang said. 'November 17. Yes, I like it. Should muddy the waters nicely.'

'Of course,' Belov said. 'You see, Mr Lang, because of the cause I serve, chaos is my main interest in life. Fear, uncertainty and chaos. I want to create as much of all these things as possible in the Western world. Then gradually the cracks begin to show and finally the system breaks down. Take Ireland, for example. We don't take sides, but we do actively help to keep the whole rotten mess going. A civil war, a descent into madness and then our friends, and there are many in Ireland, take over.'

'Another Cuba, only in Britain's backyard,' Lang said. 'Interesting.'

'I've been very frank,' Belov said. 'But it doesn't seem to bother you.'

'Very little in this life does, old sport.'

'Fine. I'll take care of this January 30 thing then.'

It was Curry who said, 'And who takes care of Ashimov? He's got to kill you now, Yuri, no choice.'

'Yes, someone should sort that bastard out.' Rupert Lang opened the briefcase beside the bed and took out the Beretta. He said to Belov, 'Fifty thousand dollars in there. I believe it's yours. I'll keep the Beretta. Just tell me where and when.'

There was a moment's silence and then Curry said, 'You can't be serious.'

Lang smiled that strange wolfish smile again. 'I killed three people on Bloody Sunday, Tom, and two others elsewhere during my service in Ulster. Never told you that. Secrets, you see, just like you.' He turned to Belov. 'Another job for January 30. First this Arab, then the Station Head of the KGB in London. That should really make the Security Services squirm and I should know, I'm on half the committees.'

He killed Colonel Boris Ashimov with absurd simplicity a week later on a rainy morning in Kensington Gardens. Belov had timed it for him. Every morning at ten Ashimov walked in the gardens, whatever the weather. On that particular Thursday it was raining heavily. Rupert Lang sat enjoying a coffee in a café opposite Kensington Palace Gardens, not expecting Ashimov to appear. But the man carrying an umbrella over his head fitted the description Belov had given him. Ashimov turned into the Bayswater Road and entered the gardens. Lang got to his feet and went after him.

He followed him along the path, keeping well back, his own umbrella raised. There was no one about. They reached a clump of trees at the centre of the gardens, and Lang quickened his pace.

'Excuse me.'

Ashimov turned. 'What do you want?'

'You, actually,' Rupert Lang said, and shot him twice in the heart, the silenced Beretta making only a slight coughing sound. He leaned down and put another bullet between Ashimov's eyes then put the Beretta in his raincoat pocket, moved rapidly across the gardens to Queen's Gate, crossed to the Albert Hall and walked on for a good half mile before hailing a cab and telling the driver to take him to Westminster.

He lit a cigarette and sat back, shaking with excitement. He had never felt like this in his life before, not even in the Paras in Ireland. Every sense felt keener, even the colours when he looked out at the passing streets seemed sharper. But the excitement, the damned excitement!

He closed his eyes. 'My God, old sport, what's happening to you?' he murmured.

He arrived at the St Stephen's entrance to the Commons, went through the Central Lobby to his office and got rid of his umbrella and raincoat and put the Beretta in his safe, then went down to the entrance to the House and passed the bar. There was a debate taking place on some social services issue. He took his usual seat on the end of one of the aisles. When he looked up he saw Tom Curry seated in the front row of the Strangers' Gallery, his left arm in a sling. Lang nodded up to him, folded his arms and leaned back.

Half an hour later the *Times* newsdesk received a brief message by telephone in which January 30 claimed credit for the assassination of Colonel Boris Ashimov.

In the three years that followed, Curry maintained a steady flow of confidential information of every description, aided by Lang. They made only three hits during the period. Two of these took place at the same time – a couple of IRA bombers released from trial at the Old Bailey on a legal technicality. The two men proceeded on a drunken spree that lasted all day. It was Curry who charted their progress until midnight, then called in Lang, who killed them both as they sat, backs to the wall, in a drunken stupor in a Kilburn alley.

The third was a CIA field officer attached to the American Embassy's London Station. He had been giving Belov considerable aggravation and, after the Berlin Wall came down, appeared to be far too friendly with the Russian's latest rival, Mikhail Shimko, who had replaced Ashimov as Colonel in Charge of London Station KGB.

The CIA man was called Jackson, and by chance, his name came up at one of the joint intelligence working parties. News had come in that he was having a series of meetings at an address in Holland Park with members of a Ukrainian faction resident in London. Curry kept a watch at the appropriate times and noticed that Jackson always walked for a mile afterwards, following the same route through quiet streets to the main road where he would hail a taxi.

After the next meeting, Lang was waiting in a small Ford

van – provided by Belov, of course – at an appropriate point on the route. As Jackson passed, Lang, wearing a knitted ski mask in black, stepped out and shot him once in the back, penetrating the heart. He finished him with a head shot, got in the van and drove away. He left the van in a builders' yard in Bayswater, as instructed by Belov, and walked away, whistling softly to himself.

It was half an hour later that a young reporter on the newsdesk of the *Times* took the phone call claiming credit for the killing by January 30.

The British Government allowed the Americans to flood London temporarily with CIA agents intent on hunting down Jackson's killer. As usual, they drew a complete blank. That the killings claimed by January 30 from Ali Hamid onwards had been the work of the same Beretta 9-millimetre was known to everyone, as was the significance of January 30. The Bloody Sunday connection should have indicated an Irish revolutionary connection, but even the IRA got no-where in their investigations. In the end, the CIA presence was withdrawn.

British Army Intelligence, Scotland Yard's anti-terrorist department, MI5, all failed to make headway. Even the redoubtable Brigadier Charles Ferguson, head of the special intelligence unit responsible to the Prime Minister, could only report total failure to Downing Street.

It was in January 1990, following the collapse of the Communist-dominated government of East Germany, that Lang and Curry attended a cultural evening at the American Embassy. There were at least a hundred and fifty people there, including Belov, whom they found at the champagne bar. They took their glasses into an anteroom and found a corner table.

'So, everything is falling apart for you people, Yuri,' Lang said. 'First the Wall comes tumbling down, now East Germany folds and a little bird tells me there's a strong possibility that your Congress of People's Deputies might soon abolish the Communist Party's monopoly of power in Russia.'

Belov shrugged. 'Disorder leads to strength. It's inevitable. Take the German situation. West Germany is at present the most powerful country in Western Europe economically. The consequences of taking East Germany on board will be catastrophic in every way and particularly economically. The balance of power in Europe will once again be altered totally. Remember what I said a long time ago? Chaos is our business.'

'I suppose you're right when you come to think of it,' Lang said.

Curry nodded. 'Of course he is.'

'I invariably am.' Belov raised his glass. 'To a new world, my friends, and to us. One never knows what's round the corner.'

'I know,' Rupert Lang said. 'That's what makes it all so damned exciting.'

They touched glasses and drank.

FOUR

Rupert lang was more right than he knew. There *was* something round the corner, something profound and disturbing that was to affect all three of them, although it was not to take place until the Gulf War was over and done with. January, 1992 to be precise.

Grace Browning was born in Washington in 1965. Her father was a journalist on the *Washington Post*, her mother was English. When she was twelve tragedy struck, devastating her life. On the way home from a concert one night, her parents' car was rammed into the kerb by an old limousine. The men inside were obviously on drugs. Afterwards, she remembered the shouting, the demands for money, her father opening the door to get out and then the shots, one of which penetrated the side window at the rear and killed her mother instantly.

Grace lay in the bottom of the car, frozen, terrified, glancing up only once to see the shape of a man, gun raised, shouting, 'Go, go, go!' and then the old limousine shot away.

She wasn't even able to give the police a useful description, couldn't even say whether they were white or black. All that mattered was that her father died the following morning and she was left alone.

Not quite alone, of course, for there was her mother's sister, her Aunt Martha – Lady Hunt to be precise – a woman of considerable wealth, widowed young, who lived in some splendour in a fine town house in Cheyne Walk in London. She had received her niece with affection and firmness, for she was a tough, practical lady who believed you had to get on with it instead of sitting down and crying.

Grace was admitted to St Paul's Girls' School, one of the finest in London, where she soon proved to have a sharp intelligence. She was popular with everyone, teachers and pupils alike, and yet for her, it was a sort of performance. Inside she was one thing, herself, detached, cold; but on the surface she was charming, intelligent, warm. It was not surprising that she was something of a star in school drama circles.

Her social life, because of her aunt, was conducted at the highest level: Cannes and Nice in the summer, Barbados in the winter, always a ceaseless round of parties on the London scene. When she was sixteen, like most of the girls she knew, she attempted her first sexual encounter, a gauche 17-year-old public schoolboy. It was less than rewarding and as he climaxed, a strange thing happened. She seemed to see in her head the shadowy figure of the man who had killed her parents, gun raised.

When the time came for Grace to leave school, although her academic grades were good enough for Oxford or Cambridge, she had only one desire – to be a professional actor. Her aunt, being the sort of woman she was, supported her fully, stipulating only that Grace had to go for best. So Grace auditioned for the Royal Academy of Dramatic Art and they accepted her at once.

Her career there was outstanding. In the final play, *Macbeth*, she played Lady Macbeth, absurdly young and yet so brilliant that London theatrical agents clamoured to take her on board. She turned them all down and went to Chichester, the smallest of the two theatres, the Minerva, to play the lead in a revival of *Anna Christie* – so triumphantly that the play transferred to the London West End, the Theatre Royal at the Haymarket, where it ran for a year.

After that, she could have everything, the Royal Shakespeare Company, the National Theatre, establishing herself in a series of great classic roles. She went to Hollywood only once to star in a classy and flashy revenge thriller in which she killed several men, but she turned down all subsequent film offers except for the occasional TV appearance and returned to the National Theatre.

Money, of course, was no problem. Aunt Martha saw to that and took great pride in her niece's achievements. She was the one person Grace felt loved her and she loved her fiercely in return, dropping out of the theatre totally for the last, terrible year when leukaemia took its hold on the old woman.

Martha came home at the end to die in her own bed, in the room that overlooked the Thames. There was medical help in abundance, but Grace looked after her every need personally.

On the last evening it was raining, beating softly against the windows. She was holding her aunt's hand and Martha, gaunt and wasted, opened her eyes and looked at her.

'You'll go back now, promise me, and show them all what real acting is about. It's what you are, my love. Promise me.'

'Of course,' Grace said.

'No sad tears, no mourning. A celebration to prove how worthwhile it's been.' She managed a weak smile. 'I never told you, Grace, but your father always believed the family tradition that they were kin to Robert Browning.'

'The poet?' Grace asked.

'Yes. There's a line in one of his great poems. "Our interest's on the dangerous edge of things." I don't know why, but it seems to suit you perfectly.'

Her eyes closed and she died a few minutes later.

★

She was wealthy now, the house in Cheyne Walk was hers and the world of theatre was her oyster, but no one could control her, no one could hold her. Her wealth meant that she could do what she wanted. Her first role on her return was in *Look Back in Anger* with an obscure South Coast repertory company in a seaside town. The critics descended from London in droves and were ecstatic. After that she did a range of similar performances at various provincial theatres, finally returning to the National Theatre to do Turgenev's *A Month in the Country*.

No long-term contracts, no ties. She had set a pattern. If a part interested her she would play it – even if it was for four weeks at some obscure civic theatre in the heart of Lancashire or some London fringe theatre venue such as the King's Head or the Old Red Lion – and the audiences everywhere loved her.

Love in her own life was a different story. There were men, of course, when the mood came, but no one who ever moved her. In male circles in the theatre she was known as the Ice Queen. She knew this but it didn't dismay her in the slightest, amused her if anything and her actor's gift for analysis of a role told her that if anything, she had a certain contempt for men.

In October 1991, Grace performed in Brendan Behan's *The Hostage* at the Minerva Studio at Chichester, still her favourite theatre. It was a short run, but such was the interest in this most Irish of plays that the company was invited to the Lyric Theatre, Belfast, for a two-week run. Unfortunately, Grace was scheduled to start rehearsals at the National for *A Winter's Tale* immediately after her stint at the Minerva, and so the director of *The Hostage* came to see her in some trepidation.

'The Lyric, Belfast, would like us for two weeks. Of course, I'll have to say no. I mean, you start rehearsing Monday at the National.'

'Belfast?' she said. 'I've never been. I like the sound of that.'

'But the National?' he protested.

'Oh, they can put things on the back burner for a couple of weeks.' She smiled, that famous smile of hers that seemed to be for you alone. 'Or get someone else.'

She indulged herself by staying at the Europa Hotel. She stood at the window of her suite and looked out at the rain driving in across the city, suddenly excited to be here, surely one of the most dangerous cities in the world. It was only four o'clock and she was not due at the Lyric until six-thirty. On impulse, she went downstairs.

At the main entrance, the head doorman smiled. 'A taxi, Miss Browning?'

Posters advertising the play with her photo on them were on a stand close by.

She gave him her best smile. 'No, I just need some fresh air and I like the rain.'

'Plenty of that in Belfast, miss, better take this,' and he put up an umbrella for her.

She started towards the bus station and the Protestant stronghold of Sandy Row, feeling suddenly cheerful as a bitter east wind blew in from Belfast Lough.

Tom Curry always stayed at the Europa during his monthly visits as visiting Professor at Queen's University. He liked Belfast, the sense of danger, the thought that anything might happen. Sometimes his visits coincided with Rupert Lang's, for Lang was now an extra Under-Secretary of State at the Northern Ireland Office, which meant frequent visits to Ulster on Crown business, and this was one of them.

Lang arrived back at the Europa at five-thirty, went into the Library Bar and found Tom Curry seated at one end, reading the *Belfast Telegraph*, a Bushmills in front of him.

Curry glanced up. 'Hello, old lad. Had a good day?'

'It's always bloody raining every time I come to Belfast.' Lang nodded to the barman. 'Same as my friend.'

'You don't like it much, do you?' Curry said.

'I went through hell here, Tom, back in seventy-three. Close to six hundred dead in one year. Bodies under the rubble for days, the stink of explosions. I can still smell it.' He raised his glass. 'To you, old sport.'

Curry toasted him back. 'As the Fenians say, may you die in Ireland.'

'Thanks *very* much.' Lang smiled. 'Mind you, you can't fault them on their attitude to culture here.' He nodded towards the wall behind the bar, where Grace's poster was displayed.

'Grace Browning, yes. She's wonderful. Strange choice of a play for Belfast, though, *The Hostage*. Very IRA.'

'Nonsense,' Lang said. 'Behan showed the absurdity of the whole thing even though he was in the IRA himself.'

At that moment Grace Browning entered. As she unbuttoned her raincoat, a waiter hurried to take it. She walked to the bar and Rupert Lang said, 'Good God, it's Grace Browning.'

Hearing him, she turned and gave him that famous smile. 'Hello.'

'May I introduce myself?' he asked.

She frowned slightly. 'You know, I feel I've met you before.'

Curry laughed. 'No, you've occasionally seen him on the television. Under-Secretary of State at the Northern Ireland Office. Rupert Lang.'

'I'm impressed,' she said. 'And you?'

'Tom Curry,' Lang said. 'He's just a Professor of Political Philosophy at London University. Visiting Professor here at Queen's once a month. Can we offer you a drink?'

'Why not. A glass of white wine. Just one, I've got to give a performance.'

Lang gave the order to the barman. 'We've seen you many times.'

'Together?'

'Oh, yes,' he smiled. 'Tom and I go back a long way. Cambridge.'

'That's nice.' She sipped her wine. There was something about them. She sensed it. Something unusual. 'Are you coming to the show tonight?'

'Didn't realize it was on,' Curry said. 'I'm only here for three days. Don't suppose there are any tickets left.'

'I'll leave you two of my tickets at the box office,' she said.

It was a challenge instantly taken up. 'Oh, you're on,' Lang said. 'Wonderful.'

She swallowed the rest of the wine. 'Good. Now I'll have to love you and leave you. Hope you enjoy it.'

As she left the bar, Curry turned to Lang and they toasted each other. 'By the way,' Curry said, 'are you carrying?'

'Of course I am,' Lang told him. 'If you think I'm going to walk the streets of Belfast without a pistol you're crazy. As a Minister of the Crown I have my permit, Tom. No problems with security at the airports.'

'The Beretta?' Curry asked.

'But of course. Lucky for us, I'd say.'

Curry shook his head. 'It's just a game to you, isn't it? A wild, exciting game.'

'Exactly, old sport, but then life can be such a bore. Now drink up and let's go and get ready.'

Grace Browning was wonderful, no doubt about it, receiving a rapturous reception from the packed house at the end of the play. Curry and Lang went into the bar for a drink and debated whether to go backstage and see her.

It was Lang who said, 'I think not, old sport. Probably lots of locals doing exactly that. We'll go back to the Europa and have a nightcap at the bar. She may well look in.'

'You like her, don't you?' Curry said.

'So do you.'

Curry smiled. 'Let's get the car.'

On their way back to the hotel, Curry, who was driving, turned into a quiet road between several factories and warehouses, deserted at night. Lang put a hand on his arm as they passed a woman walking rapidly along the pavement, an umbrella up against the rain.

'Good God, it's her.'

'The damned fool,' Curry said. 'She can't walk around the back streets of Belfast like that on her own.'

'Pull in to the kerb,' Lang said. 'I'll get her.'

Curry did so. Lang opened the car door and saw two young men in bomber jackets run up behind Grace Browning and grab her. He heard her cry out, and then she was hustled into an alley.

Grace wasn't afraid, just angry with herself for having been such a fool. On a high after her performance, she'd thought that the walk back to the hotel in the rain would calm her down. She should have known better. This was uncharted territory. Belfast. The war zone.

They hustled her to the end of the alley, where there was a dead end, and a jumble of packing cases lay under an old streetlamp bracketed to a wall. She stood facing them.

'What do you want?'

'English, is it?' The one with a ponytail laughed unpleasantly. 'We don't like the English.'

The other, who wore a tweed cap, said, 'There's only one thing we like about English girls, and that's what's between their legs, so let's be having you.'

He leapt on her and she dropped the umbrella and tried to fight back as he forced her across the packing case, yanking up her dress.

57

'Let me go, damn you!' She clawed at his face, disgusted by the whiskey breath, aware of him forcing her legs open.

'That's enough,' Rupert Lang called through the rain.

The man in the tweed cap turned and Grace pushed him away. The one with the ponytail turned, too, as Lang and Curry approached.

'Just let her go,' Curry said. 'You made a mistake. Let's leave it at that.'

'You'd better keep out of this, friend,' the man in the tweed cap told him. 'This is Provisional IRA business.'

'Really?' Rupert Lang replied. 'Well, I'm sure Martin McGuinness wouldn't approve. He's a family man.'

They were all very close together now. There was a moment of stillness and then the one with the ponytail pulled a Smith & Wesson .38 from the pocket of his bomber jacket. Rupert Lang's hand came up holding the Beretta and shot him twice in the heart.

At the same moment, the man in the tweed cap knocked Grace sideways, sending her sprawling. He picked up a batten of wood and struck Lang across the wrist, making him drop the Beretta. The man scrambled for it, but it slid on the damp cobbles towards Grace. She picked it up instinctively, held it against him and pulled the trigger twice, blowing him back against the wall.

She stood there, legs apart, holding the gun in both hands, staring down at him.

Rupert Lang said, 'Give it to me.'

'Is he dead?' she asked in a calm voice.

'If not, he soon will be.' Lang took the Beretta and shot him between the eyes. He turned to the one with the ponytail and did the same. 'Always make sure. Now let's get out of here.' He picked up the umbrella. 'Yours, I think.'

Curry took one arm, Lang the other, and they hurried her away.

'No police?' she said.

'This is Belfast,' Curry told her. 'Another sectarian killing. They said they were IRA, didn't they?'

'But were they?' she demanded as they took her down to the car and pushed her into the rear seat.

'Probably not, my dear,' Rupert Lang said. 'Nasty young yobs cashing in. Lots of them about.'

'Never mind,' Curry told her. 'They'll be heroes of the revolution tomorrow.'

'Especially if January 30 claims credit.' Rupert Lang lit a cigarette and passed it to her. 'Even if you don't use these things, you could do with one now.' She accepted it, strangely calm. 'Do you need a doctor?'

'No, he didn't penetrate me if that's what you mean.'

'Good,' Curry said. 'Then it's a hot bath and a decent night's sleep and put it out of your mind. It didn't happen.'

'Oh, yes it did,' she said and tossed the cigarette out of the window.

When they reached the Europa, Lang, a hand on her arm, started towards the lifts.

'Actually,' she said, 'I'd like a nightcap.'

Lang frowned, then nodded. 'Fine.' He turned to Curry. 'Better make the call, Tom.' He led her into the Library Bar.

A few minutes later the phone rang on the desk of the night editor at the *Belfast Telegraph*. When he picked it up, a gruff voice said, 'Carrick Lane, got that? You'll find a couple of Provo bastards on their backs there. We won't be sending flowers.'

'Who is this?' the night editor demanded.

'January 30.'

The phone went dead. The night editor stared at it, frowning, then hurriedly dialled his emergency number to the Royal Ulster Constabulary.

★

Curry joined them in the bar at a corner table. They were drinking brandy and there was a glass for him.

Lang said, 'You seem rather calm considering the circumstances.'

'You mean why am I not crying and sobbing because I just killed a man?' She shook her head. 'He was a piece of filth. He deserved everything he got. I loathe people like that. When I was twelve I was driving back from a concert in Washington one night with my parents. We were attacked by armed thugs. My parents were killed.'

She sat staring down into her glass and Curry said gently, 'I'm sorry.'

'You handled the gun surprisingly well,' Lang said. 'Have you had much training?'

She laughed. 'One Hollywood movie, just one. I didn't like it out there. There were a few scenes where I had to use a gun. They showed me how.' She finished the brandy and raised the empty glass to the barman. 'Three more.' She smiled tightly. 'I hope you don't mind, but we do seem to be rather tied in together, don't we?'

'Yes, you could say that,' Curry agreed.

She turned to Lang as the barman brought the brandies and waited until he'd gone. 'You said in the car something about January 30 claiming credit. I've read about them. They're some sort of terrorist group, aren't they?'

'That's right,' Lang said. 'Of course, in this sort of case, revolutionaries and so on, all sorts of groups like to claim credit. Very useful fact of life. We're just making sure somebody does.'

'I've already spoken to the night desk at the *Belfast Telegraph*,' Curry said. 'By tomorrow, you'll find the Ulster Freedom Fighters or the Red Hand of Ulster claiming credit, also. They're Protestant Loyalist factions.'

'But you'd prefer January 30 to get the credit?' she said.

There was a moment of silence. It was Lang who said, 'You're a remarkably astute young woman. Is there a problem here?'

'Not in the slightest. As I said, it would seem we're tied together in this.'

'Invisible bonds and all that.'

'Exactly.' She opened her handbag, took out a card and passed it to him. 'That's my address and phone number. Cheyne Walk. I'll be back in London in twelve days. Perhaps we could meet?'

'I think you can count on that.'

She stood up. 'You'll have to excuse me now. I have a matinee tomorrow.'

She walked out of the bar.

Curry said, 'My God, what a woman.'

'Yes, quite remarkable. You know, Tom, I think this is going to be the beginning of a beautiful friendship.'

When she put out the light and pulled up the covers, Grace Browning lay there, strangely calm, staring up through the darkness, looking for him, the shadowy figure with the gun in his hand, but he seemed to have gone. She closed her eyes and slept.

It was four weeks later that Rupert Lang received a call from her in response to a message he had left on her answering phone a week earlier.

'Sorry I haven't called you before,' she said. 'But some friends had a problem at Cross Little Theatre in the Lake District. They had a week unexpectedly vacant. Someone let them down so I went up and did my one-woman show.'

'That sounds interesting.'

'No big deal. Shakespeare's heroines – that sort of thing.'

'Can we meet? Tom's in town. I thought we could have dinner.'

'That sounds fine. You could come here for drinks first. Six-thirty suit you?'

'Smashing. We'll look forward to it.'

At the Cheyne Walk house she opened the door to them herself. She wore a deceptively simple Armani trouser suit in black crepe and her black hair was tied at the back of the neck with a velvet bow.

Rupert Lang took her hands. 'You look fabulous.'

'That's a bit over the top,' she said.

'Not at all.' He kissed her on both cheeks. 'Don't you think she looks fabulous, Tom?'

Curry took her hand briefly. 'Don't mind Rupert. Extravagant in everything.'

They went through into a panelled drawing room. It was furnished in Victorian style – dark velvet drapes at the windows, a basket fire on the hearth, four paintings by Atkinson Grimshaw on the walls.

'My goodness, they're worth a bob or two,' Curry said as he inspected them.

She took a bottle of champagne from an ice bucket and Rupert Lang moved in fast. 'Allow me.'

'Yes,' she said, 'my aunt loved Grimshaw, loved everything Victorian in fact. Lady Hunt, Martha Hunt. She raised me from the age of twelve when my parents were killed. This house was her pride and joy.'

Rupert Lang poured the champagne. 'I remember her husband, Sir George Hunt. Merchant banker in the city. My father used to do business with him.'

'He died before I arrived,' she said, 'and Martha only the other year.'

'I'm truly sorry.'

She went and opened the French windows. A cold, February night outside, a slight drizzle, some fog and some barge traffic, their red and green lights clear in the murk as they passed down river.

'I love the Thames at night.'

'Heart of the city,' Lang said. 'Lovely to see you.' He raised his glass. 'Now, what shall we drink to?'

'Why not January 30?' she said. 'I read about that in the *Belfast Telegraph*. I also noticed, just as you said, that some Protestant terrorist organizations also claimed credit.' She moved to the fire and sat down in a wing-backed chair. 'And those two thugs were IRA after all. There were details of their military funerals.'

Lang and Curry sat on the long sofa opposite her. 'That's right,' Curry said. 'Irish tricolour on the coffin, black beret and gloves neatly arranged.'

'Weeping relatives, lots of women in black,' Lang said. 'Always looks good. Keeps the glorious cause going.'

'And you don't approve?'

'Only one solution. The British Army should leave.'

'But that would lead to civil war and total anarchy.'

'Exactly, but this time we'd build from the ashes. A new state entirely,' Curry said.

'Run on the political lines he approves of,' Lang told her. 'Which is Marxist–Leninist to the core. I should warn you, Tom is the Communist equivalent of a Jesuit.' He went and got the bottle of champagne and replenished their glasses.

'I've looked you up,' she told Curry, 'mentioned you to one or two people. All I heard was that you were a brilliant academic who serves on all sorts of Government committees. Not a hint of this Marxist–Leninist thing.'

'Well, thank God for that,' Curry said.

She turned to Lang. 'You were easier. I just asked my press agent to check the newspaper libraries. He confirmed what you'd told me, that you two were at Cambridge together. Afterwards, you served briefly in the Grenadier Guards and transferred to 1 Para. Rather a notorious outfit. Bloody Sunday and all that.'

'So they tell me.'

'You served again in Ireland before leaving the Army when your father died. Interesting. There was only one mention of your Military Cross and that was tucked away in a decoration list in *The Times*. No reason for the award given and you never mention it, not even in election speeches.'

'Natural modesty.' Lang smiled.

'You never even told me,' Curry said.

'Secrets again, old sport, we all have them.'

'I certainly do, I killed a man,' Grace said.

'Perhaps not. I was the one who made sure with both of them.'

'I killed him,' she insisted. 'I know it and so do you.'

'Has it been a problem coming to terms with it?' Curry asked.

'Not really. Looking back it seems to have been like a performance in a play or film and it merges into all my other performances.' She shook her head. 'Heaven knows what a psychiatrist would make of that, and anyway, those men were scum.'

'Exactly,' Lang said. 'There was, as the courts put it, reasonable cause.'

'A good point,' she said. 'I got all the press cuttings on January 30. There was Ali Hamid, an Arab terrorist, a KGB colonel called Ashimov, two IRA bombers some silly judge released, an American here in London reputed to be a CIA agent and now our two friends in Belfast. I'd say the one weak link would be the American.'

'I see,' Curry said. 'You accept the killing of the KGB colonel, but the CIA man is a different proposition.'

'I see the logic in what you're saying. I suppose it's a question of your point of view.' She finished her champagne and put the glass down on a side table. 'Of course it didn't

64

take the authorities long to work out that January 30 was the date of Bloody Sunday in Londonderry — and you were there, Mr Lang. Interesting coincidence.'

'Rupert,' he said. 'Please. Yes, I was there along with a couple of thousand soldiers and large numbers of IRA supporters.'

There was a long silence. She opened a silver cigarette box and took one out. Lang gave her a light and she blew out a feather of smoke. 'Why do you do it?'

'Do what exactly?' Lang asked. 'I mean just because we arrived in that alley at an opportune moment, and as a Minister of the Crown on service in Ulster, I do have a permit to carry a weapon.'

'A silenced Beretta 9-millimetre Parabellum,' she said. 'In all the newspaper reports they constantly mention the fact that all January 30 hits have been committed with the same weapon.'

'Many people think of it as the best handgun in the world these days,' Lang said. 'The American Army uses it — there are thousands of them around.'

She opened a drawer in the side table and took out a newspaper clipping. 'This is the *Belfast Telegraph* report on the deaths of those two animals in Carrick Lane. They state that the credit for the killings claimed by January 30 is substantiated by the forensic tests on the rounds removed from the bodies, which indicated that they were killed by the same weapon used to assassinate the other victims, a Beretta 9-millimetre, silenced version.'

'Amazing what they can do these days,' Lang said. 'The scientific people, I mean.'

Curry emptied his glass. 'What are you going to do? Turn us in?'

'Don't be stupid, Tom. I'd be turning myself in, however much a good lawyer tried to argue my case. No, I haven't the slightest intention of doing that, but there is one thing I would like to know. Why do you do it?'

'For me it's simple,' Curry said. 'I've been a Marxist-Leninist since boyhood. It's my faith, my religion if you like. I think the world needs to change.'

'And Communism is the answer?'

'Yes, but change comes out of chaos and anarchy, which is where we come in.'

'And you?' she said to Lang.

'Well, life can be such a bloody bore. Helps to have a little excitement once in a while.'

'Rupert never takes anything seriously,' Curry told her.

Lang smiled. 'All right, father. *She* can play good women or bad, great queens, murderers, the worst harlot in the world. Now that's really getting your rocks off.' He turned to Grace. 'But it isn't enough, is it, and never will be.'

'You bastard,' she said. 'You clever, clever bastard.'

'But I'm right. You'd like to join in.'

She sat there, looking at him and for a moment had a quick glimpse of that shadowy figure in Washington, gun raised high, and her stomach crawled with excitement.

Two weeks later Curry turned up at the Old Red Lion, a pub fringe theatre where she was doing her one-woman show for a week. She was sharing a cramped little dressing room with two young girls acting as assistant stage managers. He glanced in and found her changing into her jeans.

'Hello, it's me,' he said.

'Tom, how nice. How was I?'

'Dreadful.'

'Bastard,' she said.

'Only sometimes. Are you free for a Chinese?'

'Why not?'

An hour later, as they worked their way through a third or fourth course, she said, 'It's lovely to see you, but to what do I owe the honour?'

66

'We saw that interview on you in the *Stage*. All about you having a month off after finishing this show until you start *Macbeth* for the Royal Shakespeare Company.'

'So?'

'There's a parliamentary break, so Rupert's free, and I have nothing on. The thing is, Rupert has this old hunting lodge in Devon – Lang Place. Been in his family for years. Moors, shooting, all that kind of stuff. On Dartmoor.'

'My dear Tom, the only time anybody bothers to go there for the shooting is August when the birds do their usual stupid thing, and deer culling is so rigid these days that it's hardly worth the effort. So – what's it all about?'

He paused while crispy duck and pancakes were served. 'The shooting could be fun – all kinds of shooting. I know Rupert might seem your effete aristocrat, but he knows his stuff when it comes to weaponry.'

She nodded. 'That does sound interesting. Anything else?'

He paused again, looking at her, then sighed. 'You've heard of Kim Philby, Burgess, Maclean?'

'Oh, yes – didn't they all go to Cambridge, too, and work for Russia?'

'Yes, well, they all had rank in the KGB. I'm a major in the GRU. That's Russian Military Intelligence. My boss would like to meet you.'

'And who might that be?'

'Colonel Yuri Belov.'

She started to laugh. 'But I know him. When I did Chekhov's *Three Sisters* last year the Soviet Embassy gave us a reception. He was chief cultural attaché or something.'

'Or something,' Curry said with an apologetic smile.

She laughed again. 'All right. When do we leave?'

And she was glad she'd gone. Rupert had a twin-engined Navajo Chieftain pick them up from an airfield in Surrey, and the flight to an old World War Two RAF landing strip near Okehampton only took an hour. Here a man with a weather-beaten face was waiting for them. He introduced himself as George Farne and escorted them to a Range Rover.

After a half-hour drive through wonderful moorland scenery and forest they reached a wooded valley and saw Lang Place. It appeared to be eighteenth century, with tall chimneys and an ornate garden behind high walls.

When they pulled up at the steps below the front door, Rupert Lang came out wearing jeans and a sweater, an Irish wolfhound at his heels. He came down the steps and took Grace's hands.

'You look wonderful, as usual.'

'Well, you don't look too bad yourself.' She kissed him on the cheek. 'What's the wolfhound's name?'

'Danger.' Lang fondled its ears.

'Bring the bags, George,' he called and took her up the steps, an arm about her waist. 'Tell me, can you ride a motorcycle?'

'One thing I've never tried.'

'Oh, you'll take to it like a duck to water. I have a couple of Montesa dirt bikes. Spanish job. Go anywhere. Good if you've got sheep in the high country. I'll show you tomorrow.'

They had an excellent, though very simple dinner, all prepared by George Farne's wife: steak, new potatoes, salad and some sort of cream tart. Afterwards, Lang opened the French windows and they stood on the terrace with their brandies, listening to the silence.

'Do you only have the Farnes working here?' she asked.

'That's right. George's dad worked for my father, so he's known this place as long as I have. He and his wife caretake. He brings in local help when he needs it.'

'What a heavenly existence,' she said.

'Don't be an idiot,' Tom Curry told her. 'You'd be screaming your head off by the second week.'

68

'Philistine,' she said and turned back to Lang. 'What now – bridge?'

'Actually, I have a shooting range in the barn. I thought you might like to try your hand.'

For a moment, she stared at him and then she smiled. 'Why not.'

When he switched on the lights in the barn they revealed a very professional shooting range with a wall of sandbags at the rear, fronted by six-foot cardboard replicas of charging soldiers. An assortment of weaponry was laid out on several trestle tables – hand guns, machine pistols and rifles.

Curry lit a cigarette and stood watching. Lang picked up the first pistol. 'Recognize this, our old friend the Beretta? This is how you load it.' He picked up an ammunition clip and rammed it in the butt. 'Would you like to try?'

'Why not.'

He ejected the clip and handed her the Beretta. She loaded it for herself. 'Good, now pull the slider and you're in business, but don't fire. Let me give you some ear muffs.' He adjusted them. 'Good. Take aim, both eyes open, then squeeze gently.'

She did as she was told, hitting the target she was aiming at in the shoulder, then firing one round after the other in a widely dispersed pattern. He showed her how to discharge the magazine.

'Not bad. At least you hit him.'

She was suddenly angry. 'Could you do better?'

Rupert slammed another magazine in the butt of the Beretta, pulled the slider and his hand swung up. He fired three times very rapidly, shooting out the target's eyes and putting the third in between.

'My God!' she said.

'He's got nothing to do with it. I've got a selection for you here. Walther PPK, Browning, both similar to the Beretta, and a Smith & Wesson revolver.'

69

She moved to the other table. 'And this lot?'

'Stun grenade, standard-type hand grenade. The rifles are an Armalite and an AK47, both with sonic noise suppressor – silencer to you. The big job is a Barret Light Fifty Rifle with a laser guide night sight – .50 round, that thing fires, guaranteed to penetrate a Kevlar at two thousand yards.'

'A Kevlar?'

'Flak jacket like the Army wears in Ireland. Actually, I've got a neater job here, rather like a waistcoat. Titanium and nylon. Should suit you down to the ground.'

She examined it. 'You were sure of me, weren't you? Do I get to try the rifles?'

'Plenty of time, we have all week, but why not.'

He reached for the AK47, unfolded the butt and Curry came forward. 'Just one thing before you two start having fun.' He picked up the Walther, slammed in the magazine and said to Grace, 'Come on.'

He walked down the range and paused about five feet from the targets. 'You want to make sure? I'll show you how.'

He walked to the centre target, held the gun to it and pulled the trigger. 'See what a brilliant marksman I am?'

He came back to her. 'But if that isn't possible, never further away than five or six feet.'

He raised the Walther and emptied it into the target.

Grace said, 'I get your point.'

Curry turned, walked to the table and put down the Walther. 'She's all yours, old lad,' he said and walked out.

FIVE

It was a bright, clear morning although rain threatened and Grace Browning was enjoying herself on a track high up above the forest. She wore black biker's leathers which Lang had provided and a rather sinister black helmet. Lang was riding behind her, wearing jeans and a bomber jacket but no helmet. Danger ran alongside with them. After his initial instruction it was fun to find how well she could handle the bike. He pulled in beside her, lit two cigarettes and passed one to her.

'You've got flair. Typical actor, I suppose. Chameleon-like ability to take on anything at short notice.'

'Nothing typical about me, darling,' she said. 'But I like physical things and this is fun.'

'Good. You've mastered the rudiments. We'll take a twenty-mile run round the moor and back to the house. You'll be amazed how quickly you'll pick it up. Just one thing. There's a very good reason why the Montesa is so popular with shepherds in mountain and moorland country. They'll do half-a-mile an hour over rough ground if you want. On the other hand, you can go rather faster.'

He turned the throttle and zoomed away and after a moment's hesitation she went after him.

Curry returned to London on the Navajo the following day. After breakfast, Lang took Grace up into the forest to give her more practice on the Montesa.

After an hour, they stopped for a break and sat on the grass. He lit two cigarettes as always and gave her one. She lay on her back. 'I like you, Rupert, I like you a lot.'

'Snap, my sweet,' he said. 'Except I love you a lot.'

'Yet you've never put a hand on me once.'

'I know, my gorgeous one,' he teased her. 'But you see, I'm terribly faithful. Fell in love with Tom first time we met at Cambridge. Women – and please don't get upset – don't do the slightest thing for me.' He turned over and kissed her. 'Having said that, I adore you. I suppose you think I've got a piece missing in my personal jigsaw.'

'Oh, Rupert, my lovely Rupert, don't we all?' she said and kissed his cheek.

He rolled away and raised himself on one elbow. 'The Navajo's doing a return; bringing an old friend of mine down just for twenty-four hours. George is picking him up.'

'Who would that be?'

'Ian McNab. Used to be my company sergeant major in the Paras. He runs a gym in London. Karate, judo, aikido – all that sort of thing for those who want it.'

He paused and she said, 'And something more?'

Rupert lit another cigarette. 'Most martial arts and defence techniques generally are designed to help you defend yourself, ward the attacker off, that sort of thing. To come to terms with those techniques takes years of training. Ian McNab offers something quite different.'

'And what would that be?'

'His self-defence system is delivered with extreme prejudice. No point in using it except to kill or maim.'

'Good God!' she said.

'There we go again, you invoking the almighty.' He stood up. 'Come on, let's get going.'

Ian McNab was surprisingly small, a grey-haired man of fifty, wearing a black tracksuit and trainers, with a broken nose and a pleasant, Highland voice.

'A great pleasure, Miss Browning. I was in Glasgow on business last year and saw you do that Tennessee Williams fella's *Cat on a Hot Tin Roof* at the Citizen's Theatre. Wonderful, you were.'

Lang said, 'Plenty of judo mats in the barn, Ian.' They left the house and walked across the yard. 'The thing is, Miss Browning was attacked by a mugger last week. Shook her up badly. Luckily someone drove by, but it occurred to me that you could help her. Your special course. The seven moves.'

'Of course, Captain.' McNab shook his head. 'The terrible times we live in.'

They went into the barn and he and Lang got a number of judo mats from a pile in the corner and laid them out together. McNab turned to Grace. 'Right, miss. My system is special and it's only to be used in extreme situations.'

'I understand.'

'You see, I can show you seven things to do which will always cripple, but may also kill. You follow me?'

'I think so.'

'For example, if you extend your knuckles in the right hand – you are right-handed, I take it?

'Yes.'

'Good. If you extend a punch under the chin at the Adam's apple, then even a sixteen-stone rugby player will go down. You can also do it with stiffened fingers. The trouble is, he could choke to death. That's why I call it my special course with extreme prejudice.'

'I see.'

'There's another. The kneecap is one of the most sensitive parts of the human body. Again, let's imagine our sixteen-stone rugby player. If you raise your foot in a struggle and stamp down on his kneecap you'll dislodge it and he'll go

73

down. You won't kill him, but you'll cripple him and very probably for life.'

'I see. Extreme prejudice again.'

'That's right. No offence meant, miss, but there's then the question of your attacker's private parts.'

Grace laughed out loud. 'There always is with men, Sergeant Major.'

Lang laughed and McNab smiled. 'Too true, miss. Then there's the reverse elbow strike. Very lethal, that.'

She turned to Rupert. 'Are you an expert in all this?'

'Now do I look the physical type, darling?' he said. 'I've got phone calls to make. Give her the works for an hour, Sergeant Major. I'll see you later.'

He went out and McNab turned to Grace. 'Right you are, miss, let's get started.'

Just before midnight she came down in her dressing gown and found Lang in the drawing room, examining some faxes.

'Problems?'

'Government business, my love, particularly the Irish mess. Never goes away. Nightcap?'

'All right.' He poured two Bushmills and gave her one. 'What about the Sergeant Major?' she asked.

'Thought you very promising. He has a gym in Soho. He'd like to see you there when you can manage it.'

'Sounds good to me.'

'I'm having the Navajo take him back to Gatwick tomorrow. It will return late afternoon, bringing Tom and Yuri Belov.'

'That should be interesting.'

The wolfhound dozed in front of the fire. 'He's lovely,' she said. 'Why do you call him Danger?'

'Well, he can be pretty ruthless when roused.'

There was a portrait of a Regency buck over the fireplace.

He wore a tailcoat, light buskins and top boots. He bore an extraordinary resemblance to Lang.

'Who is that?' she asked.

'An ancestor of mine. He was a Rupert, too. He was the Earl of Drury and a great friend of the Prince Regent. The title was lost in the eighteen sixties when the male line died out. I'm descended from the female side.'

'What a shame – you could have been Earl of Drury.'

'True.'

'He looks very arrogant, and there's a restlessness to him. I sense it in you, Rupert.'

'He killed two men in pistol duels. Once faced up to the Duke of Wellington, who shot him in the shoulder.'

'You'd rather have been him than you?' she said with sudden insight.

'Yes, why not? Action, colour, excitement. I mean life's such a bore, politics a joke.'

'But what about when you were in the Army? That must have had its moments?'

'Not real soldiering, Ireland. A sordid, bloody mess. Woman poured a chamberpot full of urine over me once from a bedroom window – but enough of that.'

Rupert poured more whiskey and sat sprawled beside her, gazing into the fire. He took her hand. 'This is nice.'

'Very pleasant,' she agreed.

'As I'm not into women and you don't exactly go for men in that way, I'd say we have a perfect relationship.'

She kissed him on the cheek and snuggled close. 'I love you, Rupert Lang.'

'I know,' he said. 'Isn't it a shame?'

The following morning she was on her own on the Montesa, high above the forest, enjoying herself. Amazing how expert she had become in so short a time. She paused to have a cigarette, sitting astride the bike, and looked up at a grey sky

75

that threatened rain. There was a droning in the distance and far away through a break in the clouds she saw the Navajo.

She finished the cigarette and took off, driving quite fast, following the track, then turning across the moor, bumping over tussocks and scattering a flock of sheep. She skidded to a halt, searching for a gap in the dry-stone wall, and there was an angry shout. She turned, still astride the bike.

The man hurrying towards her wore an old tweed suit and cap and heavy boots. He looked about fifty, with a brutal unshaven face, and carried a shepherd's crook.

'And what in the hell is your game?' he demanded. 'Frightening my sheep. You've run pounds off them.'

'I'm sorry,' she said.

'Sorry, is it? You need seeing to, you do.'

He lunged with the crook, catching the front wheel. The bike toppled and went over. As she scrambled sideways her helmet came off and he paused, astonishment on his face.

'My God, a woman.' And then there was something else there. 'Now, what if I put you over my knee and give you a bloody good hiding?'

'Don't be so stupid,' she said and reached down for her helmet.

He dropped his crook and grabbed her from behind. 'You posh bitch, I'll have to teach you some manners.'

She delivered a reverse elbow strike to his mouth and as he cried out and released her swung round and drove her knee into his crutch, all exactly as Ian McNab had shown her. He lay on his back, knees up in agony, blood on his pulped mouth.

She looked down at him, conscious of a fierce exhilaration. 'Here endeth the first lesson,' she said as she replaced her helmet, then picked up the Montesa, got astride it and drove away.

Ten minutes later she drove into the garage at Lang Place, shoved the Montesa up on its stand beside the Range Rover, hung her helmet on a peg and crossed the courtyard. Lang opened the front door.

'You looked pretty dashing as you shot into the courtyard, one boot trailing. You'll be on the dirt track circuit next.'

'That sounds fun.'

'Come into the drawing room. Yuri and Tom have arrived.'

They were standing in front of the log fire in the great stone hearth. Tom Curry kissed her on both cheeks. 'You're looking very dramatic.'

'I've been having fun.'

Rupert said, 'Yuri, I believe you two have met.'

'Last year at the Soviet Embassy,' she said. 'When we did *Three Sisters* at the National.'

Belov was dressed for the country in a light brown thorn-proof suit. He looked fit and well and smiled with great charm as he took her hand and kissed it.

'I saw you three times. I now believe with great regret that Chekhov can only be played at his best by the English. Your performance as Masha was fantastic.'

'Half-English in my case,' she said, 'but my thanks for the compliment.'

'Mrs Farne has prepared lunch in the conservatory,' Rupert said. 'Do you want to change?'

'Five minutes.'

She went out. Lang opened a bottle of Bollinger and poured. 'Her performance on the firing range has been superb and Ian McNab was more than impressed with the way she took to his instruction. She's to go to his gym when she's back in town.'

'What did you tell McNab?' Belov asked.

'I said she'd had a close shave with a mugger and wanted to know how to take care of herself.'

Belov sipped some champagne. 'Amazing, this whole business of acting. The ability to be the role. As Masha she was

77

totally convincing as a Russian woman, and yet I saw her in a TV showing of that Hollywood movie she made where she shot several men quite convincingly.' He accepted a cigarette from Rupert. 'Will she join us?'

'Oh yes, I think so,' Lang said.

At that moment Grace entered the room dressed in jeans and sweater. She took the glass Lang offered her. 'Tell me, Rupert, the sheep above the forest. Are they yours?'

'That's right, why?'

'Oh, a rather unpleasant man was up there. Shabby old tweed suit, shepherd's crook. Took exception to me riding through the fields.'

'That would be Sam Lee.' Rupert wasn't smiling now. 'What happened?'

'When I stopped, he pushed the Montesa over, then he grabbed me from behind.'

'He what?' Lang's face was suddenly bone white, his eyes blazing. 'Did he harm you in any way?'

'Well, the fact is I'm afraid I harmed him,' she said. 'I tried something the Sergeant Major showed me. Reverse elbow strike to the mouth, swivel and put a knee to the crutch. When I last saw him he was in the foetal position on the ground.'

Lang laughed out loud. 'Oh, my God, that's bloody marvellous.' He shook his head. 'I'll have George deal with him. He's out.'

'No,' she said. 'He'll behave better next time. Give him a chance, Rupert.' She smiled. 'Shall we go in to lunch?'

They had cold salmon, a mixed salad and potatoes, and Lang opened another bottle of Bollinger. Rain drummed against the conservatory glass.

'Sorry about the weather,' he said. 'That's Dartmoor for you. Starts to improve from March into spring.'

'All the joys of country living,' Grace told him.

Curry saw to the coffee and Belov said, 'I saw a late-night showing on television of a Hollywood film you made, Miss Browning.'

'Grace,' she said. 'Please, and it was my only Hollywood film. I didn't like it there. They had me wear a series of incredibly short skirts and I killed rather a lot of men. It was what's known as a revenge movie in the trade.'

'Yes, in the film you killed more than efficiently,' Belov said. 'As I recall, the police nicknamed you Dark Angel.'

'My one contribution to the script. One of my great grandmothers on my father's side was Jewish. I recall the stories she told me as a child. Judaism teaches that God is the master of life and death, but he employs angels as his messengers.'

'So there was an Angel of Death?' Curry said.

'When God inflicted the ten plagues on the people of Egypt in Exodus the Jews were instructed to put blood on either side of the doorpost so the Angel of Death would pass over them. To this day that's why Passover is celebrated.'

'An interesting legend,' Belov said.

'In Hebrew the Angel of Death is Malach Ha-Mavet. In the old days the word was used to frighten children. The film people, when I suggested it, thought it too melodramatic and came up with Dark Angel.'

'Interesting,' Belov nodded. 'The revenge concept.'

'Revenge gets you nowhere. Let's stop fencing, gentlemen. We all know pretty much all there is to know about each other. If at some time I'd caught up with and killed the man who murdered my parents it wouldn't have brought them back.'

'But it might have afforded a certain satisfaction,' Rupert told her.

'True.'

'I mean, things happened in a hurry back there in Belfast, but you didn't regret shooting that swine, did you?'

79

'Not at all. In fact it rather exorcized a ghost in my machine. I sleep better now.'

There was a long pause and rain rattled the windows. Finally Belov spoke. 'Do I take it you are prepared to join us, Grace?'

'Yes, I think so, but on my terms. You and Tom have a political commitment and I understand that, but it means nothing to me.' She ran a hand over Lang's hair. 'Rupert can't take life seriously. He bores easily, likes the excitement. I relate to that more.'

'In what way?' Curry asked.

'My father's family believed they were kin to the Victorian poet, Robert Browning. There's a line in one of his poems. "Our interest's on the dangerous edge of things." I can relate to that. It's like a performance, if you like, and performance is what my life is about.'

'Exactly,' Belov said. 'But always fantasy, always except for that alley in Belfast. That was real and earnest, razor-sharp. I should imagine that afterwards on reflection it must have seemed like one of your finest performances.'

'Very perceptive, Colonel, but I have one stipulation. If I don't like the sound of something I don't do it.'

'But of course, my dear.' He smiled at the other two and raised his glass. They all followed suit. 'To us, my friends, to January 30.'

Back in London, Grace was free for most of March. She went to Ian McNab's gym three times a week and bought herself a BMW motorcycle which she used to explore parts of the city she'd never been to before. Towards the end of the month she began rehearsals for *Macbeth*. It was in the third week of rehearsals that Curry asked if they could all meet and she invited them to Cheyne Walk.

As she handed round coffee Belov said, 'I'm having problems with the KGB here in London, not that they call themselves that since the break-up of things in Russia. The latest title is Federal Service of Counter Espionage. At the moment the London Station is being run by a Major Silsev. Here's his photo.' He passed it across. 'A crook of the first water, involved with the Russian Mafia. He's into illegal trading in weapons, various currency rackets, drugs – particularly drugs.'

Grace examined the photo and passed it to Lang. 'He looks mean.'

'He is.' Belov passed her another photo. 'Frank Sharp, one of the most notorious gang bosses in the East End of London. Silsev intends to make a deal with him. If Sharp meets his terms Silsev will bring in heroin with a street value in excess of a hundred million pounds.'

'Why should you mind? I didn't think you were in the business of doing good,' Grace said.

'I take your point. In my own defence, I hate drugs, and people who trade in them disgust me, but the feud between my people of the GRU and the KGB – by whatever name they choose to call themselves, is of prime importance. The kind of money Silsev would make from this deal would give them too much power.'

'I see.'

'My sources at the Embassy tell me that Silsev and Sharp are to meet tomorrow afternoon at four o'clock at the Karl Marx Memorial in Highgate Cemetery.'

'I know where that is. I've been there.'

'It's face-to-face stuff, no one else allowed, so Sharp won't have his minders with him.'

There was a short silence. Grace Browning turned to the others. Curry's face was pale and even Rupert Lang looked grave.

'Moment of truth, my friends,' she said and turned back to Belov. 'How do you want it done?'

★

It was raining hard when the Mercedes limousine drew up by the main gates of Highgate Cemetery shortly before four o'clock on the following afternoon.

The man in the chauffeur's uniform at the wheel said, 'Sure you don't want me to come, guv?'

'No need, Bert, this guy's kosher. Too much in it, for him not to be. Give me the umbrella. I won't be long.'

He got out of the car, a large, fleshy man of fifty in a dark blue overcoat, put the umbrella up and went in through the gates. Dusk was already falling and what with the rain, the cemetery was deserted. He followed the path through a jumble of graves, monuments and marble angels. There were trees here and there and all rather overgrown. Sharp didn't mind. He'd always liked the place, had always liked cemeteries if it came to that. Up ahead was the monument with the huge head, Karl Marx.

Sharp stood looking up at it, took out a cigarette and lit it. 'Commie bastard,' he said softly.

Major Silsev stepped round from the other side. He was small, eyes close set, wore a trilby hat and raincoat and like Sharp held an umbrella.

'Ah, there you are, Mr Sharp.

'Yes, here I bleeding well am,' Sharp told him. 'Wet and cold and I don't like all this cloak and dagger stuff, so let's get on with it.'

At that moment an engine roared into life and as they turned, a motorcycle emerged from a clump of trees and came towards them, the rider wearing black helmet and leathers.

'What the hell?' Sharp cried as it skidded to a halt.

Silsev turned to run, but Grace pulled the Beretta from the front of her leather jacket and shot him in the back.

'Bastard!' Sharp shouted and his hand came out of his overcoat pocket clutching a revolver. Before he could raise it, she shot him between the eyes and he went down. Silsev was still twitching. As she moved past, she leaned over and finished him with a headshot.

A few moments later she emerged through the main gate, a dark and anonymous figure as she drove past the Mercedes where Bert sat behind the wheel reading the *Standard*.

She moved through the evening traffic of Highgate Road into Kentish Town and then to Camden, finally turning into a yard in a side street near Camden Lock. There was a large truck, the rear door open, a ramp sloping up inside. As she ran the motorcycle up and put it on its stand, Curry, behind her, closed the yard gate.

He didn't say a word, simply stood waiting while she stripped off the leathers and helmet, revealing jeans and a tee-shirt underneath. He opened a holdall bag he was carrying and offered her a nylon anorak and a baseball cap and she put them on quickly.

'Right, let's get out of here.' Curry closed the truck door and opened the gates. 'Belov's people will clear up.'

She handed him the Beretta and he slipped it in the holdall. 'Everything okay?'

'If you mean did I kill Sharp and Silsev, yes. What with Ashimov, London's not going to be a favoured KGB posting.'

'I expect not.' They were approaching a telephone kiosk. He said, 'Give me a minute.'

A few seconds later the newsdesk at *The Times* received the call claiming responsibility for the deaths of Major Ivan Silsev and Frank Sharp by January 30 as a direct response to their involvement in the drug trade.

Curry paused on the corner of Camden High Street and hailed a cab. 'You all right?' he asked.

'Never better.'

'Good. Rupert's got tickets for *Sunset Boulevard*. We're eating at Daphne's afterwards. Does that suit?'

83

'Fantastic. Just get me home. As a great writer once said, a bath and a change of clothes and I can go on forever.'

A cab slid in to the kerb and he opened the door for her.

When Grace entered the piano bar at the Dorchester it was just before seven. Giuliano the manager met her with pleasure, kissed her hand and took her down to the far corner beside the piano where Lang, Curry and Belov waited. She looked quite spectacular in a black beaded shift, black stockings and shoes.

Belov waved off a waiter and started to pour from a bottle of Cristal champagne. 'You look wonderful.'

At that moment Giuliano came up. 'The late edition of the *Standard*. I thought you might like to see it. A double shooting in Highgate by some terrorist group. Isn't it terrible? Not safe to be out these days.'

He walked away. Rupert Lang laughed; even Tom Curry was having difficulty keeping a straight face. Belov raised his glass, looked at Grace and she smiled slightly.

'What can I say after that except to you, my friends.' He toasted them.

Beirut

1994

SIX

THE LEBANON WAS A KIND of Arab Belfast, a setting for destruction unparalleled in modern world history. The country had once been the Switzerland of the Middle East, with Beirut its capital as popular with the wealthy of the world as the south of France, and yet since 1975 when serious fighting had broken out between members of the Christian Phalangist Party and the Muslim Militia, only death and destruction had followed.

In his room on the fourth floor of the Al Bustan Hotel Sean Dillon poured out a small Bushmills from the bottle he had brought with him. He'd need to conserve it. He was just adding a little mineral water when there was a knock on the door. He put down his glass and went to open it. Hannah Bernstein stood there, wearing a linen suit the colour of pale straw and tinted glasses.

'Ah, Miss Cooper,' he said.

'Mr Gaunt.'

'Come in.'

He went back to the window and picked up his drink and she joined him.

'It looks quite a place,' she said.

'Used to be the most sophisticated place in the Middle East. Nearly three million people, Christians, Muslim and Druse.'

'And what went wrong?'

'Emerging Arab fundamentalism. It was originally French, which gave it a very sophisticated base, then in seventy-five the Christians and Muslims got stuck into each other, then Palestinian refugees moved in and made things worse. After that, the Israelis, then the Syrians, then the Israelis again, but there's always that Arab fundamentalism eating away at the heart of things in the Middle East. Don't know the answer.' He raised his glass. 'Here endeth the lesson.'

'Very unhealthy,' she said. 'Poor old Dillon. You're a doer, not a philosopher. Let's remember that and get on with it.'

'I'll do my best.'

'Now, if you'll put your jacket on and come next door to my room Walid Khasan is on his way up.'

'Why didn't you say?'

He picked up a lightweight navy-blue blazer and followed her next door. Her room was exactly like his and he checked the French windows to the terrace. There was a knock at the door. When Hannah opened it, a man in his mid-forties stood there. He wore a crumpled white suit, had long black hair, a wrinkled face and olive skin.

'Good afternoon. I am Walid Khasan.' He spoke with a strong foreign accent.

'Amy Cooper,' Hannah told him, 'and this is Harry Gaunt. Do come in.'

'Please, this is not necessary,' he said as he entered and placed a briefcase on the table. 'I am very well aware of who you are, Miss Bernstein, and you, Mr Dillon.'

She closed the door and Dillon said in fluent Arabic, 'So Ferguson filled you in totally?'

'Yes, but then he usually does,' Walid Khasan replied in the same language.

'Good.' Dillon switched back to English. 'I'm afraid the Chief Inspector has no Arabic.'

'Hebrew only, I'm afraid,' Hannah said.

Walid Khasan replied at once in excellent Hebrew. 'Oh, I

88

can speak that also, but it is not to be recommended in Beirut. The Israelis are not popular here.'

'What a pity,' she said in Hebrew. 'I'll remember that, of course. We have enough problems.'

Walid Khasan opened the briefcase, took out two Walther PPK pistols with silencers and several clips of ammunition. 'I trust these will hold you. I can supply heavier artillery, Mr Dillon, if necessary, but I'll require notice.'

'You'll get it when necessary.' Dillon checked the Walther and put it in his waistband at the rear and an extra clip in his blazer pocket. Hannah put hers in her shoulder bag.

'So,' Dillon said, 'what about our friends from Belfast?'

Walid Khasan opened the French windows and sat down in a wicker chair. 'Francis Callaghan is staying here on the floor below and uses his own name. He's supposed to represent an Irish electronics firm from Cork. I've checked and the firm is genuine. They specialize in hotel contracts, security and that sort of thing.'

Hannah leaned on the rail and Dillon sat opposite him. 'And Quinn?'

'I've seen him only once and he certainly isn't staying here.'

'What happened?' Hannah asked.

'I've had Callaghan followed by people working for me. He seems to have spent his time as any tourist would. Visiting historic remains, shopping.' He smiled. 'It may surprise you, but there is still a certain normality here.'

'And he's done nothing out of the ordinary?' she asked.

'Oh, yes. One day when I was following him myself, he had lunch at a café right on the waterfront. The sort of place dock workers might use. He met Daniel Quinn there.' He smiled. 'The Brigadier supplied me with colour faxes of these men. It was definitely Quinn.'

'You're sure?' Hannah demanded.

'Oh, yes. More interesting was the fact that they were

joined by two men I am familiar with: Selim Rassi, a very important figure in the Party of God movement, and a man from the Russian Embassy called Ilya Bikov. He's supposed to be in public relations, but he's a captain in the Federal Service of Counter Espionage.'

'KGB,' Dillon said.

'Change the name, but the same smell. They went down to a dock, boarded a high-speed boat and took off. I couldn't follow so I don't know where they went. There's a lot of shipping out there.'

'So what happens now?' Hannah Bernstein asked.

Walid Khasan smiled. 'Callaghan always has a drink in the bar around six o'clock.' He checked his watch. 'Which is in about ten minutes. Shall we go?'

The lounge bar was very pleasant, with windows open to a terrace which overlooked the city and the harbour crowded with shipping. The blue waters of the Mediterranean sparkled in the fading sunshine as evening fell. There was no sign of Callaghan, but there was a sudden call to prayer from a mosque down there in the city, then another and yet another, the sounds echoing across the rooftops.

'Very pleasant,' Hannah Bernstein said. 'And yet in the middle of all this, people have to kill each other.'

'A very old-fashioned habit in this part of the world,' Walid Khasan told her.

At that moment Francis Callaghan came up the steps from the garden and sat down at a table at the other end of the terrace. Dillon, Hannah and Walid Khasan sat down at a table at their end of the terrace. When a waiter approached Walid Khasan ordered a pitcher of lemonade for all of them.

'You can't get alcohol until after seven,' he said to Dillon apologetically.

'I'll do my best to hang on,' Dillon said.

Francis Callaghan waved a waiter away and took what

looked like a diary from his pocket. He flipped through the pages, put it back into his pocket and lit a cigarette.

'He's waiting for someone,' said Hannah. 'Perhaps Quinn?'

'I doubt it,' Walid Khasan told her. 'As I told you, the only time Quinn has surfaced was at that dockside café. I think our friend Callaghan is simply filling time. He may have an appointment to see Quinn later.'

'Fine,' Dillon said. 'When he goes we follow him.' He turned to Hannah. 'You stay here and hold the fort.'

'Thanks very much,' she said indignantly.

'Don't be so sensitive. You need to make a progress report to Ferguson, don't you? That link is essential, especially if we need to move fast to get out of Beirut.'

'Yes, I suppose you're right.' She made a face. 'Damn you, Dillon. Next time round I'm going to be a man.'

Callaghan made his move about twenty minutes later, passing them on his way into the hotel.

'Here we go,' Dillon said to Hannah. 'See you later.'

Callaghan crossed the foyer, went out of the front entrance and hailed a taxi. As it took off Walid Khasan led the way across to another taxi. He pushed Dillon into the rear and scrambled in after him.

'If you lose him, Ali,' he said to the swarthy Arab behind the wheel, 'I'll have your manhood.' He leaned back and smiled at Dillon. 'One of my men.'

Charles Ferguson listened to what Hannah Bernstein had to say.

'So far so good,' he said. 'With any luck Callaghan could lead us straight to Quinn. You could be out of there in twenty-four hours.'

'I suppose so, sir.'

'We'll see. Keep me posted and watch your back, Chief Inspector.'

He put down the phone, sat there brooding for a moment, and then rang through to Simon Carter's office.

'Ferguson here,' he said. 'The Prime Minister insists I keep you informed, so here's where we are.'

It was really quite pleasant sitting under an umbrella at one of the tables of the waterside café Callaghan had led them to. Coloured lights were strung overhead, the tables were crowded, and there was a buzz of conversation.

'Plenty of booze being consumed here,' Dillon observed.

'Ah, but Beirut is a mixed society, my friend,' Walid Khasan reminded him.

Callaghan was at a table by the far rail, drinking a beer. He appeared totally unconcerned, looking over the crowd and then out into the harbour.

'And this is where he met Quinn and Bikov?' Dillon asked.

'Yes. Actually he sat at the same table.'

'Excellent. If this thing works as it should do I could be in and out like Flynn.' He waved to a waiter and ordered two lagers.

At that moment Quinn got up and crossed to the door marked Men's Room. 'Is there another way out of there?' Dillon asked.

'No, definitely not. I've been in.'

'Good.' Dillon relaxed and lit a cigarette as the waiter arrived with the lagers.

Francis Callaghan stood at the urinal, and as he adjusted his trousers and turned, the door to one of the stalls opened and a young Arab in khaki shirt and pants emerged holding a Sterling sub-machine-gun, silenced version.

'Good evening, Mr Callaghan,' he said in good English. 'I could blow your spine off with this thing and they wouldn't even hear out there in the café, but we wouldn't want that, would we?' He reached in Callaghan's right pocket and removed a Colt automatic. 'That's better. Now stand on that stool we have so thoughtfully provided and climb through the window where my colleagues are waiting to receive you.'

Callaghan did exactly as he was told. His years of involvement in the struggle of Ulster had taught him the advisability of playing it cool in a situation like this. He clambered through the window and was pulled down by two more young Arabs. There was a van backed up behind them, the door open. One of them handcuffed his hands behind him.

Callaghan said, 'Look, if it's money . . .'

He got no further. One of the men slapped him across the face. 'Shut up!' He pulled a linen bag over Callaghan's head.

He was pushed into the back of the van, the door slammed and they drove away.

After fifteen minutes with no sign of Callaghan returning, Walid Khasan got up. 'I'll check it out,' he said and eased his way through the tables to the Men's Room. He was out again in seconds.

'Don't tell me,' Dillon said. 'He's gone.'

'I'm afraid so. He must have used the window. The only other way out.'

'You think he knew he was being followed?'

'I'd be surprised. We've been very careful and I was told he didn't know you by sight.'

'That's true enough.'

'Then I think it more likely he was just being careful and taking precautions in case he was being followed.'

'So what do we do now?'

Walid Khasan frowned, considering the matter. Finally he said, 'I'll go for a run in the taxi with Ali, circle the area, see if we can spot him. You stay here in case Quinn shows up.'

'Somehow I doubt that,' Dillon told him.

'Yes, well, there's not much else that we can do, my friend. I'll see you in half an hour.'

He left and Dillon sat there waiting. A young woman was working her way through the tables. She had hair as black as night, long to her shoulders, good breasts and hips in a clinging silky dress, dark eyes and a full red mouth. She finally reached him after much lewd comment from men at the surrounding tables.

'You are tourist?' she said in English with a heavy accent.

'You could say that, me darling.'

She put a hand on his shoulder. 'You need a nice girl, then, or a bad girl? Whichever is okay by Anya. Fifty dollars American. My place is close by.'

'Oh moon of my delight, heaven is here in your presence,' Dillon told her in Arabic. 'Unfortunately business requires me to wait here for a friend.' He took a twenty-dollar bill from his wallet and handed it to her. 'This is for the pleasure of looking on you.'

She smiled her delight, tucked it down her cleavage and made off.

In London, Rupert Lang rang the bell of Yuri Belov's mews house and was admitted instantly.

'Something important?' Belov asked as he led the way into the sitting room.

'Yes, I tried to get you the other day, but they told me you were in Paris. Some very interesting developments. The Belfast thing went extremely well. In fact Grace probably saved Dillon's life.'

'I heard that January 30 had claimed responsibility for several deaths,' Belov said. 'IRA it wasn't. The Protestant factions must be furious. Dillon certainly doesn't pull any punches.'

'The whole thing was a set-up,' Lang said. 'He took care of them, of course, but there was an extra man in the shadows.

94

He'd have got Dillon in the back if Grace hadn't intervened, so we thought we might as well claim the whole lot while we were at it.'

'And what's happened now?'

'Dillon made Daley talk before killing him. It seems that Quinn is in Beirut to do a deal for a supply of plutonium. He's dealing with a man called Selim Rassi of the Party of God and a KGB captain called Bikov.'

'Bikov?' Belov shook his head. 'I don't know him, but these Party of God people are pretty ruthless.' He shook his head. 'Plutonium. All my sources indicate that the Protestant para-militaries in Ulster have reached a new mood of desperation, but plutonium brings in the threat of nuclear devices. That's a whole new dimension.'

'Yes, but see it from their point of view. Sinn Fein, which is really the same as the IRA, get three per cent of the vote in the Republic of Ireland and ten per cent in Ulster, and yet, as the product of a ruthless campaign of terrorism, they end up having achieved peace negotiations which could mean the Protestants being thrown to the wolves, the Army packing in and the threat of some sort of departure by the British Government. It could be a recipe for civil war.'

'Another Bosnia, my friend,' Belov said. 'But the threat that could be imposed if this plutonium could be used in a nuclear device would be incalculable. A whole new and terrible world.' He walked to the sideboard, poured a couple of whiskies, came back and gave one to Lang. 'Let's hope our friend Dillon has the right kind of luck.'

At that moment Francis Callaghan was standing in front of a desk in a rather gloomy room illuminated by a single light bulb. They had only just pulled the bag off his head and he was dazzled after the darkness. He was also, for the first time, beginning to feel thoroughly frightened. The young man who had kidnapped him in the toilet at the café sat behind the desk, smoking a cigarette, the Uzi machine gun in front of him. He was examining Callaghan's passport.

'You are from Cork, I see. You represent an electronics firm?'

'That's right,' Callaghan told him eagerly. 'Francis Callaghan. I'm at the Al Bustan. If you look in my wallet there's a permit from the Ministry of Supply.'

'You're a liar.' The young man nodded and someone standing behind Callaghan punched him in the kidneys so that he went down on one knee. 'You're an Irish terrorist, Protestant variety, here with Daniel Quinn to acquire a supply of plutonium from a KGB agent named Bikov and Selim Rassi of the Party of God.'

'There's been a mistake,' Callaghan said.

The young man nodded again. This time a rifle butt thudded into Callaghan's back and he went down again. The two men who had been standing behind him started to kick him in the body savagely.

'Not his face,' the young man ordered.

After a while they stopped, pulled Callaghan up and sat him in a chair. He was in considerable pain and half sobbing as he said, 'You've got the wrong man.'

'Really.' The young man leaned back and lit another cigarette. 'I don't think so, but we'll see.' He nodded to the others. 'Let's save some time. Put him in the well. I don't think he'll last long down there.'

They grabbed Callaghan by the arms, picked him up and hustled him out, along a passage, across a courtyard and into a barn. There was the round low stone wall of a well in the centre. One of the men fished a key out of his pocket and unfastened Callaghan's handcuffs. The other picked up a rope with a loop on the end and slipped it over his head and beneath his arms.

'Now, look here,' he protested.

One of them slapped him, then they ran him across the

barn and shoved him over the wall, hanging on to the rope, bracing themselves as he swung against the stonework. They lowered him quickly and after about thirty feet, he splashed into water. He had a moment of panic as he went under but it was only about four feet deep. The bottom was a thick and slimy ooze and the stench was terrible.

'Loosen the rope,' one of them called.

Callaghan did as he was told, looking up at the faces peering down at him, watching the rope going up. It was bitterly cold and he shivered and then the light went out and there was only the darkness.

Dillon leaned over the rail at the edge of the terrace, looking out at the shops in the darkness of the harbour and waiting for Walid Khasan. There had been no sign of Quinn, not that he'd really expected one. He went down some steps to a lower level where motor boats were moored. As he lit a cigarette, there was a footfall and he turned and found Anya the prostitute there.

'So here you are,' she said in Arabic.

'So it would appear,' he said. 'And the answer is still the same.'

'What a pity.' She reached in her shoulder bag, produced a Colt .32 automatic with a silencer on the end and rammed it into his side. 'No one will hear, Mr Dillon, so I suggest you do as I say.' She reached in his pocket and found the Walther. 'So, now we walk to the other end and mount the steps, all very sensibly. You follow me?'

'Oh, if needs be, I'm the most sensible man in the world, girl dear,' he told her in English.

'Good, then let's get moving.'

There were several cars parked at the top of the dock and she took him across to the other side, where the van which had transported Callaghan earlier was waiting. Two men moved out of the shadows. One of them pulled a bag over

97

his head and the other handcuffed him. They pushed him in the rear and joined him. Anya got behind the wheel and drove off.

When they took the bag off his head he was standing in the same room Callaghan had found himself in earlier and the same young man sat behind the desk. The two men stood behind Dillon and the girl went and leaned against the wall, smoking a cigarette.

'You do good work,' Dillon told her. 'I'm only sorry I didn't take you up on your offer.'

The man behind the desk said, 'My sister, Mr Dillon, so mind your mouth.'

He nodded and one of the men put a rifle butt into Dillon's back, sending him down on his knees. They lifted him up and put him in a chair.

The young man said, 'You are Sean Dillon, an ex-IRA enforcer now working for Brigadier Charles Ferguson of British Intelligence. You are staying at the Al Bustan with a good-looking lady called Amy Cooper who is really Chief Inspector Bernstein of Scotland Yard's Special Branch.' He shook his head. 'Jewish. We don't like Jews here in Beirut. They've given us a lot of trouble.'

'Well, good for them,' Dillon said.

One of the men clouted him across the side of the head and the young man said, 'My name is Omar, that is all you need to know. I'm with the Dark Wind group. You've heard of us?'

'Yes, I've heard of you.'

'I know why you are here. To find an Irish Protestant terrorist called Daniel Quinn who is here to do a deal with Selim Rassi of the Party of God and a piece of KGB slime called Ilya Bikov.'

'You've a vivid imagination.'

One of the men hit Dillon again and Omar continued,

'You were following Callaghan tonight, Quinn's right-hand man. You were a nuisance, Mr Dillon. You see, we of Dark Wind don't care for the Party of God at the best of times, but in this case, we would like the plutonium for ourselves.'

'So what's stopping you?'

'Like you, I don't know where Quinn and Selim are hanging out. However, we do have Callaghan at the bottom of the well on the other side of the courtyard. He won't like it down there, he won't like it at all, and neither will you.'

'I see,' Dillon said. 'I'm to have a bath, too?'

'You will end up dirtier than you went in, Mr Dillon. It's rather unpleasant. I don't think Callaghan will last the night. He'll talk by morning.

'You seem sure about that.'

'Oh, I am. You see, I've had a rather ingenious idea. I've nothing against you, so I'll have a message sent to Walid Khasan and the Chief Inspector offering to sell you back.'

'Now, isn't that kind of you,' Dillon said.

'Ah, but there's a catch. Once down there with Callaghan you go to work on him. I don't care how you do it, but you get him to tell us where Quinn may be found.'

'Is that all?' Dillon said.

Omar got up, came round, put a cigarette in his mouth and lit it. 'Enjoy it, Dillon – your last for some time – and be sensible. You see, if you don't get Callaghan to talk, I won't sell you back. I'll have you shot.'

Dillon smiled at Anya. 'See where an interest in good-looking women gets you? I should have listened to my Aunt Mary.'

Anya laughed out loud and Omar smiled. 'I like you, Dillon, but business is business.' He nodded to the two men. 'Take him.'

They led Dillon along the passage, across the courtyard and into the barn. They paused at the well while one of them removed his handcuffs, then slipped the loop over his head.

99

'Over you go,' he ordered.

Dillon climbed over the wall and they lowered him down into the darkness. He was aware of the water, cold and clammy, the stench. He glanced up as he slipped out of the rope and saw them peering down. They pulled up the rope.

Dillon turned, aware of the other man against the wall. 'Would you be Francis Callaghan?'

'Who in the hell are you?'

One of the men called in English, 'Have a good night,' and the light was turned out, leaving only the darkness.

Dillon said, 'I'm supposed to be Harry Gaunt working for the United Nations and staying at the Al Bustan.'

'Supposed to be.'

'I'm Sean Dillon. Does that name mean anything to you?'

'My God, I can't believe it. The big IRA gunman that turned sides and works for Brit Intelligence?'

'The same. I was following you.'

'And why would you do that?'

'I want Quinn, Francis me boy. We know all about this plutonium deal and Selim Rassi and Bikov, so don't bother to deny it.'

'Screw you,' Callaghan said.

'Have you heard from Belfast lately? Daley, Jack Mullin and four more of your lads, all dead, Francis. Six at one blow, just like the tailor in the fairy tale, only his were flies on a slice of jam and bread.'

'You're a bloody liar.'

'Sorry, old son, but it's the truth. I stiffed five of them myself.'

There was a silence for a moment, then Callaghan said, 'Jesus!'

'He can't help and neither can I. You see, they don't need me. They're going to sell me back to my people, turn the odd pound. But you – either you come up with the right answers or they'll have your balls.'

'I've got to think this out.' Callaghan sounded desperate.

'Well, you've got a long, cold night ahead of you to make a decision.' Dillon waded across the well, feeling at the wall. 'My God, this place stinks.' There was a movement in the water. 'Rats, too. All the comforts of home.'

Callaghan said, 'I hate rats.'

'Well, son, I think you'll be used to them by morning.'

Dillon found a ledge, sat down, water up to his waist, and folded his arms.

SEVEN

I<small>T WAS PERHAPS AN</small> hour later that the light came on again above. Dillon glanced up and saw Walid Khasan peering over the wall.

'Are you there, Mr Dillon?'

'Yes,' Dillon called. 'And Callaghan's with me.'

'I'm sorry, my friend, they picked me up when I returned to the café.'

'Are you joining us?'

'No. Omar, their leader, has decided he'll ransom you for one hundred thousand English pounds. I'm being released to go back to the hotel to inform Chief Inspector Bernstein. I just wanted to assure myself you were alive and well.'

'I'm alive and in the well, as you can see,' Dillon told him. 'I don't know for how long. Double pneumonia coming up, I shouldn't wonder, it's rather cold down here.'

'Try and hang on. I'll be back, and don't worry. I know this Omar. Whatever else, he's a man of his word.'

'And Callaghan?'

'Out of our hands now. Omar has made it clear. Either he comes up with the information as to Quinn's whereabouts by morning or he stays down there till he dies. Goodbye for the moment.'

The light went out and Callaghan said, 'The bastards. All right for you, Dillon.'

'There's always a choice, Francis. You can come clean and tell them what they want to know.'

'They'll kill me anyway.'

'Maybe not. Quinn's their business now, not mine, but you could still be of use to my boss, Brigadier Charles Ferguson, and you must know who he is.'

'Become an informer, you mean?'

'Absolutely. I'm sure you could tell him a great deal about all those friends of yours in the UFF and the UVF. You see, if the IRA agree to a ceasefire it's the Protestant Loyalists the British Government are going to have to worry about.'

'And so they should. We'll give them hell for selling us out.'

'Not from the bottom of a well in Beirut. Tell me where Quinn can be found and I'll see if we can do a deal with Omar. You'll be of no further use to him, but to us . . . That's a different story.'

'I'll see you in hell first.'

'Suit yourself, son. You'll be a long time dead.'

There was a swishing in the water. Callaghan said, 'Oh, Christ, the rats are back.'

Hannah Bernstein had been worried for some time. It was taking too long. She sat in her room at the Al Bustan gazing out to the bright lights of the city below.

'Damn you, Dillon, where are you?' she said softly.

Born into a wealthy upper-class Jewish family, her father a famous surgeon, her grandfather a rabbi, the best schools, then Cambridge, she had astounded everyone by joining the police, and her rise to Detective Chief Inspector in Special Branch had been meteoric. On two occasions she had shot people in the line of duty, so violence was not unknown to her, but her weakness was a rather rigid moral code that made it difficult for her to cope with the Dillon of the old days, the legendary IRA gunman. She could never see his slate as wiped clean, no matter what he was doing now on the side of right.

Having said that, the truth was she liked him too much.

The empty hotel room had begun to feel oppressive. She went downstairs to the bar, waved a waiter away and went out on the terrace. Leaning on the balustrade, she looked down over the gardens to the brightly illuminated car park. At that moment, a taxi drove up and Walid Khasan got out.

He started up the steps to the terrace and she called, 'Over here.'

He paused, glanced up, then hurried to join her. 'We've got trouble, I'm afraid,' he said. 'Serious trouble.'

Her stomach knotted. 'Tell me.'

When he was finished, she said, 'Can this Omar be trusted?'

'Oh, yes, but judge for yourself.'

Walid turned and waved to the taxi. The rear door opened and Omar got out. He paused halfway up the steps to light a cigarette, then joined them, smiling pleasantly.

'Chief Inspector, what a pleasure.'

She became very formal, very much the police officer. 'Can we rely on your good faith?'

'Absolutely. We of Dark Wind always keep our word.'

'See that you do.' She glanced at Walid Khasan. 'I'll speak to the Brigadier. Obviously you'll act as our contact in this matter.'

'Of course.'

She turned to Omar. 'We'll be in touch, then.'

'A pleasure meeting you, Chief Inspector,' he said, turned and went down the steps.

Beirut was three hours ahead of London, so it was just before eight at the Cavendish Square flat and Charles Ferguson was about to leave for dinner at the Garrick Club when the phone rang.

'Bernstein,' she said. 'Bad news, I'm afraid.'

Ferguson listened to what she had to say, then sighed. 'Oh, dear, what a bloody mess.'

'Can anything be done, sir?'

'Oh, yes, plenty of cash in the contingency fund. Anticipating the possible need to get you out in a hurry I ordered the RAF to respray one of our Lear jets in United Nations strip. That way it can land at Beirut International Airport. We'll fly via Cyprus.'

'We, sir?'

'Yes, I'd better come myself. I'll be with you tomorrow, Chief Inspector.'

'Thank God for that.'

'One thing you can do. You demand to see Dillon personally, to assure yourself he's still in one piece. You also tell this chap Omar that I want Callaghan, too. This present job's blown, of course, but he could be very useful to us – fountain of knowledge as regards the Protestant movement.'

'Right, sir.'

'Be of good heart, Chief Inspector, I'll be with you soon.'

When Walid Khasan and Hannah were led into the room, Omar stood up behind the desk. 'A pleasure to see you again, Chief Inspector, and so soon.'

'Let's make this brief.' She was as cold and formal as if charging someone at West End Central Police Station. 'Brigadier Ferguson arrives tomorrow and your terms will be met.'

'Excellent.'

'Just one thing. You give us Callaghan too.'

'That could be arranged.' He shrugged. 'Depending on his willingness to give us the information we need.'

'Right, I'll speak to Dillon now and I'll make that point clear.'

The lights came on and Dillon glanced up to see her peer down. 'You all right, Dillon?

'I've been better, girl dear, but you shouldn't be here in such bad company.'

'We'll have you out tomorrow. The Brigadier's flying in.'

'Now, isn't he the grand man?'

'Are you there, Callaghan?' she called.

'And where else would I bloody be?'

'We've struck a deal. Tell them where to find Quinn and they'll let you leave with us.'

'And then what?'

'You'll fly back to London and sing your heart out.'

'Screw you.'

'Then they'll leave you down there to rot. Your choice.' She leaned over further. 'Bye for now, Dillon, see you soon.'

The lights went out and Callaghan said, 'Lousy, stinking bitch.'

'Oh, she can be all of that.' Dillon laughed. 'But I like her.'

It was unbelievably cold down there. After a few hours Dillon found that he'd somehow got used to the stench, but not the cold – that was mind-numbing. Sitting on the ledge, leaning back, he actually dozed off and came awake in a split second to hear Callaghan.

'Get away from me, damn you!'

There was a splash in the water and Dillon felt a rat scurry across his arm. 'Are you all right, Francis?'

'No, I'm bloody well not.'

Dillon checked his watch, a Rolex Divers, the face phosphorescent. 'Seven-thirty. Break of a new day. They'll be starting to serve a traditional English breakfast at the Al Bustan. Fried eggs, bacon, sausage, toast and marmalade, nice hot pot of tea or coffee.'

'Shut your mouth,' Callaghan said.

'I can dream, can't I? That's exactly what I'm going to have when the Brigadier arrives and gets me out of here. Nice long hot shower to get rid of the stink, clean clothes and then that breakfast. Doesn't matter what time of day it is, I want the breakfast.'

'Screw you, Dillon, I know what you're trying to do.'

'I'm not trying to do anything, Francis. Our operation to catch Quinn is blown. It's Dark Wind's business now. We're out. You could have been useful back in London, but if you prefer to be a hero of the glorious revolution – if that's how you see yourself – well, that's your problem.'

'Shut up, will you? Just shut up!'

Beirut International Airport was served only by the national carrier MEA, but when Ferguson arrived at nine o'clock in the morning after a night flight via Cyprus, the Lear jet in its United Nations colours was accepted without question as were the papers the forgery department at the Ministry of Defence in London had supplied at such short notice. Hannah Bernstein and Walid Khasan met him as he came through into the terminal. He wore a linen suit, Panama hat and Guards tie, and carried his malacca cane. He handed his overnight bag to Walid Khasan and kissed Hannah on the cheek.

'You're looking agitated, my dear.'

'I've a right to be.'

'Not at all.' He nodded to Walid Khasan. 'It's been a long time.'

They went out to the yellow taxi, where Walid's man, Ali, sat behind the wheel. Walid sat in the front, and Ferguson and Hannah in the rear.

'Shall we go straight there?' Walid asked.

'Good God, no,' Ferguson said. 'I need a shower and some breakfast. Do this fellow Omar good to wait.'

'And what about Dillon, sir?' Hannah demanded.

'And since when did you get worked up about his welfare, Chief Inspector? He'll survive.' He opened his briefcase and took out some coloured faxes which he passed to Walid Khasan. 'Is this them?'

Walid nodded. 'That's Selim Rassi and the other is the Russian, Bikov.'

'Good.' Ferguson took them back and put them in the briefcase.

Hannah Bernstein said, 'But does that matter, sir? I don't understand.'

'You will, my dear,' Ferguson told her. 'You will.'

It was still very dark down there in spite of the fact that it was eleven o'clock in the morning when Dillon checked his watch. He hadn't heard a sound from Callaghan for a while.

'Are you still with us, Francis?'

There was a splashing sound, then Callaghan said warily, 'Only just.' He sounded terrible. 'I can't take much more, Dillon.'

At that moment the light was turned on up above and Omar leaned over. 'Your friends are here, Mr Dillon. Our business has been concluded satisfactorily so we'll bring you up now. We'll drop the rope.'

'What about Callaghan?'

'Has he spoken?'

'No.'

'Then he stays. Here comes the rope now.'

As it dropped down Callaghan surged through the water and grabbed at Dillon. 'Don't leave me. I've had enough, Dillon. Can't take any more, not on my own.'

'Steady, son.' Dillon put one arm around him and reached for the rope. 'Just tell me about Quinn.'

'He's on a freighter called *Alexandrine*, Algerian registration. It's anchored about a mile out of the harbour. There was a meeting arranged on board for seven o'clock tonight with Selim Rassi and Bikov. The Russian's delivering the plutonium then.'

'The truth, is it?' Dillon said. 'If you're lying these lads up above will skin you.'

'I swear it.' Callaghan sounded desperate. 'Just get me out, Dillon. Take me to London with you. I've had enough.'

'Sensible lad.' Dillon pulled the loop over him and under his armpits. 'Haul away,' he called.

He waited as Callaghan rose above him and was pulled over the edge of the well. The rope came down again. Dillon pulled it over his head.

'Here we go.'

He went up quickly, pushing his feet against the side, and hands reached to pull him over the round wall. They were all there – Omar and his two men, Anya, Walid Khasan, Hannah, Ferguson, and Callaghan draped in a blanket.

'Good God, Dillon, you stink like a sewer,' Ferguson said.

'I think it *was* a sewer,' Dillon told him.

Hannah passed him a blanket, concern on her face. 'You look terrible.'

'So, our friend here decided to speak up, did he?' Ferguson said.

'Freighter called the *Alexandrine* about a mile out of the harbour. Algerian flag. Quinn's out there now. There's a meeting with Rassi and Bikov at seven when the plutonium passes over.'

Ferguson smiled fiercely. 'Excellent. Everything comes to he who waits.' He turned to Walid Khasan. 'Don't you agree, Major?'

'I certainly do.' Khasan's English had lost its accent.

'Major?' Hannah Bernstein said, looking bewildered.

'Yes, allow me to introduce Major Gideon Cohen of Mossad.'

'Israeli Intelligence?' she said. 'You didn't tell me.'

'What's more to the point, he didn't tell me,' Dillon chipped in.

'Yes, well, I didn't want to spoil your performance, dear boy. I mean, we all know what a brilliant actor you were at RADA.'

'And still am, you old bastard.'

'Yes, well, I thought the real thing would give you an edge and I knew you would cope. You always do, Dillon.'

'And what about me, Brigadier?' Hannah demanded. 'You didn't trust me, that's what it came down to.'

'Not at all. Thought you'd give a better performance if you thought it was for real, just like Dillon.'

They were all laughing and Omar lit a cigarette and put it in Dillon's mouth. 'Captain Moshe Levy.'

'All Mossad?' Dillon asked.

'I'm afraid so.'

'Even Anya?'

She laughed. 'And still Anya. Lieutenant Anya Shamir.'

'You're mad, the lot of you,' Dillon said. 'Operating here in Beirut like this. Israelis. They'd hang you in the market place.'

'Oh, we manage,' Gideon Cohen said.

'Will somebody tell me what's going on here?' Francis Callaghan asked and turned to Dillon. 'This whole thing was a fucking set-up, is that what they're saying?'

'So it would appear, Francis.'

'You rotten, lousy bunch of bowsers.' Callaghan jumped up, the blanket slipping down to reveal the filth that covered his clothes. He was almost in tears.

Ferguson said, 'Don't be a silly boy. You've really done rather well. You'll fly back to London and answer every question the Chief Inspector here asks you.'

'And what if I tell her to stuff it?'

'Ah, well, in that event you'll just have to stand trial at the Old Bailey as a participant in numerous bombings and murders. Plenty unsolved on the files that we can hang on you. I'd say you could draw about four life sentences.'

Callaghan slumped in the chair, mouth open, staring at Ferguson. It was Dillon who said with surprising gentleness, 'It's coming to an end, Francis, twenty-five years of slaughter.

Be sensible and help that end to come about. You do what the Brigadier wants and you won't end up in a cell for the rest of your life.'

Callaghan nodded, looking dazed. 'But I should have met Daniel last night. How do you know how he's reacting to my disappearance? Maybe he's changed the meet.'

'Leave that to us, boy.' Ferguson nodded to Moshe Levy and he and his two men lifted Callaghan up and Anya followed.

'Now what?' Dillon demanded.

'Well, I think it would be useful if Major Cohen arranged for a little reconnaissance, just to check that the *Alexandrine* is still at anchor out there. Once we know that position we'll decide on what to do tonight.'

'I'll go out myself in a speedboat,' Cohen told him and wrinkled his nose. 'You really do stink, Dillon.'

'You realize there were rats down there?' Dillon said 'One bite and you could get Weil's disease. I mean, forty per cent of people who get that die.'

'Not you, Dillon,' Hannah Bernstein said. 'You've so much Bushmills Irish Whiskey in your blood it's the rat who would die. Now for God's sake let's get you back to the Al Bustan and a bath.'

Dillon stood in a hot shower for a solid thirty minutes, lathering his body with showergel, shampooing his hair several times. Finally, he turned the bath taps on and padded to his suite to find the ice box. There was a half-bottle of Bollinger champagne inside. He opened it, found a glass, went and climbed into the bath and just lay there, stewing in the hot water and savouring the ice-cold champagne.

After a while, the wall phone sounded and he picked it up. 'Dillon.'

'It's me,' Hannah said. 'Are you decent?'

'How dare you suggest such a terrible thing.'

'Very funny. Major Cohen's turned up. The Brigadier's meeting him on the terrace. He wants both of us there.'

'Ten minutes,' Dillon said. 'I'll see you down there.' He replaced the phone, finished the champagne, climbed out of the bath and reached for a towel.

The terrace was bright in the afternoon sunshine, the awnings billowing in the breeze. When Dillon arrived, Ferguson, Hannah and Cohen were sitting at a table under an umbrella by the balustrade.

'Well, I must say you smell better,' Ferguson observed.

'I'll ignore that.' Dillon turned to Cohen. 'All right, Major, what's the situation?'

'The *Alexandrine* is there all right. There are quite a few ocean-going ships at anchor that far out so it was easy to have a run round in a speedboat and check the situation.'

'Anything unusual?'

'Definitely. Security lights rigged all the way round the entire ship. I'd say it's going to be very difficult to get anywhere near in darkness and it will be dark at seven.'

'Look, what if we forget about the *Alexandrine*?' Hannah suggested. 'What if we concentrate on intercepting Bikov and Rassi before they actually get out there?'

'Not possible,' Cohen said. He took a map from his pocket and unfolded it. 'This is Beirut. Now, out there is the *Alexandrine* and here,' he tapped a finger, 'here are three yacht basins and two areas of high density for small craft. If Quinn has been alerted to Callaghan's disappearance, the last thing he will do is take a speedboat from the area I first saw them.'

There was silence. Hannah spoke again. 'Then what do we do? If the ship is protected by security lights, we couldn't make an approach.'

'Oh, yes we could,' Ferguson said. 'We could go in underwater.'

Dillon groaned. 'You mean I could.'

'He's really too modest, Major,' Ferguson said. 'He actually blew up some PLO boats the other year in this very harbour and on behalf of your people.'

'Yes, I'm very well aware of that fact,' Cohen said. 'I've studied the file.' He smiled at the Irishman. 'I'll be honest, Dillon, none of my people are underwater specialists. You'd be on your own.'

'Jesus!' Dillon said. 'Tell me something new.'

'I can get you anything you want as regards Scuba equipment.'

'How kind,' Dillon said. 'I'll call again. Could you also get me a little Semtex and a few timer pencils?'

'Yes, that would be no problem.'

'What on earth is this, Dillon?' Ferguson put in. 'Semtex? We don't need to blow the damn ship up.'

'Maybe we do,' Dillon said. 'Maybe we do.' He turned to Cohen. 'Now, let's see how we're going to do this.'

It was already dark by six-fifteen when Ferguson, Dillon and Hannah Bernstein, on a small private dock next to a yachting marina, watched Cohen and Moshe Levy check the diving equipment. There were two air tanks, an inflatable jacket, a pair of nylon fins, an underwater torch and a dive bag.

Dillon was already wearing a black nylon diving suit and cowl. He opened the dive bag and took out a Browning Hi-Power. There was a Carswell silencer which he screwed on the end and a twenty-round clip.

'You're going to war again,' Hannah said.

'That's right.' He took a block of Semtex from the bag and two pencil timers. 'Three minutes?' he asked Cohen.

'Yes,' the Major said. 'That's what you asked for and that's what I've done, but I think you're crazy.'

'I usually am.'

'You're sure you'll recognize them?' Hannah demanded.

'Jesus, girl, I saw those fax pictures the Brigadier brought, didn't I?'

Ferguson, who had been a silent observer, said, 'Let him get on with it, Chief Inspector.'

'And save the free world?' Dillon laughed. 'Isn't it interesting that it's always sods like me that have to do it, Brigadier?' He turned to Cohen, who had finished loading the large inflatable that was tied to the dock. 'You and me, Major,' Dillon said and climbed down.

Levy untied the line securing them to the dock, and at that moment, Hannah stepped down.

'Chief Inspector,' Ferguson said. 'What are you doing?'

'I'm going along for the ride, sir, just for once. I'm tired of being a bystander.'

Dillon laughed out loud and she nodded to Cohen. He started the twin outboard motors and they slipped away from the dock into the darkness.

All the security lights were on view as they coasted in towards the *Alexandrine*. Cohen cut the engines about a hundred yards out and they came to a halt and just floated, virtually motionless. The Israeli produced a night sight and had a look towards the general harbour.

'Something coming. A motorboat.'

It appeared from the shadows into the pool of light surrounding the *Alexandrine* and coasted in to the ship's ladder. Two men clambered over and started climbing up.

'That's them, Bikov and Rassi.' He passed the sight to Dillon. 'See for yourself.'

Dillon had only seconds to catch them before they reached the deck. He nodded. 'Looks like them to me. Let's do it.'

He passed the sight to Cohen, went and put on a weight belt, then clamped a tank to his inflatable and pulled it on, fastening the velcro tabs across his chest. He hooked the diving bag at his waist. He took out the Hi-Power, and slipped the weapon inside his jacket.

'I don't like it, this diving,' Hannah whispered. 'It's not natural.'

'The only danger is from going deep,' he said. 'The air we breathe is part oxygen and part nitrogen. The deeper I go the more nitrogen is absorbed and that's when the trouble starts, only I'm not going deep. I'll cross to the *Alexandrine* at fifteen or twenty feet. No sweat.' He pulled on his mask. 'Do you still love me?'

'Go to hell, Dillon!' she said.

'I've been doing that for a long time now, dear girl,' he said and fell back into the water.

Dillon's approach took only a few moments. He surfaced by the platform at the bottom of the steel stairway at the side of the ship. He eased out of the inflatable and tank and clipped them to the rail beside the platform, then clambered up on to the platform. He opened his jacket and took out the Browning and cocked it. At that very moment, an Arab seaman holding an AK47 appeared at the top of the stairs and started down. He saw Dillon and tried to bring the gun to bear, but Dillon shot him instantly, the silenced weapon making a dull thud as it hit the Arab in the chest and knocked him over the rail into the water.

Dillon started up the stairway and a voice called in Arabic, 'Achmed, where are you?'

Dillon paused. Another Arab appeared, also armed with an AK47. He stood there quite unconcerned and Dillon took careful aim and shot him in the head. The man dropped his rifle, and went over the rail into the water.

A hundred yards away in the darkness Hannah Bernstein, looking through the night sight, shuddered. 'My God, there were guards, two of them.'

'What did he do?' Cohen asked.

'He shot them both.'

'Well, he would, wouldn't he?' and he took the night sight from her gently.

Dillon moved along the deck, keeping to the shadows. He heard laughter, peered through a porthole and found half-a-dozen sailors playing cards, smoking and drinking.

'And merciful Allah wouldn't be too pleased about that,' he said softly and moved on.

He came to some sort of salon, glanced in through a square window and found Selim Rassi and Daniel Quinn sitting on either side of a table. There was a small briefcase between them. There was no sign of the Russian.

Dillon opened the salon door and stepped inside. Quinn had his back to him but the Arab saw him at once and reached inside his jacket. Dillon shot him twice in the heart, sending him backwards in his chair.

Quinn turned, his own chair going over, and Dillon said, 'Easy, Danny boy, easy.'

'Who in the hell are you?' Quinn demanded.

'Oh, we go back a long way, you and me – Derry in the old days. Sean Dillon, Danny, your worst nightmare.'

'Dillon.' Quinn's face was pale. 'You fucking bastard. Working for the Brits now.'

'But I thought that was your side, Danny? Make your mind up. Now, open the case.'

'You go to hell.'

Dillon's hand came up, he fired and part of Quinn's right ear disintegrated. He lurched against the table, a hand to his ear.

'Open it!' Dillon snapped.

Quinn unclipped the briefcase. Inside were two objects resembling thermos flasks. Dillon picked one up and slipped it into his dive bag. He did the same with the other.

'What have I got here?'

'Plutonium 239. Three hundred grammes.'

'That could take out half of Dublin.'

'For God's sake, Dillon, you're not with the IRA any more. We can show the fucking Fenians we mean business.'

'It's finished, Danny,' Dillon said. 'Peace is coming whether you like it or not. We've got Callaghan. He'll sing like a bird. I killed Daley in Belfast and five of your foot soldiers. You're finished, me ould son.'

The door opened behind him. He turned, dropping to one knee, and found Bikov there. Dillon fired twice, knocking him out to the deck. Behind him, Quinn dropped behind the desk, drew a pistol and fired, at the same time shouting at the top of his voice.

Dillon went out, crouching low in time to catch the seamen emerging on to the deck further along. Several of them were armed and when they saw him they fired.

He darted to the other side of the ship, paused beside the engine room and took out the Semtex block. He activated both three-minute timers, raised the engine room hatch and dropped them in, then he went up a ladder to the top deck.

Cohen had been watching through the night sight. As gunfire cracked, Hannah said, 'What is it?'

'He's in trouble.' Cohen dropped the night sight, picked up an Uzi, cocked it and gave it to her. 'I hope you can pull a trigger, because we're going in to get him.'

As the first seaman emerged at the top of the ladder behind him, Dillon turned and fired twice, knocking him down, then he vaulted over the stern rail into the water. As he surfaced the inflatable surged forward, Cohen at the tiller, Hannah Bernstein spraying the deck above with the Uzi.

'Hang on!' Cohen cried and threw a line.

They sped away into the darkness, the odd angry shot

117

pursuing them, and finally slowed. Cohen leaned over. 'Did you get it?'

'Oh, yes, it's here in the dive bag.'

Cohen gave him a hand on board and at that moment, the *Alexandrine* blew up in a great eruption of orange flames, the sound echoing towards the land.

'Oh, my God!' Hannah Bernstein said.

'They must have had trouble in the engine room.' Dillon shook his head. 'And the Sons of Ulster are going to need a new leader. Just shows you can't depend on anything in this wicked old life.'

It was exactly two hours later that the Lear lifted off the runway at Beirut International Airport and started a steady climb to thirty thousand feet. Callaghan, dressed in slacks and a polo neck sweater, sat by himself looking decidedly unhappy. Ferguson, Hannah Bernstein and Dillon were grouped together.

'You did well, Chief Inspector,' the Brigadier told her.

'Better than well,' Dillon said. 'When Cohen came in to get me, she stood up in that boat and gave us covering fire with an Uzi. Annie Oakley come back to haunt us. Time you made her Superintendent, Brigadier.'

'Out of my hands. It's a Scotland Yard matter.'

'And you with no influence,' Dillon mocked.

'And what about Dillon, sir?' Hannah demanded. 'If anyone did well it was he.'

'Yes, well, I had every confidence in him, as usual, which was why I brought this.' Ferguson opened the small ice box in one of the cupboards and produced a bottle of Krug. 'You open it, dear boy.'

'You old sod,' Dillon said and eased off the cork while Hannah got out the glasses. He turned to Callaghan. 'Will you join us in a glass, Francis?'

'Go stuff yourselves, the lot of you,' Callaghan said.

London

1994

EIGHT

T HE PRIME MINISTER at the debriefing the following morning was absolutely delighted. 'So Dillon's done it again.' He
turned to Carter. 'I know you don't like him, but you must
admit he gets results.'

'Yes, the little swine manages that all right.'

'Oh, come on, Simon,' Rupert Lang told him. 'It's results
that count. The Protestant terrorist movements have been
dealt a crippling blow. Ferguson's unit has not only foiled the
worst bomb threat possible, a threat that would have added
an entirely new dimension to the Irish problem, they've also
got rid of one of the most dangerous leaders there was.'

'And that is of crucial importance,' the Prime Minister told
them. 'President Clinton is giving us all his support in an
effort to produce a final and lasting peace in Ireland. Senator
Edward Kennedy has brought his considerable influence to
bear in Congress and several other prominent Irish-Americans, such as Senator Patrick Keogh and former Congressman
Bruce Morrison, have been working behind the scenes for
months to persuade the IRA to come to the peace table.'

'I'll believe it when it happens,' Carter snorted. 'I mean,
how can we deal with people who've bombed the hell out of
us for twenty-five years?'

'We dealt with Kenyatta in Kenya after the Mau Mau
rebellion and gave them independence,' Ferguson told him.
'Same thing in Cyprus with Archbishop Makarios.'

'I think Ferguson's right,' Rupert Lang said. 'We have to travel hopefully.'

'Quite right,' the Prime Minister said. 'Look, gentlemen, I'm the last person to look favourably on the IRA. I don't forget the Brighton Bombing when they almost got the entire Government, but twenty-five years is long enough. The chance for peace is overwhelming and we must seize it, but it does mean keeping the lid on the Protestant hard men. It's the most volatile of situations. Let me put it this way. I don't want us on the very brink of peace to see it all destroyed by the wrong kind of incident.'

'I think we're all agreed on that,' Ferguson told him.

'Now, I intend a flying visit to Washington quite soon to see President Clinton. The Irish Prime Minister, Mr Reynolds, will be joining us. This is all very hush-hush and you gentlemen will respect my confidence.'

'Of course, Prime Minister,' Carter said and they all nodded.

'One other matter. You may have heard of Mr Liam Bell?'

'I know him,' Rupert Lang said. 'Met him in Washington when he was a Senator before he gave up politics and became president of some huge electronics firm.'

'He's also Irish-American and was much involved with fund-raising for the IRA through NORAID, the Northern Ireland Aid Committee,' Carter added.

'Yes, well, he's seen the error of his ways there. He's genuinely committed himself to achieving peace. He's coming over on a fact-finding mission on behalf of President Clinton on Thursday. He'll spend one night in London at his house in Vance Square, then proceed to Belfast. He'll be coming in by private jet.'

'Do you want us to look after him, Prime Minister?' Carter asked.

'No publicity, that's essential. As it happens there's a Conservative Party fund raiser on Thursday night at the Dorchester. Six o'clock for drinks, you know the sort of thing? I'll have to show my face and I've seen that Mr Bell has an invitation so that I can have a private word with him.' He turned to Ferguson. 'I'd like you to keep an eye out for him, Brigadier.'

'Of course, Prime Minister.'

John Major stood up. 'Hard times, gentlemen, dangerous times.' He smiled. 'But we shall come through. We must.'

Rupert Lang and Yuri Belov had lunch in the pub opposite Kensington Gardens – Shepherd's Pie washed down with lager.

'So civilized, London,' Belov said. 'You English are unique. The French say you can't cook, but your pub grub is wonderful.'

'They've never forgiven us for Waterloo,' Lang said.

Belov sat back. 'Ferguson and Dillon are a rare combination.'

'You can say that again and this Bernstein girl is pretty hot stuff, too.'

Belov nodded. 'So where do we stand? The Sons of Ulster destroyed, Daniel Quinn eliminated, the plutonium threat taken care of . . .'

'And Francis Callaghan singing like a bird.' Lang smiled. 'So where does that leave us?'

'With the prospect of peace looming up in Ireland and that doesn't suit.'

'I see. You mean you and your people would prefer another Bosnia? A civil war?'

'I've told you before, Rupert, out of chaos comes order.'

'And the kind of Ireland you'd like to see based on sound Marxist principles?'

'Something like that, but the most important factor in the equation will be how well the Protestants react to the peace proposals.'

123

'I think there's a fair chance they might react violently,' Lang said.

'It's essential,' Belov told him. 'To provoke not so much the IRA, but the Catholics.'

'Yes, I see the logic in that, so what are you thinking of?'

'That perhaps we should do it for them. After all, January 30 have hit the IRA before this.'

'And the Prods.'

'It doesn't matter. It's consequences that are important. For example, this Irish-American, Liam Bell, here on behalf of Clinton. What if something unpleasant happened while he was here in London?'

'There'd be hell to pay.'

'Exactly. I mean, never mind President Clinton – I don't think the great American public would be pleased.'

'So where is this leading to?'

'What's Grace doing at the moment?'

'A Noël Coward thing, *Private Lives*, at the King's Head. That's a pub theatre. You know the sort of thing – fringe.'

'What time does she go on stage?'

'Eight-fifteen. I went last night.'

'Excellent. Speak to her and Tom. Get them invitations for this affair at the Dorchester on Thursday. Let's see what we can come up with.'

When Dillon called at Ferguson's office at the Ministry of Defence just after lunch on Thursday, the Brigadier was busy, but Hannah came to the outer office to greet him. Dillon wore a bomber jacket, navy-blue sweater and jeans.

'How is he?' he said. 'Your message on my answer machine said urgent.'

'It is. He'll speak to you in a moment.'

Dillon lit a cigarette and she sat down at her desk, her tan wrapover skirt opening.

'I love that fashion,' he said. 'Lets a fella see what grand legs you've got.'

'Well, get used to it,' she said, 'because that's all you're going to see.'

'The hard woman, you are. Have we got far with Francis Callaghan?'

'Oh, yes, he's behaved himself. The trouble is most of his hard-core information concerns the Sons of Ulster, so it's out of date. The other stuff concerning the UVF, the UFF and the Red Hand of Ulster is very generalized. He's not told us much that we didn't know.'

'What about January 30?'

She shook her head. 'He seems as much in the dark as the rest of us.'

'Do you believe him?'

'Our interrogation team do and they haven't left it to chance. They've used a pretty advanced lie detector test and it certainly shows he was telling the truth.'

'Another dead end there, then.' He walked to the window. 'Strange, that.'

'Oh, I don't know. It could simply indicate a terrorist group operating very privately on a cell system.'

'Good sound Marxist principles, that.'

She frowned. 'That's an interesting point. You could be right.'

The buzzer sounded. She got up and Dillon followed her into Ferguson's office, where they found him seated at his desk.

'Ah, there you are so we can get on,' he said as if Dillon had kept him waiting.

''Tis sorry I am,' Dillon said doing his stage Irishman. 'Ten miles I've walked from the Castledown Bridge in my bare feet, my boots tied round my neck to save the leather, but an honour it is to serve a grand Englishman like yourself. In what way may I be of service?'

'There are times, Dillon, when I think you're quite mad, but never mind that now. I see you're dressed in your usual careless way. Well, it won't do. Decent suit, collar and tie and be at the Dorchester ballroom for six.' He pushed an engraved card across his desk. 'That gets you in. You as well, Chief Inspector. I'll meet you there. I want you both armed, by the way.'

It was Hannah who said, 'Do we get to know why, sir?'

'Of course. As you can see from the card, fund raiser for the Conservative Party. The Prime Minister will be looking in. There will be one unexpected guest.'

'And who would that be, sir?'

He told them about Liam Bell. When he was finished he said, 'He'll just be a face in the crowd. Highly unlikely anyone would recognize him.' He pushed a photo across. 'There he is. No press release. He'll arrive at six-fifteen. I'll greet him when he comes in and take him to a private room where he and the PM will have a little chat. He has a house in Vance Square. I presume he'll return there afterwards. He has an onward journey by private jet in the morning at seven o'clock from Gatwick so he's hardly likely to go out on the town.'

'And what would you like us to do, sir?'

'Keep an eye on him, that's all.'

'Fine, sir,' Hannah said. 'We'll see you there, then.'

She and Dillon went out and Ferguson opened a file and started to go through some papers.

Dillon arrived at the Park Lane entrance to the Dorchester at ten minutes to six. There was quite a crowd pressing to get in and he pushed his way through, taking off his navy blue Burberry trenchcoat to reveal a rather smart grey flannel suit by Yves St Laurent, with blue silk shirt and dark-blue tie. He saw Hannah Bernstein standing beside the uniformed security guards and she waved.

'Here, give me your coat. I'll put it with mine. Don't use the cloakroom. It would take an hour to get it back.' She turned to the head security guard. 'He's with me. Ministry of Defence.'

Dillon produced his ID card and the man nodded. 'That's fine, sir.'

They moved towards the entrance to the ballroom and found Ferguson standing talking to Rupert Lang.

'Ah, there you are,' Ferguson said and turned to Lang. 'Chief Inspector Hannah Bernstein and Sean Dillon. This is Rupert Lang, an Under-Secretary of State at the Northern Ireland Office.'

'A pleasure, Chief Inspector.' Lang took in her black silk trouser suit with obvious approval. 'Mr Dillon.' He didn't hold out his hand. 'Your fame precedes you.'

'What you really mean is ill-fame,' Dillon said cheerfully.

'For God's sake, Dillon, I can't take you anywhere,' Ferguson said. 'Clear off and get yourself a drink while the going's good and be back here in fifteen minutes.'

Dillon and Hannah pushed through the crowd to the champagne bar. 'Not for me,' she said.

'Good God, girl, is it the Sabbath or something?' He reached for one of the glasses of champagne and drank it down. 'Of course, I was forgetting. You only drink kosher wine.'

'I shall kick you very hard if you don't behave yourself,' she told him.

At that moment there was a flurry of movement at the entrance and they turned to see the Prime Minister enter, followed by several members of the Cabinet. The crowd parted and started to applaud. He smiled his acknowledgement and waved.

'The great and the good and the not so good,' Dillon said. 'They're all here.'

He turned to reach for another glass of champagne and saw Grace Browning and Tom Curry at the other end of the bar.

'Jesus!' he said, 'Would you look who's here?'

'Who?' Hannah asked.

'Grace Browning and that professor fella from the Europa. I told you I spoke to her after you'd gone to bed. I'll have a word with her.'

'No you will not. It's just on six-fifteen. We're needed,' and she turned and moved towards the entrance.

As they arrived, Ferguson was greeting Liam Bell, a tall, grey-haired man with a fleshy face who seemed to smile easily.

'That's real kind of you, Brigadier,' he was saying as Ferguson took his coat.

Ferguson passed the coat to Dillon. 'Sean Dillon, who is on my staff.'

'A good Irish name.' Liam Bell held out his hand and Dillon warmed to him.

'And Detective Chief Inspector Hannah Bernstein.'

Bell smiled. 'I've always approved of women police officers, but never more than now.'

Before she could reply Ferguson said, 'The Prime Minister is waiting. I'll take you to him.' He nodded to Dillon and Hannah. 'Be available.'

They moved off through the crowd. Dillon said, 'Did you come in your car?'

'Yes, I have priority parking right outside on the kerb.'

'See what having great legs gets you?'

'You offensive little jerk.' She punched him in the side.

'Only some of the time. Now let's one of us have another drink.'

Grace Browning stood at the bar with Tom Curry and sipped a glass of Perrier.

'You're sure you don't want a glass of champagne?' he asked.

'Don't be silly, Tom, I have to perform, don't I? What about transport?'

'A black cab just for us, with one of Yuri's boys at the wheel. He knows what we look like. He'll be straight across the road the moment we appear.'

'That seems all right.'

An arm went about her shoulder and Rupert Lang kissed her hair. 'You're looking rather delicious.'

'Rupert darling.' She kissed him on the mouth.

'Stop trying to make Tom jealous,' he said. 'Bell has just arrived and Ferguson's taken him to see the PM in a side room. You know what he looks like.'

'Of course I do. I've been shown enough pictures.'

Yuri Belov moved out of the crowd, urbane and charming, a glass of champagne in one hand.

'Hello, Colonel, good to see you,' Rupert Lang said.

'Mr Lang – Professor.' Belov took Grace's hand and kissed it. 'Miss Browning, you look as charming as ever. You're looking forward to your performance this evening?'

'Of course.'

Rupert said softly, 'By the way, Ferguson has Sean Dillon here and the Bernstein woman. Just your type, Tom, she went to Cambridge, too.' He kissed Grace again. 'See you later.'

'After the show at my place.'

He walked one way and Belov another.

Dillon, who had observed the whole scene, said to Hannah, 'I'll be back,' and pushed through the crowd.

'Miss Browning.' He gave her his best smile. 'You won't remember me.'

'But I do,' she said. 'The Europa in Belfast. You'd been to see my show and were very charming about it.'

'You were wonderful.'

'You remember Professor Curry?'

'Of course.' Dillon nodded.

'But you didn't tell us your name.'

129

'Dillon – Sean Dillon.'

'And you were at RADA?'

'A long time ago. I worked at the National briefly. Played Lyngstrand in *Lady from the Sea.*'

'One of my most favourite plays. But I've never heard of you?'

'Oh, I gave it all up a long time ago.'

'Ah, I see, you found something better?'

'No, you might say the theatre of life called. Are you working at the moment?'

'I'm doing *Private Lives* at the King's Head.'

'Not a bad play,' Dillon said. 'He had a way with words, old Noël.'

At that moment he was tapped on the shoulder and turned to find Hannah Bernstein there. 'Sorry to interrupt, but our friend's ready to go.'

Dillon smiled, took Grace Browning's hand and kissed it. 'I'll try to get in to see the show. I'd hate to miss it.'

Curry said, 'Actually, we'd better make a move, too. Grace hasn't a lot of time. Good night.' He led her away through the crowd.

'Come on, Dillon,' Hannah said and pulled on his arm.

As Dillon and Hannah reached the foyer Ferguson led Liam Bell through the crowd. 'I hope everything went well,' the Brigadier said.

'Fine, just fine. The Prime Minister was most helpful. I hope things are as constructive in Belfast and Dublin, but you must excuse me now. I'm kind of jet-lagged and I've an early start. I'll get a cab.'

'Good God, no,' Ferguson said. 'My Daimler's outside. My chauffeur can run you home. It's Vance Square, isn't it? Islington?'

'That's right. I have this rather nice old house on the other side of the churchyard. Used to be the minister's.'

'Good, we'll take care of that.' As Bell walked to the door Ferguson dropped back slightly. 'Follow him, Chief Inspector, just to make sure, and you, Dillon.'

'Right, sir,' she said.

Ferguson and Bell paused in the doorway while the Brigadier waved to his driver.

Grace Browning, from the back of the black cab Belov had provided, saw them. 'There he is,' she said, 'Let's go — I want to be there before him,' and the cab moved out into the Park Lane traffic.

As Liam Bell got into the Daimler, Dillon and Hannah turned to her Rover saloon. She got behind the wheel, Dillon scrambled in and they were away.

'Hold the bag open,' Grace told Curry.

He did as he was told. She removed her high-heeled shoes, took out a pair of loose muslin trousers and pulled them on, tucking the short skirt of her dress inside. Next came a pair of slippers and a cheap three-quarter length raincoat. Then she found a long scarf and wrapped it round her head, the chador worn by most Muslim women. Finally she took out a Harrod's plastic bag with the Beretta inside. She checked the action, then put it in her shoulder bag.

'Ready to go. I didn't tell you, Tom, but I've changed the plan. I went and had a look at this place Vance Square this afternoon. Bell lives in the old rectory and the easiest way to get there is to walk through St Mary's churchyard. I'm banking that's what he'll do, so you drop me there and clear off.'

'Now look here,' he protested.

'It's only a quarter of a mile to the King's Head. I'll walk. No problem.'

'I can wait.'

'No way,' she said fiercely. 'I'll see you at the theatre. It's how I want it, Tom.'

The cab turned into Vance Square and she tapped on the window. The driver pulled in at the kerb. She turned, smiled at Curry and got out. She crossed to the entrance to the churchyard and the cab moved away.

The churchyard was a jumble of Gothic monuments and gravestones, great crosses and here and there a marble angel. There was a path running through to the old rectory, with a light at the entrance and one at the other end. In between was a place of shadows. She walked about halfway along the path, positioned herself between a mausoleum's bronze doors and waited.

It started to rain in a sudden rush as the Daimler deposited Liam Bell at the kerb by the entrance to the churchyard.

'Good night,' he said to the chauffeur and turned.

The Daimler drove away and Hannah Bernstein coasted into the square and slowed down. 'There he goes,' she said as Bell entered the churchyard. 'We can go now.'

She started to increase speed but Dillon grabbed her arm. 'Just a minute, I think I saw someone in there up ahead of him.'

'Are you sure?' She braked to a halt.

'Yes, I damn well am.'

He was out of the car in a second and running for the entrance to the churchyard, a silenced Walther in his hand.

Liam Bell pulled up the collar of his raincoat and hurried on as the rain increased. He reached the centre of the churchyard, was aware of a movement up ahead in the shadows. He paused and Grace Browning moved out of the shadows. At the same moment, Dillon ran through the entrance gates. In the half-light, he saw Grace and shouted at the top of his voice.

'Mr Bell, get down!'

Bell paused, bewildered, turned to look at Dillon, turned

again and she levelled the Beretta and fired twice, hitting him in the heart, knocking him to one side of the path. He fell against a tombstone and hung there for a moment.

Dillon dropped to one knee and fired the Walther, but she had already slipped into the shadows of the mausoleum. He emptied his gun into the darkness of the bronze doorway, but unknown to him, Grace had dropped flat on her face on the ground. He ejected his magazine and reached for another. As he rammed it into the butt, she stepped into the light and took deliberate aim, her arm extended.

'Very foolish, Mr Dillon.' Her voice was perfect Pakistani English in its inflection. 'And you don't often make mistakes. I admire that.'

Dillon stood there, frozen, awaiting the bullet, then suddenly she raised an arm in a kind of salute and slipped into the shadows. He pulled the slider on the Walther and fired twice. Behind him, Hannah ran up the path, gun in hand.

'See to him,' he said and ran along the path into the darkness.

Grace Browning was already on the other side of the rectory, the church to one side. There was another, older part of the cemetery there. As she went round the end of the church, a side door opened, light flooded out and an old man in a cassock appeared. She ran past him, head down, to where she knew there was a gate in the wall, opened it and darted along the street outside. She paused in a doorway at the far end, removed the chador from her head, slipped off the muslin trousers and pulled down her skirt. She put the Beretta into her shoulder bag, rolled up the muslin trousers and put them and the chador in her plastic Harrod's bag. At the end of the street there was a rubbish bin at the base of a streetlight. She dropped the plastic bag inside, turned into the High Street and walked calmly away along the pavement.

★

133

As Dillon entered the other part of the cemetery the side door was still open, light flooding out, and the old man in the cassock stood there.

'What on earth's going on?' he demanded.

'Police,' Dillon told him because it was the easiest thing to say. 'Who are you?'

'Father Thomas.'

'Did you see anyone?'

'A woman ran past a few moments ago, Muslim, I think. She wore one of those headscarves. Oh, and baggy cotton trousers. What's happened?'

'There's been a shooting, a neighbour of yours, Liam Bell.'

The old man was shocked. 'Oh, dear Lord!'

'Back there on the path. You'll find a young woman there. She's a Chief Inspector Bernstein. Tell her I'll contact her on my Cellnet phone.'

Dillon hurried away, found the gate in the wall and ran to the end of the lane.

Grace Browning reached Upper Street ten minutes later. There were already large numbers of people crowding into the King's Head, one of the most celebrated pub theatres in London, and a poster on the wall featured her prominently. She walked through the crowd. Many people recognized her, smiled and said hallo, but she kept on going until she reached Curry, who was at the far end of the bar.

'Oh, there you are, Tom,' she called brightly.

'Thought you were going to be late,' he said. 'And I've never known you do that.'

All this was for the consumption of those standing nearby. She said, 'Come through and talk to me while I dress.'

Dillon hesitated on the corner of the lane and the High Street. It was quite busy in spite of the rain, plenty of people hurrying by and lots of traffic. Hopeless really and then he noticed the plastic shopping bag sticking out of the rubbish bin at the base of the streetlamp in front of him. It was the Harrod's name that caught his eye, common enough in the right place, but not here. He took it out, opened it and found the muslin trousers and the chador.

'Would you look at that, now,' he said softly.

He replaced them in the bag and pushed it inside the front of his trenchcoat, then he called Hannah on his Cellnet phone. She answered at once.

'I'm on the High Street,' he said. 'You've seen Father Thomas?'

'Yes, he's here. Two police cars arrived already and I can hear the ambulance. A waste of time, I'm afraid. Liam Bell is dead.'

'Poor sod,' Dillon said. 'Didn't stand a chance. Did the priest tell you about the woman dressed like a Muslim?'

'Yes.'

'I've just found a Harrod's shopping bag sticking out of a rubbish bin here on the corner of the back lane and the High Street. Inside are a pair of muslin trousers and one of those headscarves, the chador.'

'Sounds like an Arab fundamentalist hit.'

'I don't think so. She called out to me, Hannah, called me by name. She had a very pronounced Pakistani accent. Another thing. I'll bet you five pounds that January 30 claim this one within the next hour.'

'But why?'

'I'll tell you later. I'm going to take a walk up the road, nothing I can do here. I'll call you.'

He put the Cellnet phone in his pocket, turned up the collar of his raincoat and walked rapidly away through the rain.

A waste of time of course. After all, he'd no reason to know whether she'd gone left or right on the High Street. The rain increased in force, clearing the pavements to a certain degree as people sought shelter. He turned into Upper Street and paused, looking across at the welcoming lights of the King's Head, remembering that Grace Browning had told him she was playing there in *Private Lives*. He could see the poster on the wall, darted across the road and paused in the doorway. He took out the Cellnet and called Hannah again.

She answered at once. 'Bernstein.'

'Dillon.'

'Where are you?'

'Took a walk up the High Street and ended up at the King's Head. What's happening?'

'All the usual things. Forensic are on to it now. They've just turned up with the scene-of-crime van.'

'Have they taken him away?'

'They're bagging him now. The Brigadier's here. I'll see if he wants a word.' She called to Ferguson. 'Dillon, sir, do you want to speak to him?'

Ferguson, who was talking to Father Thomas, called, 'Tell him to come to Cavendish Square. I'll see you there as well. I'm waiting for the American Ambassador.'

'Dillon?' she said. 'Stay there. I'll pick you up.'

He got himself a Bushmills and moved to the door giving access to the theatre section. The young girl on duty had the door half-open and was peering through it.

She half-turned as Dillon appeared at her shoulder. 'It's a sell-out, I'm afraid.'

'That's all right, I just wanted a peek, I happen to know Grace Browning.'

He looked over her shoulder across the darkened room, the audience seated at the tables, to the brightly lit stage area, where Grace Browning, dressed in a costume from the nineteen thirties, was vigorously denouncing her leading man. She turned and stormed off and the audience applauded.

The young girl said, 'Isn't she wonderful?'

'You could say that,' Dillon said and smiled. 'Yes, I think you could.'

He turned away as the interval crowd started to come out to the bar, and saw Hannah enter. He went to her, draining his glass and putting it on the bar.

'I might have known. I meant you to wait outside, not inside,' she said. 'Let's get going.'

'Jesus, girl, the bad mood you're in.'

'I got both barrels from the Brigadier. In his opinion you and I have fallen down on the job rather badly.' They got into her car and drove away. 'Now, what happened back there?'

'She stepped out from a mausoleum doorway on the other side of Bell. There wasn't much light and she had the scarf around her head. I shouted to Bell to get down, but she shot him twice – silenced weapon, of course. As I fired in return, she faded away.'

'And then.'

'Rather stupid. I emptied my gun hoping for a lucky hit. While I was reloading she stepped into the path, levelled her gun and called to me.'

'What did she say?'

Dillon told her. 'And the accent was very Pakistani, no doubt about that. When she made off, I opened fire again, which was when you arrived.'

'So we're looking for a Muslim woman?'

'Or someone pretending to be one,' Dillon took the Harrod's shopping bag from inside his trenchcoat and opened it. 'A pair of muslin trousers and one chador.'

'Good,' she said. 'You can get good fingerprints from a plastic bag, did you know that?'

'No, I didn't.'

'But why didn't she shoot you?' Hannah shook her head. 'It doesn't make sense. And how did she know who you were?'

He lit a cigarette. 'Oh, that's easy. You see, I think we've met before.'

NINE

Ferguson was sitting by the fire, the telephone in his hand, when Kim showed them in. He waved them to sit.

'Yes, Prime Minister, of course, I'll be there in an hour.' He nodded. 'We'll have a complete update for you.' He put the phone down. 'What a balls-up. God knows what President Clinton's going to say.'

'Yes, it's bad news, I'm afraid,' Hannah said.

'Bad news?' His face was purple. 'It's bloody disastrous. I mean, you two were supposed to watch out for him.'

'She was ahead of him, waiting in ambush in the cemetery,' Dillon said. 'It was only chance that I noticed her as we drove off.'

'What happened? Tell me everything.'

Which Dillon did. When he was finished he said, 'A bit of luck finding the muslin trousers and the chador, not that they'll help much in my opinion.'

'Which doesn't count for very much at the moment,' Ferguson told him.

Hannah said, 'Dillon has a theory that January 30 will claim this one, sir.'

Ferguson, in the act of taking a cigarette from a silver box, paused, frowning a little. 'But they just have. Phoned the BBC about an hour ago. That's one of the things the Prime Minister wants to see me about.' He lit his cigarette. 'All right, Dillon, let's have it.'

'I think we've met before, that's why she knew me.'

'Where?'

'Belfast when the Sons of Ulster set me up, the lone motorcyclist in black leathers who took out the lookout man. I said at the time, if you recall, that he made a strange gesture. Raised an arm in salute before riding off.'

'And?'

'She did exactly the same tonight. So it was no man on that motorcycle in Belfast; it was her.'

'Another thing, sir,' Hannah said. 'The night she saved Dillon in Belfast she used an AK, but all the other hits have been with the same weapon, the Beretta. I've a hunch that the rounds that come out of Mr Bell will match.'

'I'm not sure that makes sense to me,' Ferguson said, 'but we'll wait and see what the lab report shows. Anyway, I've got to go and see the PM now to discuss this whole unfortunate affair and the possible repercussions. You two will just have to wait here until I get back. Not much sleep for anyone tonight, but that's the way it is.'

Simon Carter and Rupert Lang were waiting downstairs when Ferguson arrived at Downing Street.

'Good God, Ferguson, what went wrong?' Carter demanded.

'I'll explain that to the Prime Minister,' Ferguson said as an aide took them upstairs. 'Are you thoroughly briefed on all this?' he asked Rupert.

Lang nodded. 'I'm afraid so. Terrible business.' He was, in fact, more up to date than any of them, for he had been at Cheyne Walk after the show discussing the night's events with Grace, Curry and Belov when the call on his Cellnet phone had summoned him to Downing Street.

The aide showed them into the study. The Prime Minister didn't bother with the courtesies. 'Sit down and let's get on with it, gentlemen. Brigadier, what went wrong?'

Ferguson explained exactly what had happened. When he was finished, Carter snorted angrily. 'So Dillon failed this time?'

'Nonsense.' It was the Prime Minister who had spoken. 'There was nothing more that Dillon or Chief Inspector Bernstein could have done, that's obvious. This woman was ahead of them, waiting to ambush Mr Bell. What I'd like to know is how she knew about him, knew he was here, knew his whereabouts.'

'Yes, a mystery that, Prime Minister, and Dillon has supplied another.' He explained briefly Dillon's theory that the motorcyclist in Belfast and the Muslim woman were one and the same person. 'And it may not be just a theory,' he concluded. 'Dillon predicted who would claim responsibility before we heard about the call to the BBC.'

'January 30,' the Prime Minister said. 'Surely to God we can do something about these people? Brigadier, I would be obliged if you'd mount a special investigation, go over everything they've ever been connected with. There must be something, some clue or other. There must be.'

'If there is, we'll find it,' Ferguson told him. 'Perhaps the Deputy Director's people can do the same. Two separate approaches might turn something up.'

'Of course, Prime Minister,' Carter told him. 'And I'd particularly like to find out why this woman didn't shoot Dillon when she had the chance.'

The Prime Minister stood up and warmed his hands at the fire. 'Events in Ireland are moving faster than I would have thought possible. Because of this, I intend to make my flying visit to see President Clinton tomorrow. With luck I'll be back before anyone knows I've gone. I do not, I repeat, not want this on the front page of the *Daily Express*.'

'We understand, Prime Minister,' Carter said.

'But I stress again how worried I am that the Protestant factions may get out of hand and ruin all hopes of peace at the most crucial stage. This January 30 business tonight will hardly help. I know they've operated across the board and appear to kill willy-nilly, but Bell was not only a good man, he was a Catholic and this won't sit well with Sinn Fein and the IRA.'

'I'm afraid you're right,' Rupert Lang said.

The Prime Minister nodded. 'Another thing. As you know, President Clinton appointed Mrs Jean Kennedy Smith American Ambassador in Dublin last year. I understand from reports from your people, Mr Carter, that there have been threats to her life from Loyalist terrorists.'

'A lunatic fringe only, Prime Minister.'

'Perhaps,' John Major nodded. 'But I need hardly point out the disastrous consequences of anything happening to the sister of the most revered American President of the century.'

At the Cavendish Square flat, Kim provided sandwiches and tea while Ferguson ~~when~~ went over the proceedings at Downing Street with Dillon and Hannah Bernstein.

'So what does he want us to do?' Dillon asked. 'We've already eradicated one of the worst Protestant factions and saved Ireland from nuclear threat. Do we work our way through the leadership of the UFF and UVF, one by one?'

'I don't think that will be necessary,' Ferguson told him. 'But coming up with an answer on January 30 would be more than helpful. I want you and the Chief Inspector to get straight on with it tomorrow. Go back through all the old files since they first struck. Check everything again. Ask the computer for answers.' He stood up. 'Good God, two o'clock. I'm for bed.'

'All right for him,' Dillon said as they went downstairs. 'Ten paces to his bedroom, that's all.'

'Come off it, Dillon, it's only five minutes' walk to your place in Stable Mews,' Hannah said.

'True, but a lot further for you. I was thinking, how about

a glass of something to warm you up on this cold night, and as you say, my place is just around the corner.'

'Well, you can think again.' She got in her car and switched on the engine. 'Night, Dillon, sleep tight.'

She drove off without waiting for his response.

They were waiting for Rupert Lang when he got back to Cheyne Walk. Grace opened the door to him and led the way into the drawing room where the others were sitting by the fire.

'Foul night,' Lang said. 'Any coffee?'

'Tea.' She nodded at the table. 'Freshly made. Much better for you at this time of night.'

'So, my friend, what happened?' Yuri demanded.

'Considerable agitation as you may imagine. The Prime Minister went through the roof. Carter got stuck into Ferguson – Dillon and Bernstein being supposed to keep an eye on Liam Bell on his way home. He felt they'd fallen down on the job.'

'And?'

'The PM pointed out that as Grace was waiting ahead of Bell in the cemetery to ambush him, it was rather unfair to blame Dillon. The thing is, Carter hates Ferguson's guts.'

'Well, he would,' Belov said. 'What was Ferguson's reaction?'

'Oh, he agreed with the Prime Minister that Dillon couldn't be blamed, especially as Dillon had actually forecast that January 30 would claim credit for the killing.'

'He what?' Tom Curry said. 'But how could he know?'

Lang turned to Grace. 'You, I'm afraid, my sweet. That Sons of Ulster thing. He said that before riding away you raised your arm in a kind of salute.'

'So?' Grace Browning said calmly.

'It seems you spoke to him tonight.'

'Quite deliberately in a very Pakistani accent,' she said. 'To use your favourite phrase, Rupert, it muddies the waters.'

'Fine, but you could have shot him and didn't.'

'But if he was dead, darling, nobody would know that the Muslim even existed, never mind had a Pakistani accent. Bernstein was too far away to see anything.'

'But according to the report, the old priest at the church saw you run past.'

'That was chance, Rupert. I didn't know I'd be seeing the priest when I confronted Dillon.'

'I follow your logic,' Belov told her, 'but the arm raised in salute – it's a trifle theatrical.'

'But then I am,' she said simply.

'Anyway,' Lang said. 'The Prime Minister has ordered Ferguson to mount a special investigation into January 30. Go right through the files. See what the computer comes up with. He's asked Carter to get his people to come up with something similar.'

'I don't think we need to worry about that,' Belov said. 'An old story. They've tried before and got nowhere.'

'I agree,' Tom Curry said.

Lang shrugged. 'If you say so.'

Belov said, 'Anything more?'

'Yes, actually.' Lang smiled. 'I was saving the best till last. The Prime Minister is flying out tomorrow in secret to Washington. The Irish Prime Minister will join him there.'

'And the purpose of the meeting?'

'To discuss the final negotiations leading to Sinn Fein persuading the IRA to call a truce of some sort. You know how it goes. Come to the peace table. All is forgiven. He'll be back in twenty-four hours.'

'Now that is interesting,' Belov said. 'You really must keep me informed on that one, Rupert.' He stood up. 'We'd better let you get to bed, Grace.'

She nodded. 'Yes, I could do with it. It's been a heavy night.'

She took them to the door and got their coats. Rupert kissed her on the cheek. 'How about lunch tomorrow? The Caprice suit you?'

'Marvellous.'

'Not me, I'm afraid,' Belov said. 'Too conspicuous.'

'I'll be there,' Curry told her. 'You can count on it.'

They stood for a moment on the pavement, waiting for Belov to adjust his collapsible umbrella. 'I'll get a taxi at the Albert Bridge,' Belov said. 'And you?'

'Going the other way. We could always walk – it's only a mile and a half to Dean Close.'

Belov hesitated. 'A pity she did what she did. I mean alerting Dillon like that. Why on earth this business of the arm raised in salute?'

'One brave acknowledging another,' Curry suggested.

'Well, it worries me,' Belov said. 'Smacks of unbalance.'

'She never guaranteed you sanity, old sport,' Rupert Lang said, 'only a performance. It's theatre to Grace, an exciting game, and you'll just have to put up with that.'

'I take your point. Still . . .' Belov shrugged. 'I'd better get off.'

They parted and Grace Browning watched them go from the parted curtains of her bedroom. She turned and moved through the quiet dark and got into bed. When she closed her eyes, the shadow man was there again, the gun raised, but only for a split second, then he disappeared. She smiled and drifted into sleep.

'But why didn't she shoot you?' Hannah asked.

It was the following morning and she and Dillon were working in one of the side offices of Ferguson's suite at the Ministry of Defence.

145

'Try this for size,' Ferguson said from the doorway. 'Many assassins stick to the target and don't deviate. Many psychological profiles agree on that.'

'He's right,' Dillon told her. 'If you take underworld killings, a professional hit man only goes for his target because that's all he's paid for.'

'Unless you happen to get in his way,' Hannah said.

'Of course.'

Ferguson said, 'I'll leave you two to sort it out, I've got other fish to fry. Check the letter file on my desk, Chief Inspector, and send them out. I'm due at the Home Office.'

The door closed and Hannah said, 'The fact is she could have killed you and didn't.'

'Even more interesting, she could have let me die in Belfast but saved my life instead, that's the real puzzle.'

'What do you mean?'

'Well, wrap your fine police brain around this. There is only one possible explanation for Belfast. She was protecting me.'

'So?'

'But there's more than one possible explanation for her action last night.'

'We've just agreed you weren't the target. What else do you suggest?'

'To start with I don't buy the Muslim woman act – it's too up front – but let's say she wanted me to see her in that guise. And calling to me in that Pakistani voice would reinforce the whole idea. Without me we wouldn't have known that the assassin was apparently a Muslim.'

'Except for Father Tom.'

'And he was an accident.'

'Exactly.'

She sighed. 'I'll have to go and see to the Brigadier's mail.' She went to the door. 'What about you?'

'I'm going to start with that first hit in Wapping, the

146

Arab. Go through the others step by step. See if there's a pattern.'

'They did all that at Scotland Yard. They even allowed the FBI to go through the files after that CIA man was killed. None of them came up with a thing.'

'When ordinary men have failed, the great Dillon may achieve much. On your way, woman.'

She started to laugh helplessly and went out.

It was just before lunch when she returned. Dillon was surrounded by files and working away at the computer keyboard.

'How are you getting on?'

'I'm treating the whole thing as if nothing's been done, punching in the facts from each case as I see them, picking out items which seem strange or unnatural to me and asking the computer to comment.'

'And?'

'Oh, nothing yet. I'll wait until everything is there before putting it into the search pattern.'

'Anything strike you particularly?'

'Well, in a general way the randomness of it all. No apparent pattern.' He reached for a cigarette. 'The first hit on the waterfront here was Wapping. That was when the Beretta was first used. The victim, Hamid, was a known Arab terrorist. The following day, it was Colonel Boris Ashimov, who our people knew was Head of Station, KGB London.'

'I can't see any connection there.'

'I think there must have been. I think the two hits were too close together not to be related. I don't believe in coincidence.'

'I see what you mean.'

'Then there were two Provisional IRA men, not important, just foot soldiers, killed in Belfast and with the same Beretta. Now I find that particularly strange.'

'Why?'

'Two reasons. First of all the fact that they weren't important. I mean, if January 30 wanted to make a statement why not do somebody of significance in the IRA framework? Secondly, how come the gun turns up in Belfast when it was last used in London?'

Hannah sat on the window seat. 'What are you getting at exactly?'

'To get from London to Belfast you either fly or go by ferry. In either case there's strict security to pass through. No way of carrying a gun. Every alarm in the place would go off. No terrorist I can think of, whether IRA or anything else, would try it.'

'If we're talking about our woman of mystery, maybe she just decided to take a chance.'

'Not this woman. It would be like committing suicide.'

'So what's the answer?'

'Maybe whoever took the Beretta through had a right to. Lots of people are licensed to carry in Northern Ireland. Prominent civil servants, members of the Judiciary, Members of Parliament.'

'Plus serving members of the armed forces.' She shook her head. 'That's a large assumption. Someone like Carter might think it just a little crazy.'

'Oh, I don't know. Think of that Greek outfit, November 17. It's an open secret in Athens that the members are doctors, lawyers, politicians. They've killed as ruthlessly as January 30 in the last few years and never been caught.'

'An interesting idea.'

'Well, never mind that now. The fact that January 30 means Bloody Sunday has no significance. We know from information the IRA have passed over that they're not a known Irish Republican group. They not only killed those two Provos in Belfast, they did the two IRA bombers released on a technicality by the courts here in London.'

148

'Yes, their operations do appear to be totally random.'

'You can say that again. They've killed Arabs, Prods, a CIA man, two KGB men here in London and a well-known East End gangster and now an ex-American Senator.'

'Yes, random it certainly is.'

Dillon nodded. 'But only in the sense that they'll do anybody.'

'It's almost as if they don't take sides,' Hannah said.

'No, I don't buy that.' Dillon shook his head. 'I don't think it's as random as it looks. I think there's a purpose.'

'It beats me.' She stood up. 'Do you feel like some lunch?'

'Give me ten minutes. I just want to tap a few more facts in.'

She went back to her desk and busied herself with some papers. After a while he came in. 'How do you fancy some pub food in Wapping?'

She sat back. 'What are you up to?'

'Remember the gangster who was shot in Highgate Cemetery, Sharp, along with that KGB man, Silsev?'

'What about him?'

'According to the file, his chauffeur found him, a man named Bert Gordon.'

'So?'

'He said he didn't see or hear a thing, said he sat in the car at the cemetery gates reading the paper until so much time had gone by he got worried.'

'So he went and found them,' Hannah said. 'I read that file, too.'

'Yes. He said his boss had a meet, but he didn't know who with or what it was about.'

'So?'

'Oh, I've a suspicious nature. I'd imagine he knows more than he's said. I mean, an East End hood meets the Head of Station KGB for London in Highgate Cemetery in the rain

149

and they both get wasted. Come on, girl dear, there's got to be a good reason.'

She nodded. 'You think you can get this Bert Gordon to tell you what he wouldn't tell Scotland Yard?'

'I can be very persuasive.'

'All right.' She stood up. 'Where do we find him?'

'He runs a pub in Wapping called the Prince Albert.'

She picked up her shoulder bag. 'We'll take the car. Come on,' and she led the way out.

As they went downstairs she said, 'Knowing how you operate I think police presence very sensible. You drive while I talk to Central Records Office at Scotland Yard. I might as well find out all there is to know about Mr Bert Gordon.'

The Prince Albert was at the end of a wharf in Wapping, overlooking the river. It looked in good order, brightly painted in green and gold. They got out of the car and Hannah looked across the cobbled street.

'It'll be like a grave at lunchtime and shoulder-to-shoulder at the bar tonight.'

'And how would you be knowing that?' he asked.

'I did my time on the pavement as a constable in Tower Bridge Division. Lots of pubs like this down there. One fight a night and two on Fridays, we used to say.'

'Shocking,' he said. 'A nice Jewish girl like you and Friday night the start of the Sabbath.'

'Very funny,' she said and led the way in.

There was a long mahogany bar, with mirrors on the wall behind fronted by bottles. Tables were scattered here and there and there were three booths by the window. The only customers were two very old men sitting on high stools, pints of beer in front of them while they stared up at a television set suspended from the ceiling in a corner.

The barmaid looked up from the newspaper she was

reading. She was middle-aged, with hair that had obviously been dyed black and a careworn face.

'What can I get you?'

'Mr Bert Gordon,' Dillon said.

There was something in her eyes as if she sensed trouble. 'He isn't here. Who wants him anyway?'

Hannah produced her ID and held it up. 'Detective Chief Inspector Bernstein.'

'So tell him to come out like a good boy,' Dillon told her.

He'd been aware of the door slightly ajar at the end of the bar. Now it opened and Gordon stepped out. Dillon recognized him from his photo in the file.

'It's okay, Myra, I'll handle it.' He took Hannah's ID card and examined it, then passed it back. 'Nice Jewish girl in a job like that. Disgraceful. You should be married with two kids. I'm Jewish myself.'

'I know, Mr Gordon. You changed your name from Goldberg years ago.'

'Anti-semitism used to be a problem when I was a kid.'

'Yes, well, a change of name didn't keep a nice Jewish boy out of prison. I calculate you've done fifteen years when you add it together.'

'So I did my time. What is this anyway?'

'We want a little information,' Dillon said. 'About the killing of your old boss in Highgate Cemetery.'

Gordon shrugged. 'I told the police everything I knew. I gave evidence at the inquest. It's all in the record.'

'I wouldn't say all was the right word,' Hannah said. 'In fact you were rather sparse on facts, so let's talk.'

'All right,' he said reluctantly and raised the bar flap. 'Follow me.' He led the way out through the door.

'Anyone like a drink?' he asked. He and Hannah were sitting on either side of a large cluttered kitchen table.

'No thank you,' Hannah answered.

'Well, I'll join you,' Dillon told him, 'just to stay friendly.'

'You don't look to me as if you've ever been friendly to anyone in your life, my old son,' Gordon said. 'Scotch all right?'

He splashed whisky into two glasses and handed Dillon one. The Irishman went and stood by the door.

Hannah said, 'Albert Samuel Goldberg, known as Gordon. I checked you out. Quite a record. Bookie's runner as a kid, professional boxer, nightclub bouncer, then you were mixed up in that gold bullion robbery at Heathrow in March, seventy-three. You served three years.'

'Ancient history.'

'Grievous bodily harm, assault with a deadly weapon. Armed robbery in seventy-nine. You got ten years and served seven. Lately you've been Frank Sharp's chauffeur and minder. He always looked after you, didn't he? But then he wasn't the one who went to prison. It was idiots like you.'

'Frank was good to me. He was good to all his boys.' He swallowed his Scotch. 'But like I said, all ancient history, so what is this?'

'You said you didn't know who your boss was meeting at Highgate and that you'd no idea what the meet was about?'

'That's what I told those guys from Scotland Yard and that's what I told the coroner's inquest.'

Hannah leaned back in her chair. 'Then why is it I don't believe you?'

'Fuck you, darling,' Gordon told her. 'And mind you, that's not a bad idea.'

'Naughty, that,' Dillon said. 'Bad language to a lady brings out the worst in me.'

'Well fuck you too,' Gordon said and reached for the whisky bottle.

Dillon's hand came out of his trenchcoat pocket, clutching the silenced Walther. There was a dull thud and the whisky bottle shattered in Gordon's hand.

'Jesus Christ!' He jumped up, soaked in whisky. 'What's going on here? I didn't count on shooters. What kind of police are you?'

He reached for a kitchen towel and Dillon said, 'Just keep thinking Gestapo and we'll get along. I'm very good with this thing. I could shoot half your right ear off.'

He levelled the Walther and Gordon put up a hand and cowered away. 'For God's sake, no!'

'Dillon, stop it!' Hannah ordered.

'When I'm finished.' He lowered the Walther. 'I could say you're going to tell me the truth because Frank Sharp was a friend of yours and you'd like to see the people responsible pay.' Gordon mopped himself shakily with the kitchen towel. Dillon continued, 'But we'll forget about loyalty, morality, all that good old English rubbish. We'll say you're going to speak up in the next five seconds because if you don't I really will shoot your ear off.'

'Dillon, for God's sake,' Hannah said.

Gordon put up a hand defensively. 'Okay, I give in. Just let me get another drink. I need it.'

He found another bottle of Scotch in a cupboard and opened it.

Dillon said, 'You knew it was this Russian Silsev that Sharp was meeting in the cemetery?'

'Yes, Frank told me. The meet was at the Karl Marx statue. I asked if he wanted me along, but he said no.'

'And you knew what the meeting was about?' Hannah said.

'It was to do with drugs. Frank said this Silsev geezer was KGB working in London but he had connections with this Moscow Mafia.'

'And what are we talking about?' Hannah asked.

153

'Heroin. Frank said a street value of maybe a hundred million.'

'I see.' She nodded. 'And that's all you know about it?'

'On my mother's life. Frank said this guy had approached him and no other mob in London. Told him he was offering him the deal of a lifetime.'

'So no one else knew?'

'Of course not. I mean, why would this Silsev geezer approach anyone else? Frank was the number one man in the East End for years.' He poured a little more Scotch, hand shaking.

Dillon said, 'You just sat in the car, waiting for him?'

'Like I told the cops and I didn't hear a thing. The gun must have been silenced. I sat there reading the paper until I got worried and went looking.'

'And you saw nobody?'

'Like I told the police, nobody.'

'Think hard,' Dillon said, 'It's raining heavily and getting dark and you're sitting there at the wheel with the newspaper and no one came out.'

'I've told you.' Gordon paused, frowning. 'Here, just a minute. Yes, that's right.' It was as if he was looking back and recreating the scene. 'Yes, this big bike came out through the gates. The guy in the saddle wore black leathers and one of those black helmets you can't see through.'

'Bingo,' Dillon said. 'Give the man the star prize.'

'God, you were a bastard in there, Dillon,' she told him as they drove away. 'Don't ever do that to me again.'

'It got a result,' he said. 'Exact description of our mystery rider from Belfast and you now know what Silsev and Sharp were up to.'

'My God,' she said. 'Heroin at a street value of a hundred million pounds. It doesn't bear thinking of.'

'Well, don't,' he said. 'Let's call in at Mulligans in Cork Street. Smoked salmon and champagne.'

'I'm driving, Dillon.'

'I know, girl dear. I'll drink the champagne for you. You can content yourself with the smoked salmon.'

He sat back, grinning, and lit a cigarette.

Washington
London
Washington

1994

TEN

It was raining in Washington, driving in from the river through the late afternoon as the large sedan moved along Constitution Avenue towards the White House. In spite of the weather, there was a sizeable crowd in Pennsylvania Avenue, not only tourists but a fair smattering of journalists and TV cameras.

The chauffeur lowered the glass screen that separated him from the rear. 'It's going to be difficult getting at the front without them recognizing you, Senator.'

Patrick Keogh leaned forward. 'Let's try the East Entrance.'

The sedan turned up East Executive Avenue, pulled up at the gate, where the guard, recognizing Keogh at once, waved them through. The East Entrance was used frequently by White House staff and by diplomatic visitors who wanted to avoid the attention of the media.

Keogh got out and said to the chauffeur, 'Don't know how long I'll be, on this one,' and went up the steps.

When he got inside he found a Secret Service agent on duty, talking to a young Marine lieutenant in razor-sharp uniform. The lieutenant snapped to attention. 'Good evening, Senator.'

'How did you know I'd use this entrance?'

'I didn't, Senator, I have a colleague at the front entrance as well.'

Keogh smiled amiably. 'Now that's what I call sound strategic thinking.'

The young man smiled back at him. 'If you'll follow me, Senator, the President's waiting.'

When they entered the Oval Office the room was in half-darkness, curtains drawn, most of the light coming from a table lamp on the massive desk and a standard lamp in one corner. It was a room entirely familiar to Keogh, with its array of service flags, a room he had visited many times to speak to more than one President. This time it was Bill Clinton behind the desk, but it was the other occupant of the room, at ease in a wing-back chair that surprised Keogh. John Major.

'Ah, there you are, Patrick, I appreciate you coming at such short notice,' Clinton said. 'I believe you two know each other?'

'Mr Prime Minister.' Keogh held out his hand as John Major stood up. 'A real pleasure.'

'Senator,' John Major said.

'Please be seated, Patrick, and we'll get to it,' Clinton told him. 'By the way, there's coffee over there if you'd like?'

'I think I would, I'll help myself.' Keogh finally returned to the desk area and took a spare chair. 'Yours to command, Mr President.'

'I'd like to believe that's true, and in a way it makes what I'm going to ask you especially difficult.'

Patrick Keogh paused, the cup to his mouth, and then he smiled, that slightly lopsided grin that had always been a personal trademark, and his face was suddenly suffused with immense charm.

'Can't wait, Mr President. I can tell this is going to be real special.'

'It is, Patrick. In fact it's probably more important than anything you've been involved in in your entire political life.'

'And what would it be concerned with?'

'Ireland and the peace process.'

Keogh paused, his face serious, and then he quite deliberately emptied his cup and put it on the small table beside him.

'Please go on, Mr President.'

'We know how hard you've worked behind the scenes with other committed Irish-Americans towards achieving peace in Ireland,' John Major said. 'And the visits to Ireland of former Congressman Bruce Morrison and his friends have proved a real help in the necessary consultations.'

'It's nice of you to say so, Prime Minister,' Keogh said. 'But it's no burden. The killing has gone on too long. This thing in Ireland must come to an end. Now, what is it you want me to do?'

'We'd like you to go to Ireland for us,' the President said.

'Good God!' Keogh's head went back and he laughed. 'Me go to Ireland? But why?'

'Because, to use that old Irish phrase, you're one of their own. You're as Irish as the Kennedy family. Hell, I've read about what happened when President Kennedy went there in nineteen sixty-three and visited the old Kennedy farm.' Clinton looked at a paper in front of him. 'Dunganstown. You were with him.'

Patrick Keogh nodded. 'His great-grandfather left there back in the nineteenth century at the same time mine did to become a cooper in Boston.' He smiled at John Major. 'No offence, Prime Minister, but the English didn't leave large numbers of Irish much option in those days except to get out.'

'True,' John Major said. 'In self-defence I'd point out that many came to England and prospered. It's estimated, at least eight million of the English population are Irish or of Irish descent.'

'That's right,' Keogh said. 'But the American tradition is especially strong. You know, that year I went to Berlin with Jack Kennedy and he made a famous speech. He challenged the Communist system. He said *"Ich bin ein Berliner"*. At that moment in time he was the most famous man in the world.'

'Absolutely,' John Major said, 'and deservedly so.'

'Then he went to Ireland, to Dublin, and stayed at our Embassy in Phoenix Park. Then Wexford and on to Dunganstown and Mary Kennedy Ryan's cottage. First cousins, second cousins, every kind of cousin.' Patrick Keogh laughed. 'They all turned up. When he visited New Ross the town shut down and then he spoke to the Irish Parliament.' Keogh shook his head. 'When he left at Shannon Airport thousands turned out to see him go. Women were crying.'

'I know,' Clinton said. 'By the way, the Irish Prime Minister sends his regrets. He'd hoped to be with us but the peace movement has gathered such momentum in Ireland, he just couldn't leave.'

'I understand,' Keogh said. 'So what is it you want me to do?'

Clinton turned to John Major. 'Prime Minister?'

'As the President has said, we'd like you to go to Ireland. Let me explain. The peace process has moved very fast. Gerry Adams for Sinn Fein and John Hume have between them started a genuine groundswell towards peace in the communities.'

'Do you believe this to be true of the Protestant Loyalists as well?' Keogh asked.

'Yes, in the generality. The hardliners on both sides will still be a difficulty and if the IRA do stand down, a further problem will be in persuading the other side that it's genuine, but we'll cross that bridge when we come to it.' John Major smiled. 'I call it the Paisley bridge.'

Keogh grinned. 'Now that is one hell of a bridge to cross.'

President Clinton said, 'But first and foremost we need a

ceasefire from the IRA. Adams and Sinn Fein have tried hard and so have Bruce Morrison and his friends, but it's a question of persuading the hardliners to agree. It can't be partial, it must be total. All or nothing.'

'The thing is,' Major said, 'there's the prospect of a secret meeting in Ireland soon, all sections of the IRA getting together, even splinter groups like INLA. Now, if you could attend that meeting, throw your weight behind Adams, John Hume and the peace movement, the effect might be incalculable.'

'Your name means a lot over there,' the President said. 'It might just tip the balance.'

Keogh shook his head. 'I'm not so sure. Why should they listen to Patrick Keogh? I've not been exactly everybody's cup of coffee for some time now.'

'It's worth a try, Patrick, don't put yourself down.' Clinton got up and paced around. 'Politics is so often just a game. No one knows that better than the three of us, but now and then – not very often perhaps – but now and then, something comes along that's worth everything. I think that after twenty-five years of war in Ireland we might just have a chance this time of doing something about it and I sure as hell would hate to see that chance go.'

There was silence for a moment. Keogh sat there, frowning, and then he sighed. 'I'd find it difficult to argue with that. So how am I going to get in on this meeting?'

'Nothing official,' Clinton said. 'Look around this office. You don't see my National Security Adviser, no CIA presence, no one from the FBI or Justice and State. The Prime Minister and I believe that this should be under wrappers until it's actually happened.'

'And how in the hell do we do that?'

'I've given the matter some thought,' Clinton said. 'And then the other day I saw something rather interesting in the *Washington Post*. There was a report that mentioned a stained-glass window of your great-great-uncle who was a Catholic bishop and which was recently installed at Drumgoole Abbey. It's a convent run by the Little Sisters of Pity, I understand.'

'That's correct, Mr President.'

'This stained-glass window is in a small chapel, the Keogh Chapel. I understand you helped create a foundation to assist in the development of the school the Little Sisters run there?'

'I was fortunate enough to be able to interest a few business associates in the work there.'

'But you've not visited the place yet?'

'I will when I can,' Keogh told him.

'Why not now, Patrick?' Clinton said. 'Let's say you go to Paris on holiday. The press won't get too excited about that. You go via Ireland, put down at Shannon Airport and proceed onwards by helicopter to Drumgoole Abbey, announcing that you want to visit the chapel.'

'You see the point,' John Major put in. 'The press and TV are caught on the hop. You're on your way before they know it's happening.'

'That's right,' Clinton said. 'If you turn up, they'll lay on a service at the abbey, turn out the kids from the boarding school and wave you off as you fly back to Shannon, only on the way you'll put down at a place called Ardmore House. That's where the Sinn Fein and IRA meeting will take place. You'll do your thing . . .'

'For good or ill,' Keogh said.

'For good, Patrick, I'm certain of it, then back to Shannon and onwards to Paris.'

Keogh nodded slowly. 'Totally secret, the whole thing.'

'Absolutely. You see, the visit to Drumgoole Abbey would take care of any reports of you being sighted at Shannon, provide an explanation. The Mother Superior wouldn't be told of your visit until you were on the way.'

'Yes, I understand that.'

There was another pause and John Major said gently, 'Is there a problem, Senator?'

'Only if this doesn't stay top secret,' Patrick Keogh said. 'I'm aware that the American Ambassador in Dublin has received death threats from hardline Protestant Loyalist groups. I understand she's been referred to as that Kennedy bitch. God knows what they'd call me.'

'Yes, we are very concerned about the other side's attitude in all this,' John Major said. 'But we can't let that stand in the way of our negotiations.'

'Of course not,' Keogh said. 'But if news got out about what I'm supposed to be trying to achieve there are those on the Orange side of the line who might think it would make sense to remove me permanently from the scene. Let's face it, the murder of Liam Bell doesn't exactly fill one with hope.'

Clinton went back to his chair behind the desk and sat down. 'God knows, this wouldn't be a picnic, and we are asking you to put yourself on the line. That's why I suggest following the procedure I've laid out. All very low key. Only a very small circle of people will know.'

'What about the IRA conference? They'll know.'

John Major said, 'Gerry Adams wants things to happen now, no doubt about that. I'm sure we can work something out. For example, what if you were introduced as a total surprise?'

'I like it,' Clinton said. 'The shock effect would be tremendous. So what do you think, Patrick?'

'I'm not sure.' Keogh sighed. 'I can't argue with the importance of all this, but you're asking me to go into the war zone and I'm getting old.' He smiled that wry smile again. 'Okay, maybe I'm kind of scared at the prospect, but I do have my family to consider. I would have to consult my wife and she's gone down to our house at Hyannis Port. We're only three miles down the beach from Ted Kennedy.'

'How long do you need?'

'Twenty-four hours?'

John Major said, 'I leave at noon tomorrow.'

'Right, I'll be in touch before then.'

He stood up and Clinton pressed the buzzer for the aide. 'I've given instructions to the commanding officer at Andrews Air Force Base to grant you every facility. If you want to go to Hyannis Port tonight they'll speed you on your way.'

'That's kind, Mr President.' Keogh held out his hand to John Major. 'Prime Minister. We'll speak tomorrow.'

The door opened behind him, the Marine lieutenant appeared and Patrick Keogh turned and left the room.

He didn't even bother to go to his Washington home, simply told his chauffeur to take him to Andrews Air Force Base and spoke to the commanding officer on the car phone to let him know he was coming. On the way he changed his mind and told his chauffeur to divert to Arlington National Cemetery. It was raining harder now, so he took the umbrella his chauffeur provided and walked to President Kennedy's grave. He stood there for quite some time, lost in thought. An ageing lady, who also held an umbrella over her head, walked up.

'What a man,' she said. 'The greatest President this century.'

'I couldn't disagree with that,' Keogh said.

'He gave people hope,' she said. 'That was his greatest gift and he had courage. On top of that he was a war hero. Amazing.'

'He certainly was.'

She glanced sideways. 'Excuse me, but do I know you? You look familiar.'

Patrick Keogh gave her that immensely charming smile. 'No, I don't think so, I'm nobody special.' He turned and walked away.

★

At Andrews they provided a helicopter, but pointed out that the Cape Cod area was not good that evening, with heavy fog at Hyannis Port. The best they could offer was a flight to Otis Air Force Base on Cape Cod itself and onward transportation by limousine. He had no quarrel with that and found himself on his way within twenty minutes, drifting out across the Potomac as dusk settled on the horizon.

He tried to read the *Washington Post* but his brain refused to take it in. He could think of only one thing, the situation outlined to him by the President and the British Prime Minister. It came to him with sudden clarity that he was faced with the most important decision of his life.

In London it was almost midnight and Dillon was working away at his desk, checking computer print-outs. It was very quiet. Suddenly the door opened and Hannah Bernstein entered. She was wearing a raincoat.

'I don't believe this. I've been trying to contact you all night. Why didn't you have your answerphone on?'

'I hate those bloody things.'

'I then had the crazy thought that you might still be here.'

He ignored her, checking a print-out. 'So you were right, then.' He put the print-out down and sat back, swivelling in the seat. 'Do you believe in coincidence?'

'Sometimes. Why do you ask?'

'Karl Jung used to speak about something he called synchronicity, events having an apparent coincidence in time and the feeling that some deeper motivation is involved.'

'And what's that got to do with January 30?'

'Oh, I don't know. The ould head's pounding from it all. All those hits with the Beretta, that's no coincidence, it's a fact. Four IRA men stiffed – that's a fact, too, no chance there.'

'So?'

He lit a cigarette. 'Two Heads of Station KGB London knocked off. Now why, I asked myself, why two? And then good old Bert Gordon gives us the reason for the Silsev and Sharp hit. Drugs.'

'And why was Ashimov killed?'

'I don't know, but it's synchronicity that we go to Beirut and find another KGB officer on the make, this time flogging plutonium.'

'You're not suggesting a connection?'

'Only in that it indicates the KGB, or whatever they call themselves now, seem to be dipping their fingers into every racket available.'

'So what does that tell you?'

'That there might be a Russian connection somewhere, so I've asked the computer to check everything for me as regards the Russian Embassy in London. Personnel – the lot.'

'Brilliant,' she said. 'Any other coincidences you want to check?'

'Strange you should say that, but there is and for the life of me I can't think what it is.'

'Are you serious?'

'Absolutely.'

'Then you really do need a night's sleep.'

He stood up and reached for his jacket. 'My place or yours?'

'Where shall I kick you, Dillon, just tell me?' she said. 'Now come on. I'll drop you off.'

When the limousine reached the Hyannis Port house from Otis Air Force Base, Patrick Keogh was tired. The last few miles through thick fog had been a real strain. The driver, an Air Force sergeant, declined the offer of a cup of coffee and started back immediately.

Keogh stood there for a moment and suddenly a wind blew in strongly from the sea, tearing the fog into tatters, and he could see the white surf on the edge of the beach. On impulse, he walked down there and stood listening to the waves thundering in, the wind in his face.

A voice called, 'Pat, are you there?' It was his wife and he turned and saw her a few yards away, a flashlight in her hand. 'Are you all right? Is anything wrong? They phoned me from Otis to say you were on your way. I heard the car.'

He put an arm around her and kissed her. 'My head was feeling a little thick. You know what helicopters are. I just felt like a blow. We'll go in now.'

In the kitchen he poured a little Scotch into a glass and added Branch water while Mary made coffee. A literary agent by profession, she was nobody's fool, but more than that she was a woman with the woman's uncanny instinct to sense when things weren't right.

She poured coffee. 'You shouldn't have this, you won't sleep.'

'I won't sleep anyway, not tonight.'

She sat on the opposite side of the table. 'Tell me about it, Pat.'

So he did.

When he was finished she said, 'It could be a can of worms. They're asking you to put yourself on the line. Even the IRA can't control all their people. There are splinter groups, real crazies. Look at those INLA people who killed Mountbatten and these Protestant Loyalists are just as bad. Ulster Volunteer Force, Ulster Freedom Fighters, then there's the Red Hand of Ulster. They're the kind of fanatics who'd kill Queen Elizabeth if they thought it would advance their cause and they'd still call themselves Loyalists while doing it.' She shook her head. 'It's a mad, crazy world over there. So much killing, so many years of brutality.'

'Which is why it has to stop.' He reached for the coffee pot. 'It takes courage to make the right decision. By the way,

I went to Arlington before I came down. After all, it was Jack Kennedy who got me into politics. I felt close.'

'You always will be.'

'But while we're on the subject of heroes.' He gave her a wry smile. 'Where I'm concerned, some would say I have made a considerable number of errors, but not this time. This time I'm going to stand up to be counted.'

'You're going to go?'

'I'm afraid so.'

'Can I go with you?'

'No.'

She sighed. 'I see.'

'Are you angry with me?'

'No, proud of you actually.'

'Good.' He stood up and reached out a hand. 'Let's go to bed. I'll fly back to Washington in the morning and inform the President and John Major of my decision.'

It was a fine bright morning with a patchy sky, the Washington streets cleared by the rain, as Keogh's sedan once again turned into the White House by the East Entrance. When Keogh went in, the Marine lieutenant from the previous evening was waiting.

'Good morning, Senator.'

'Don't they ever give you any time off?' Keogh asked.

'Seldom, sir.' The young officer smiled. 'I'm a fourth generation Marine, Senator, Path of Duty and all that. If you'll come this way, the President and the Prime Minister are in the Rose Garden.'

As Keogh joined them, Clinton turned and smiled. 'You must have got up early.'

'You could say that, but I wanted to catch you both together before the Prime Minister left.'

'You're going to go?' Clinton said.

'Yes, I think you can count on that. What kind of time scale are we talking about?'

Clinton turned to John Major, who said, 'Quite soon. The next few days. Obviously the Irish Prime Minister must know, and Gerry Adams.'

'We'll let you know at the soonest possible moment, Patrick,' Clinton told him.

'That's fine. I'm at your disposal.'

'There is of course the question of your personal safety,' Clinton said.

Patrick Keogh smiled wryly. 'Mr President, I'm a big target. Having said that, I don't take kindly to the idea of a dozen Secret Servicemen surrounding me at all times.'

'But you must have some security.' Clinton was shocked.

'Yes, well, maybe we should look to our British cousins for that. They are, after all, the experts where Ireland is concerned.' He turned to John Major. 'Wouldn't you agree, Prime Minister?'

'I'm afraid so,' John Major replied.

'Right, let's examine the problem. I land at Shannon, helicopter to Drumgoole, drop in at Ardmore House, then back to Shannon. I hardly need the SAS to take care of that. Who would you recommend, MI5?'

'No, as the operation takes place in a foreign country, it would be MI6, Senator.'

'You don't sound too enthusiastic,' Keogh said. 'Come on, Prime Minister, I'm putting myself on the line, so who have you got? Who's your best?'

'My best is rather unusual,' John Major said. 'What some people call the Prime Minister's private army. For some years now there has been such a group specifically targeting terrorism and responsible to the Prime Minister only.'

'I like the sound of that. Are they any good?'

'Extremely good, though rather ruthless. The unit is commanded by Brigadier Charles Ferguson.' John Major

171

hesitated. 'There is one unusual thing I should tell you. Ferguson's right-hand man is called Sean Dillon. He was a feared IRA enforcer for years, then in ninety-one he tried to blow me up at Downing Street when the War Cabinet was meeting.'

Patrick Keogh laughed his delight. 'The dog. And now he's working for you?'

'And Ireland in his way. Like most of us, he thinks it's gone on too long.'

'Good.' Keogh nodded and turned to Clinton. 'Mr President, I've agreed to go, but these are my terms. I want Ferguson and this man Dillon taking care of me when I'm there.'

Clinton glanced at Major and the Prime Minister nodded. 'No problem.'

'To that end I'd like to meet them as soon as possible. Can you have them over here fast?'

'Would tomorrow suit?' John Major asked and they all started to laugh.

In London, Charles Ferguson sat in his office and listened to the Prime Minister on the secure phone as he crossed the Atlantic.

'Of course, Prime Minister,' he said. 'I'll take care of it.'

He put the phone down and sat there frowning for a moment. Finally he picked up the internal phone and spoke to Hannah Bernstein. 'Get in here and bring Dillon.'

He got up, went to the map wall, fiddled around until he was finally able to pull down a large-scale map of Ireland. He was examining it when Hannah Bernstein and Dillon entered.

'Do you know where Drumgoole Abbey is?' Ferguson asked Dillon.

'And what decent Catholic doesn't?' Dillon moved beside him and pointed. 'Have you taken to religion, Brigadier? Little Sisters of Pity there. Very holy.'

Ferguson ignored him. 'Ardmore House.'

Dillon frowned slightly. 'Naughty, Brigadier, very naughty. The Provisional IRA have been known to meet there on more than one occasion.'

'And will again, only this time they'll have a special guest whose welfare we'll be responsible for.'

'May I ask who that might be, sir?' Hannah Bernstein asked.

'Of course you may, my dear. It's Senator Patrick Keogh,' he told her.

ELEVEN

THE FOLLOWING MORNING Ferguson reported for a break-fast meeting at Downing Street. When he was shown into the study the Prime Minister, Carter and Rupert Lang were having coffee.

'Ah, there you are, Brigadier. I've already filled in the Deputy Director and Mr Lang on my discussions with the President and Senator Keogh.'

'I see,' Ferguson said gravely. 'I would remind you that you stressed absolute secrecy in this business. As I understood you, both the President and Senator Keogh were adamant about that.'

'I can assure you that no one else outside of this room will know about the affair,' the Prime Minister said. 'To be frank, I'm not mentioning it to the Cabinet, not even to the Secretary of State for Northern Ireland. That may seem strange considering the fact that I've informed Mr Lang, but he, after all, is here in another capacity as a member of this rather special committee.'

'Don't you trust us, Ferguson?' Carter demanded belligerently.

'Silly questions don't need an answer,' Ferguson said. 'But as I see it, Senator Keogh's offered to put his head into the mouth of the lion. That shows considerable courage. I want to make sure he has every chance of taking it out again.'

'You really do think he could be in danger?' Rupert Lang asked.

Ferguson sat there frowning. The Prime Minister said, 'Brigadier?'

'Well, let's look at it this way, Prime Minister. Say you were a Protestant terrorist group who didn't want the peace initiative to work, can you think of a better way of ruining it than killing Patrick Keogh, one of the Kennedy old guard, perhaps the most respected Senator in Washington?'

Simon Carter nodded. It was almost with reluctance that he said, 'He's right, and it wouldn't just be the IRA up in arms, but the entire Irish nation.'

Rupert Lang said, 'I'd have thought the same argument would apply where IRA extremists are concerned.'

'Explain,' the Prime Minister said.

'I've seen the reports, we all have. There are plenty of hardliners in the IRA who don't agree with Gerry Adams and his supporters politicizing the struggle. There are plenty who still want to go down the path of the gun and the bomb. There might well be amongst them people who would see the advantage in killing Keogh.'

'And why would that be?' John Major asked.

'Because the automatic assumption would be that the Protestants were responsible,' Ferguson said. 'I think you'll find all negotiations would break down and pretty permanently.'

'I'm afraid he's right,' Carter said.

The Prime Minister nodded thoughtfully. 'Then we'll just have to see that it doesn't happen and that's your department, Brigadier.'

Carter interrupted. 'The Security Services would be happy to help. We do have considerable expertise on the ground in Ireland, I hardly need to stress that.'

'But not in the Republic,' John Major said and smiled slightly. 'That would be illegal, wouldn't it?'

'A technicality, as you know, Prime Minister. MI6 operates there all the time.'

'Not on this occasion. Senator Keogh has been specific about his security, as I told you.' He turned to Ferguson. 'Does the assignment give you any problems?'

'Not at all, Prime Minister. Senator Keogh arrives out of the blue at Shannon. Helicopter trip to Drumgoole, where the Mother Superior won't even know he's coming until he's on the way. Let's say half an hour on site, then on to Ardmore House, where only Gerry Adams will be expecting him.'

'And what about security there?' Rupert Lang demanded.

'General security will be as good as you want,' Ferguson said. 'The IRA run a tight ship at these affairs. All the delegates will be shocked out of their socks when Adams produces him. He'll have finished his speech before they have time to recover, and back to Shannon and away.'

'Put that way it all sounds terribly simple,' the Prime Minister said.

'It could be,' Ferguson told him, 'but with one proviso. Total secrecy. Nobody must know he's coming; at any point in the trip, Shannon, Drumgoole, Ardmore. Nobody must know.'

'And just you and Dillon guarding him?'

'No, I'll take Chief Inspector Bernstein as well. The three of us should suffice.'

The Prime Minister nodded. 'Right, let's pray it works.' He turned to the other two. 'This meeting at Ardmore should take place in a matter of days. I'll notify you, of course, but for now, we'll adjourn. The Brigadier is due in Washington.' He shook Ferguson's hand. 'Good luck, Brigadier. You've never handled anything of greater importance.'

The Lear jet left Gatwick at ten-thirty with the usual two RAF pilots, Ferguson and Dillon in the rear. The Brigadier worked his way through two newspapers for half an hour while Dillon read a magazine. Later, as they crossed the Welsh coast and moved out to sea, the Irishman made tea.

176

'Plenty of sandwiches in here, Brigadier, if you feel peckish.'

'Not now, later. Chief Inspector Bernstein didn't seem too happy.'

'She feels left out of things.'

'Well, that's just too bad. I mean, someone's got to mind the shop.' He shook his head. 'Women are so unreasonable, Dillon. They don't think like us. Different species.'

'My God, if the sisterhood heard you say that, they'd tear you limb from limb. Sexist, racist, chauvinistic and of the male variety.'

'My dear boy, you know exactly what I mean. Here's Bernstein, brilliant and capable. First-class honours from Cambridge, marvellous police record. I mean, she's shown herself capable of shooting a man when necessary.'

'And a woman,' Dillon said.

'Yes, I was forgetting that. So why does she now have to go into a pet because she isn't going to Washington?'

'Maybe she just fancied meeting Pat Keogh?'

'Well, she will eventually.'

'You should have made that clear.'

'Nonsense.' Ferguson handed back his mug. 'Another cup of tea and tell me what you think of all this.'

'You mean whether Keogh turning up at Ardmore House would have any effect on Sinn Fein and the IRA?'

'Well, would it? You should know. You were in the bloody movement for long enough.'

'Times change.' Dillon lit a cigarette. 'And men change with them. Irish people north and south of the border, Protestant and Catholic, want peace. Oh, there are still the traditional hardliners on both sides, but if we stick with Sinn Fein and the IRA, I think you'll find there's groundswell support for peace. Twenty-five years is too long. Having said that, Gerry Adams, Martin McGuinness, people like that who want to take the whole thing into the political arena, need all the help they can get and yes, Keogh could help.'

'Why particularly?'

'He worked with President Kennedy in the old days for one thing and that's a special kind of Irish legend. For another, his credentials are good. He's a Catholic. Nobody can query him, which could be important if he makes the right speech.'

'Well, let's hope he does. How have you got on with the January 30 investigation?'

'Fine. I've disregarded all previous investigations, sifted through every piece of information, put it all on the computer and instituted various searches. The Chief Inspector is going to check the results as they come through while I'm away.'

'Well, let's hope you turn something up,' Ferguson said and reached for another newspaper.

At that moment in the office at the Ministry of Defence the printer was churning out the latest batch of information from one of Dillon's searches, his enquiry about staff at the Russian Embassy. Hannah put the sheets together, mainly text information, but also photos. Amongst them was Yuri Belov's, not that his face meant anything to her. She placed them in neat piles and left them on Dillon's desk.

She went back into her own office, rather disconsolate, annoyed that she'd missed out on the American trip, but there was nothing to be done about that. Rain drove against the window. She wondered how Dillon and the Brigadier were getting on out there over the Atlantic, then sat down at her desk with a sigh and started to sort through the day's mail.

When Grace Browning answered the door at the Cheyne Walk house she found Tom Curry on the doorstep. 'This is a nice surprise,' she said as she led the way through to the kitchen. 'I was just making coffee.'

'Business, I'm afraid. Rupert phoned me,' Curry told her. 'Something very big's come up. He and Yuri will be round directly.'

'Have you any idea what it is?' she asked as she made the coffee.

'No. Can't help. Just as much in the dark as you.'

'I'll put some extra cups out, then.'

At that moment the doorbell rang. 'I'll get it,' Curry told her and went out.

By the time she'd prepared a tray and carried it through to the drawing room they were there, the three of them, standing by the fire.

Rupert kissed her on the cheek. 'Ravishing as always.'

'Save the compliments. What's this all about?' she asked as she poured the coffee.

'Tell them, Rupert,' Belov said.

When Lang had finished recounting the details of his meeting at Downing Street, there was silence for a moment, then Curry spoke.

'Very interesting, but what are we talking about here?'

'Sinn Fein and the IRA are very close to calling at least a truce and going to the peace table,' Belov said. 'If that happens there would be enormous pressure on the various Protestant groups also to call a ceasefire.'

'International pressure,' Lang said. 'I'll tell you that for nothing.'

'Peace in Ireland?' Grace said. 'That wouldn't suit you, would it, Yuri? What you'd like to see is another Bosnia.' She laughed. 'What a shame. All your hopes of Ireland descending into chaos and a good Communist state emerging at the other end have gone up in smoke.'

'Not necessarily,' he said. 'If Keogh was assassinated on this trip, the effect would be incredible, especially if one of the Protestant Loyalist factions was to blame.'

'And you think that's a possibility?' Tom Curry said. 'Why, they wouldn't even know he was there.'

'Yes, but we would.' Belov smiled. 'And this time January 30 wouldn't claim credit. We'd give that to the UFF or the Red Hand of Ulster.'

There was total silence now until Lang said, 'The ultimate hit. My God, Yuri, you *are* ambitious.'

Grace Browning's heart was beating fast, her mouth dry with excitement. Belov turned to her. 'When does your show finish at the King's Head?'

'Saturday.'

'Two days.' Belov nodded. 'Since Rupert first phoned me I've spoken to my Dublin sources. The word is that this IRA conference will take place on Sunday afternoon.'

Grace took a deep breath. 'How would I get there?'

'Very simple. Straight in and out. There's a man who does the occasional flight for me, highly illegal, of course. His name is Jack Carson. He operates a small air-taxi service from a little airfield in Kent near a village called Coldwater. He owns a couple of twin-engined planes.'

'And he could do the Irish run?'

'No problem. He's mainly done France for me in the past, but he did Ireland once before a year ago. It's just like England. Scores of small landing strips out there in the countryside. I'm sure he could find one very close to this Drumgoole place. I say Drumgoole because I imagine that will be the soft spot. You can't go after Keogh at Ardmore House with Provisional IRA gunmen all over the place.'

'But what about air traffic control and so on?' Curry asked. 'I mean, you have to log flights and get permission.'

'Oh, Carson's used to that. No flight plan means you're a bogey on someone's radar screen, but there are lots of bogeys up there, including birds, and if you know where to go there's a lot of airspace that's not controlled.'

'But the approach to the Irish coast?' Rupert Lang said. 'Surely that presents a difficulty?'

'Not at all. If he hits the coast at six hundred feet he'll be below their radar screens.' Belov shrugged. 'This man is good and he knows his business. It will work.'

'And what happens at the other end?'

'Once we know where Carson will land I'll arrange for my people in Dublin to leave a car.'

'And then what happens?' Grace asked.

'I don't know, but we're talking about an Abbey, nuns, schoolchildren, not Fort Knox.'

'I still need to get close.'

'You'll come up with something.'

'No, we will.' Tom Curry put an arm around her shoulder. 'No arguments, Grace, I'm coming, too.'

She turned to Lang. 'What do you think?'

'He always did like his own way.' He smiled wryly. 'Wish I could come along, but I rather obviously can't on this occasion. It sounds like fun.'

Belov said, 'Right, I'll get things started with Carson and it only remains for Rupert to keep us informed.' He smiled and held out his cup. 'Could I have some more coffee?'

When the Lear jet landed at Andrews Air Force Base and Dillon and Ferguson disembarked they were met by a young air force captain.

'Brigadier General Ferguson? Right this way, sir. There's a helicopter waiting to take you to Otis Air Force Base. You'll be taken from there by limousine to Senator Keogh's house at Hyannis Port. I'll see your bags are delivered to your hotel.'

Within five minutes they were strapped in and taking off.

'Brigadier General,' Dillon said. 'You've been promoted.'

'No, that's the American terminology,' he said. 'We stopped using the general bit years ago.'

181

'I thought we'd be seeing Keogh in Washington.'

'So did I until we were halfway across the Atlantic.'

'I wonder why the change?'

'I expect he'll tell us when he wants us to know.' Ferguson opened his briefcase, produced a map of Ireland and unfolded it. 'Now show me Ardmore House and Drumgoole again.'

When the limousine deposited them outside the Hyannis Port house, it was Mrs Keogh who met them at the front door.

'Brigadier Ferguson? I'm Mary Keogh.'

'A pleasure, ma'am.'

'Sean Dillon.' He held out his hand and she shook it, eyeing him curiously.

'Now, you I've heard a great deal about, Mr Dillon.'

'All bad, I suppose.'

'I'm afraid so.'

'Ah well, you can't win them all.'

She turned to Ferguson. 'Actually, my husband's walking on the beach.'

'I see,' Ferguson said. 'Perhaps we could join him?'

'Why not. I'll see you in a little while.'

'Of course.'

As they turned to go she called, 'Brigadier?'

Ferguson paused. 'Ma'am?'

'I'm not happy about this.'

'I understand, ma'am, believe me.'

She closed the door and went in. Dillon lit a cigarette. 'A good woman, that one.'

'Yes, I'm inclined to agree,' Ferguson said, 'Now let's go and find the Senator.'

On the beach, the surf pounded in with a great roaring and it was very windy. They saw Patrick Keogh in the distance, walking towards them, occasionally stopping to throw a stick for a black dog that ran in circles around him. As he got closer, they could see he was wearing heavy corduroy trousers and an Aran sweater.

'Brigadier Ferguson?'

'Yes, Senator.' Ferguson shook hands. 'A pleasure, sir.'

'And this must be the great Sean Dillon.' Keogh held out his hand.

'Jesus, Joseph and Mary, Senator, and isn't that overdoing it?' Dillon said.

'Ah, but isn't that what we Irish always do? Let's walk awhile.'

'Of course, sir,' Ferguson said.

'I'm sorry to make John Major rush you two across the Atlantic at such short notice, but with my wife being concerned that I might get my head blown off, I decided that where security was concerned I wanted the best and your Prime Minister said that was you two.'

'Very flattering,' Ferguson said.

Dillon cut in. 'No false modesty needed, Brigadier. We'll do as good a job as anyone and better than most.' He lit a cigarette in cupped hands. 'I'm a plain man, Senator, so one Irishman to another. Why are you doing this? Because if the wrong people got on your case you really could get your head blown off.'

'Dillon!' Ferguson said sharply.

'No.' Keogh put up a hand. 'I'll answer that. Jack Kennedy once said something about good men doing nothing. You know, just standing by. Well, maybe I've stood by on too many occasions.'

Ferguson said, 'I remember when you made the cover of *Time* magazine during the Vietnam War. When Khe San was besieged you insisted on flying in on a fact-finding mission and ended up manning a heavy machine gun as I heard and took a bullet in the shoulder.'

'There were those, especially my political opponents, who thought I was grandstanding, Brigadier. I could never compare with Bobby Kennedy. I worked closely with him. He never shirked an issue, helped guide us through the Cuban missile crisis, had the guts to stand up to the Mafia, served his country and gave his life.'

He stood gazing out to sea and Dillon said, 'You think you should do the same?'

'Good God, no!' Patrick Keogh rocked with laughter. 'Sean, my friend, just for once I want to get something absolutely right, something that I myself can respect, but I sure as hell don't want to finish up face down doing it, which is why I want you and the Brigadier.' He laughed again. 'Now let's go and have something to eat and then we can talk some more.'

They had a light meal in the kitchen – salad, salmon and new potatoes – just the four of them around the kitchen table.

Afterwards over the coffee Keogh said, 'So let's go over it again, Brigadier.'

'Well, as I told the Prime Minister, it can all be very simple. You drop in at Shannon totally unexpected. I believe that for political reasons it's essential that your appearance at the IRA conference at Ardmore House should be kept secret for as long as possible.'

'I agree.'

'But even arriving at Shannon in a private Gulfstream doesn't mean you won't be recognized. Ground staff, baggage handlers, who knows? And someone will talk, rumours will start and the media will get to hear of it.'

'But too late to be able to do anything about it,' Mary Keogh said.

'Exactly.' The Brigadier nodded. 'It can be said afterwards that the sole reason for the stop at Shannon was that the Senator, on a sudden whim, decided he wanted to see the Keogh Chapel. At that stage no one will know about the stop-off at Ardmore House on the way back.'

'It's certainly slick,' the Senator said.

'But what about security?' his wife said. 'I'm concerned about that.'

'No need to be. Dillon, myself and Detective Chief Inspector Hannah Bernstein, my aide, will be with him at all times. I need hardly stress that the usual IRA efficiency will ensure security at Ardmore House.'

'And I know Drumgoole Abbey,' Dillon said. 'It's miles from anywhere in a beautiful valley. There's the abbey itself, and the convent with its school. Just nuns and children.'

'It'll work.' Keogh patted his wife's hand reassuringly. 'We'll have some more coffee on the porch, then I'll let you gentlemen go.'

Sitting there, looking down at the beach, the sea wild beyond, Mary Keogh said, 'I'm intrigued, Mr Dillon. My husband asked for your background. He's told me about you, but there are things I don't understand. You went to the Royal Academy of Dramatic Art in London and acted with the National Theatre?'

'That's right,' Dillon said.

'But then you joined the IRA?'

'I was nineteen years of age, Mrs Keogh, and living in London with my father. Nineteen seventy-one it was. He went to Belfast on a holiday and was killed by crossfire. British paratroopers and IRA. An accident.'

'Only you didn't see it that way?' There was real empathy in her eyes.

'Not at nineteen.' Dillon lit a cigarette. 'So I joined the glorious cause.'

'And never looked back,' Ferguson said. 'On the most-wanted list for years.'

'Is it true you tried to blow up the British War Cabinet in February, ninety-one?' Keogh asked.

'Now, do I look the kind of fella that would do a thing like that?' Dillon said.

Keogh roared with laughter. 'Yes, actually you do, my fine Irish friend.'

Mrs Keogh said, 'I'm still puzzled. How come you changed sides?'

'I fought for what I believed in, I'm not ashamed of that, although I never approved of the bomb as a weapon. For me that was the greatest weakness in the IRA campaign. Not just the dead, but fifty thousand ordinary people maimed or injured. Women in a shopping mall, kids.' He shrugged. 'In the end nothing's worth that, not even a united Ireland. Something goes click in your head. You change.'

'I finally caught up with him in a Serb prison,' Ferguson said. 'They were going to shoot him for flying medical supplies in for children. I managed to make a deal.' He shrugged. 'Now he works for me.'

'And I'll say amen to that. I couldn't be happier that he is on this occasion,' Patrick Keogh told them. 'I'll go and tell your driver to bring the limousine round and I'll inform Otis you're on your way.' He got up, moved to the door and turned. 'Oh, by the way, the President wants to meet you when you get back to Washington.'

Mrs Keogh said her goodbyes and went inside. Ferguson, Dillon and Keogh stood by the limousine for a moment.

'Tell me, Dillon,' Keogh said. 'Do you really think it will work, peace in Ireland?'

'A lot is going to depend on Protestant reaction,' Dillon said. 'On how threatened they feel. There's an old Prod toast, Senator: Our country, too. If they think the other side will allow them that observation there might be hope.'

'Our country, too.' Keogh nodded. 'I like that. It has a ring to it.' He looked solemn. 'Perhaps I could use that at Ardmore.'

Ferguson said, 'We'll be seeing you soon, sir, at Shannon.'

'Only a matter of days, Brigadier.'

'And you're happy, Senator?'

'Am I hell.' Keogh laughed. 'Frightened to death.'

'Ah well, we all get like that,' Dillon told him. 'It's a healthy sign.'

'You know, I once made a speech that for various reasons didn't appeal to a lot of people, but it appealed to me,' Keogh told them. 'I said something about a man doing what he must in spite of personal consequences, that whatever sacrifices he faces, if he follows his conscience, he alone must decide on the course he must follow.'

They stood there in silence and it started to rain. Keogh flung back his head and roared with laughter. 'Hell, that sounded like a campaign speech. Off you go, gentlemen, and I'll see you at Shannon.'

He turned and went inside.

In the helicopter, Ferguson busied himself with papers from his briefcase and hardly said a word. It was later when they were being driven from Andrews in an air force limousine through the heavy Washington traffic that he finally put the papers away and leaned back.

'Interesting man, Patrick Keogh. Triumphs on occasion, but also tragedies and mistakes.'

'But he's still here,' Dillon said. 'He's a survivor. He doesn't whine when something goes wrong. He picks himself up and gets on with it.'

'You liked him?'

'Oh yes, I think he's a man who can look in the mirror and not be afraid.'

'I didn't know you had an artistic soul, Dillon.'

At that moment they reached the White House and were delivered to the West Basement entrance.

★

When an aide showed them into the Oval Office there was no one there.

'Please wait, gentlemen,' he said.

Outside, darkness was falling and Ferguson moved to the window and looked out. 'My God, but we're part of history here, Dillon, from Roosevelt to Clinton and everything in between.'

'I know,' Dillon said. 'The performance continues relentlessly. It's like the Windmill Theatre during the Blitz in London during the Second World War. The motto was: *We never closed.*'

A private door clicked open and Clinton appeared. 'Sorry to keep you waiting. Brigadier Ferguson?' He held out his hand.

'Mr President.'

'And Mr Dillon?'

'So they tell me,' Dillon said.

'Be seated, gentlemen.' They did as they were told and Clinton sat behind the desk. 'You've seen Senator Keogh, I understand, and everything's in place?'

'Yes,' Ferguson said. 'Or as far as it can be at this moment in time.'

'He's spoken with me on the phone and seems more than happy with your plans.'

'Good,' Ferguson said.

Clinton got up and walked to the window. 'A fact of life when you hold high office, gentlemen, is that in the eyes of the media everything becomes political.'

'I'm afraid it has always been so,' Ferguson told him.

'I know.' Clinton nodded. 'Anything I do must have some political advantage. This has already been said about the efforts I've made to help with the Irish situation.' He came back to the desk and sat down. 'Not true, gentlemen. Politicians are accused of many things, but for once I can say hand on heart that I'm interested in the outcome for its own sake and in this case that means peace in Ireland.'

'I believe you, sir,' Ferguson said.

'Thank you, and please believe Senator Keogh also. There is no personal advantage for him in this business. He's putting himself on the firing line here because he believes it's worth doing. As I said, I've talked to Senator Keogh and he seems satisfied with your plan of campaign. I'd appreciate it if you'd go over it with me now, Brigadier.'

When Ferguson was finished Clinton nodded. 'It makes sense to me.' He turned. 'Mr Dillon?'

'It could all be beautifully simple,' Dillon said, 'but surprise is everything, the Senator arriving out of the blue and so on. Secrecy is essential to the whole thing.'

'Yes, I agree.' Clinton checked his wristwatch. 'Midnight in London, gentlemen, which means it's now Friday there. I'm expecting news of the timing of the IRA meeting at Ardmore House quite soon now. I'd go to your hotel and catch a little sleep now while the going's good, Brigadier. I'll be in touch on the instant.'

'Of course, Mr President.'

Clinton pressed the buzzer on his desk and stood. 'Once again, I can't impress on you enough the importance of this mission.'

An aide came in and held the door open for them.

It was in fact only four hours later that Dillon came awake with a start in his hotel room and reached for the telephone.

'Ferguson here. I've got the good word so stir yourself, Dillon, and let's get out of here. I've phoned Andrews and the Lear will be ready to leave by the time we get there. I'll see you downstairs.'

The phone went down and Dillon hauled himself out of bed. 'Wonderful,' he said. 'Bloody marvellous. There must be a better way of making a living.' He headed off to the shower.

★

189

As the Lear lifted and turned out over the Atlantic, Dillon unbuckled his seat belt and altered his watch. 'Five-thirty in the morning London time.'

'Yes, with luck we should hit Gatwick by noon. Flight Lieutenant Jones tells me we'll have tailwind all the way across.'

'So, what about the Ardmore House meeting – when is it?'

'Sunday afternoon at two.'

'That's all right, then. Is it okay if I sleep now?' And Dillon dropped his seat back and closed his eyes.

London
Devon
London

1994

TWELVE

Hᴀɴɴᴀʜ ʙᴇʀɴꜱᴛᴇɪɴ was working in her office when Dillon went in. She took off her glasses and rubbed her forehead.

'Where's the Brigadier?'

'Dropped off at Cavendish Square to change clothes. He'll be here directly, then he wants to see the Prime Minister again.'

'Has anything been finalized?'

'You could say that. The IRA meeting is at Ardmore House on Sunday afternoon at two. Keogh will arrive at Shannon in a private Gulfstream. He'll proceed by helicopter at once to Drumgoole.'

'And security?'

'The good Senator will be quite content with you, me and the Brigadier.'

She smiled in delight. 'So he hasn't left me out? I thought he might.'

'Now, why would he do a thing like that to you?' Dillon grinned and lit a cigarette.

'How do you get on with Keogh?'

'Fine. A decent enough stick and not at all the way some of these reporters write him up. He's got plenty of guts to take this thing on.' Dillon nodded. 'I liked him. How have we got on with the January 30 investigation?'

'I've run off the print-outs for you. I think it's all done.

Here, I'll show you.' She got up and walked into the office Dillon had been using. The print-outs were neatly stacked by the computer. 'That lot there is the Russian enquiry you asked for, details of personnel at the Russian Embassy.'

'Good, I'll have a quick look.'

'A long look, Dillon, there's a lot of it. Of course senior personnel are at the top.' She smiled. 'I'll make some tea.' She disappeared into her office.

As she waited for the kettle to boil there was a step behind her and she turned. Dillon stood in the doorway, his face pale and excited. There was a computer print-out in his hand. He laid it on her desk.

'What is it?' she demanded.

'A nicely coloured photo and full details on a man called Colonel Yuri Belov, Senior Cultural Attaché at the Russian Embassy.'

'So?' She carried on making the tea.

'It's been suggested he's Head of London Station for the GRU, that's the Russian Military Intelligence.'

'I know what it is, Dillon.' She came and stood at his shoulder. Belov, in the photo, smiled up at her.

'Does he look familiar to you?' Dillon asked.

'No.' She shook her head. 'I can't say that he does.'

'Well, he does to me.'

At that moment the outer door opened and Ferguson entered. 'Ah, is that tea on the go? Jolly good. I'll have a quick cup, then I'll get off to Downing Street.'

Hannah Bernstein handed him a cup of tea. 'Dillon thinks he's come up with something to do with the January 30 enquiry, sir.'

'Oh, and what's that?'

'Colonel Yuri Belov.' Dillon indicated the print-out. 'Do you know anything about him?'

'Senior Cultural Attaché at their Embassy. I've seen him around on the Embassy party circuit.'

'It says here he may be Head of Station, GRU.'

'That suggestion has been mooted, but never proved, and we've never been involved with the GRU over here in any kind of a conflict of interest. Our dealings with the KGB, of course, have been very different.' Ferguson sipped some of his tea. 'But what is this, anyway?'

'I've only seen him once, but it was an important once.' He turned to Hannah. 'Remember when we were at the Europa? I told you I spoke to Grace Browning, the actress, and a Professor Curry?'

'So?'

'I saw them at the Dorchester the night Liam Bell was killed. She and Curry were at the champagne bar. Rupert Lang appeared, all very affectionate. Old friends kissing, that sort of thing.'

'Good heavens, man, so Rupert Lang is a friend of hers, so what?' Ferguson demanded.

Dillon held up the print-out. 'This man joined them, Colonel Yuri Belov, possibly Head of Station GRU. Now you must admit that would make a grand scandalous plot for the Sunday papers, a Minister of the Crown and a Russian agent.'

'But I've told you I've seen the man myself on the Embassy party circuit. These people are always around.' Ferguson put down his cup. 'Politicians are constantly invited to such affairs. They meet everybody, Dillon.'

Dillon said, 'Just hear me out, then you can give me the sack if you want.' He turned to Hannah. 'And you use your fine policewoman's mind on it, too.'

'All right,' Ferguson said. 'Come into my office and get on with it.'

He sat behind the desk. Dillon said, 'I was talking to Hannah about coincidences the other night. It got a little academic what with Karl Jung being mentioned, but what I was really getting at was that I don't believe in them.'

Ferguson was interested now. 'Go on.'

'As I said to Hannah, all those hits with the Beretta in the January 30 murders, that's no coincidence. Four IRA men stiffed and that's no coincidence, either. Two Heads of Station KGB London knocked off. Was that chance? I think not and that's why I asked for a computer print-out on all staff at the Russian Embassy.' He smiled. 'Which brings us to Yuri Belov at the champagne bar at the Dorchester.' Dillon turned to Hannah. 'I've always heard a good copper develops a nose for crime that's nothing to do with facts. Are you beginning to smell something unusual here, Chief Inspector?'

She turned to Ferguson. 'I'd like to hear more, sir.'

'There is more,' Ferguson said. 'I too can smell it. Carry on, Dillon.'

'My meeting with Daley that night in Belfast, the Sons of Ulster business. My supposed meeting with Daniel Quinn when they set me up. Who knew about it? Hannah, though she didn't know where I was to meet them. You, Brigadier, the Prime Minister, Simon Carter and Rupert Lang.' He turned to Hannah. 'Let's hear what a brilliant detective has to offer on this one.'

She glanced at Ferguson and he nodded gravely. 'Carry on, my dear.'

'Right, sir. Let's accept that January 30 knew Dillon was having a meet and didn't know where, but the mystery woman knew enough to follow him and was armed and ready for action. My question would be how did she know it was all going to happen?'

'And what is your conclusion, Chief Inspector?'

'You can discount yourself, Brigadier, me, Dillon.' She smiled. 'Now we come to the Prime Minister, Simon Carter and Rupert Lang.'

'We can hardly imagine the Prime Minister to be the source of the leak,' Ferguson said. 'And the idea that the

Deputy Director of the Security Services would seems inconceivable.'

'Which leaves us with only one probable source, sir.'

'It doesn't seem possible.' He shook his head. 'A Minister of the Crown, an Under-Secretary of State at the Northern Ireland Office.' He shook his head. 'Rupert Lang served in my regiment, the Grenadier Guards. After that, I Para. He received a Military Cross in Ireland, was wounded.'

'Just bear with me,' Dillon said. 'The Liam Bell killing. The whole thing was kept under wraps, his stop-off in London, I mean. We knew, and as usual, you, the PM and the Deputy Director and Lang.'

There was a pause. 'They were ready for Bell's presence at the Dorchester that night, Brigadier, ready enough to be able to wait ahead of him in ambush in that cemetery in Vance Square.'

Dillon was full of energy and very insistent. Ferguson raised a hand. 'Enough, you've made your point.' He turned to Hannah. 'What's the police view, Chief Inspector?'

'Not strong enough to make a case, sir, but worth pursuing enquiries.'

'And you, Dillon?'

'At this point in time I'd say your little ad hoc committee of you, Carter and Lang should cease functioning. There should be no further opportunity of Lang receiving secret and valuable information until we sort this out. For example, he knows about the Keogh affair.'

'But doesn't at this moment know when Keogh will be arriving at Shannon or the time of the IRA meet at Ardmore,' Hannah said. 'I'd say it should remain that way, sir.'

'But what on earth can I say to the Prime Minister?' Ferguson asked.

'Oh, come on, you ould sod,' Dillon said impatiently. 'You've been lying beautifully for years. Why stop now?'

'Dear God!' Charles Ferguson said. 'But you're right, of course,' and he reached for the red phone.

The Prime Minister received the call in his study at Downing Street.

'Ah, Brigadier. I've just heard from President Clinton that the IRA meeting at Ardmore is scheduled for two o'clock on Sunday afternoon. I presumed you would be coming round to fill me in on your meeting with Senator Keogh.'

'Something of supreme importance has happened, Prime Minister, a question of a leak of vital information.'

'Serious?' John Major asked.

'I'm afraid so and it could have a bearing on Senator Keogh's visit. As you know, secrecy is of the essence there.'

'Well, of course it is, we all accept that.'

'Then may I very earnestly beg you to take my advice on this, Prime Minister. I know of the Sunday meeting because President Clinton has told me, just as he has told you. Dillon and Chief Inspector Bernstein know because they must. Will you leave it at that for the moment?'

'You mean don't tell the Deputy Director and Rupert Lang? Are you suggesting this leak you mention comes from one of them?' There was total astonishment in the Prime Minister's voice. 'Surely that's inconceivable?'

'Prime Minister, be advised by me in this matter. It's a question of checking all avenues. Give me a few hours only.'

There was a pause and John Major said, 'Of course. I'm disturbed, Brigadier, because you're usually right and this time I don't want you to be, but carry on and speak to me at your soonest.'

When Ferguson went into Dillon's office the computer was humming, Dillon and Hannah beside it. Ferguson was full of energy now, brisk and businesslike.

'All right, what are we up to?'

'We're just checking on Tom Curry,' Hannah said.

Ferguson nodded. 'You know, that name is familiar. There's a Professor Curry from London University who sits on a number of Government committees.'

The printer started to eject paper and Dillon tore it out and laid it on the desk. Tom Curry's picture stared up at them. The details from the data bank did not only mention his academic qualifications but as usual with those engaged in Government work referred to his private life in intimate detail.

'Cambridge,' Ferguson said and frowned. 'Good God, Moscow University researching a PhD.'

The printer kept working. 'Rupert Lang coming through now,' Hannah said.

'Good God, he doesn't need to,' Ferguson told her. 'It says here that Curry and Lang have been living together for years at Lang's house in Dean Close. That's within walking distance of Westminster. Homosexual relationship since they were at Cambridge together.'

'Yes, but look further down,' Hannah said. 'It's Curry's academic record that's interesting. He's worked at Yale, Harvard, is a professor at London but look at that, sir. He's a visiting professor at Queen's University, Belfast, three or four days a month.'

'How interesting.' Ferguson was all business now. 'We know Curry was in Belfast when you and Dillon were handling the Sons of Ulster business, Chief Inspector.'

'Yes, sir.'

'Then there's those two provisional IRA foot soldiers in the alley that January 30 claimed the other year. It would be interesting to know if Professor Curry was in Belfast then.'

'And it would be interesting to know if Rupert Lang was,' Dillon put in.

'Easy enough to find out,' Ferguson said.

'It also raises an interesting point about the famous Beretta

January 30 used in all of their killings except the Sons of Ulster thing,' Dillon said. 'The fact that a weapon used in London could have turned up in Belfast, security restrictions into Ulster being so tough. I suggested to Hannah that the explanation might be that the owner of the Beretta might have a permit to carry.'

'That would certainly apply to a Minister of the Crown, but we can check on that soon enough.' Ferguson frowned and rubbed the bridge of his nose. 'Something's just occurred to me. Those two KGB Heads of Station, getting knocked off. Apparently, since the changes in Russia in the last few years, the long-standing feud between the GRU and the KGB has intensified. There could be a connection there with Belov. I'll look into it.'

'I'll phone Queen's University and check if the date of the killing of those two IRA men coincided with Curry being there,' Hannah said. 'And I'll get a run-down on the times Lang's visited Belfast from the Northern Ireland Office.'

'What about you, Dillon?' Ferguson demanded.

'Oh, I'll just ring Grace Browning's agent.'

Ferguson, in the act of reaching for the phone, stopped. 'Why?'

'It was a woman who saved me in the Sons of Ulster affair; it was a woman who killed Liam Bell – someone in my opinion, giving a rather excellent performance as a Pakistani woman. I'd like to remind you that she was performing in Belfast when I had my meeting with the Sons of Ulster and I did see her at the champagne bar at the Dorchester with Curry, Lang and Belov.'

'No, that really would be too much,' Ferguson said. 'What are you going to do?'

'Find out from her agent if she's performed in Belfast before the time Hannah and I were there. I'll also have a look at the files. Check her background.'

'Do that.'

Dillon paused in the doorway and turned to Hannah. 'Remember the other night when we were talking about synchronicity and you asked me if there were any other coincidences I wanted to check?'

'Yes. You said there was, but for the life of you, you couldn't think what it was.'

'I finally discovered. The night in Belfast when our mystery woman saved me and then raised her arm in salute. I'd seen Grace Browning's picture on a theatre poster at the Europa. After the same woman didn't shoot me and gave me that identical salute in the cemetery at Vance Gardens, I walked up to the King's Head in Upper Street and saw Grace Browning's face on a theatre poster.'

There was silence. Ferguson said, 'That's pretty slim evidence, Dillon. Circumstantial to say the least.'

'I know, Brigadier, but it's what Karl Jung meant by synchronicity,' and Dillon went into the other office.

Within an hour he and Hannah were back at Ferguson's desk.

'Well, what have we got?' he demanded.

Hannah turned to Dillon. 'You start.'

'Right,' Dillon said. 'In October, ninety-one, Grace Browning did a short run at the Minerva in Chichester of Brendan Behan's *The Hostage*. The company were asked to do a two-week run of the play at the Lyric Theatre in Belfast. The first and second weeks in November.'

He paused. 'Go on,' Ferguson said.

'The killing of those two IRA men that January 30 claimed credit for took place during the first week of the run.' He turned. 'Hannah?'

She said, 'Tom Curry was there for four days covering the time in question and also Rupert Lang. He was there for two days, but one of them was the day in question.'

'Dear God!' Ferguson said.

'More bad news,' Hannah Bernstein told him. 'According

to the record, Lang is licensed to carry a handgun when in Northern Ireland.'

'And the weapon?'

'A Beretta 9-millimetre Parabellum. We'd need to check the rounds it's fired.'

'Of course,' Ferguson said, 'but there's increasingly little doubt about what we'd find.' He shook his head. 'I don't understand.'

'One slight clue,' Dillon told him. 'It seems Curry came from Dublin. There was a history of Irish nationalism in the family, but his mother became a card-carrying member of the Communist Party.'

'All right, that might explain Curry, but what about the Browning woman, one of our finest actresses, and Rupert Lang?'

'There is one link, sir,' Hannah Bernstein said. 'A violent one. When she was twelve her parents were murdered in a street robbery in Washington. She was present. Saw it all.'

'Good Lord.'

'After that she came to London and lived with her aunt in the house she presently occupies in Cheyne Walk.'

'And Rupert Lang isn't just Mr Savile Row,' Dillon said. 'He was at Bloody Sunday with 1 Para, wounded. He has killed at least three times according to his army record and was awarded a Military Cross for undercover work.'

Ferguson sighed and turned to Hannah. 'Is it still a circumstantial case, Chief Inspector?'

'Oh, yes, sir, but a strong one.'

He nodded. 'I can see that, but I'll have to speak to the Prime Minister.'

'And Lang, sir?'

'We'll see. Leave it to me.'

At around the same time, Grace Browning and Tom, driving down from London into Kent, found a sign to Coldwater.

The village wasn't much – a line of cottages on either side of the road, a village green, a pond, a small inn called the George and Dragon. They carried on through and found another sign a quarter of a mile further on that indicated Coldwater airfield to the right.

They found it at the end of a narrow lane: a couple of old hangars, a control tower and a single tarmac runway that was crumbling badly. There was an old Land Rover parked outside a Nissen hut. They parked alongside it, and as they got out, the door of the hut opened and a man emerged.

He was of medium height, in his late forties, with a greying beard and tangled hair. He wore black flying overalls and an old American air force flying jacket.

'Mr Carson?' Curry asked.

'That's me.'

'Don't let's bother with names.'

Carson didn't offer to shake hands. 'Colonel Delov said you'd be around. Better come in.'

Curry opened the boot of his car and took out two suitcases. He followed Carson into the Nissen hut, Grace behind him. Inside, he put the cases down and looked around. There was a stove for heating, a desk, charts pinned to the wall.

'You know the flight's planned for Sunday?' Curry asked.

'That's right.' Carson unrolled a flying chart across his desk. It covered Ireland across to the Galway coast. 'I've found an old flying strip about ten miles from this Drumgoole place. Here at Kilbeg.'

'Do you envisage any problems with the flight?' Grace asked him.

'Only with the weather. Ireland's a sod. Too much rain. Flight time to County Clare could be anything between three and four hours depending on the wind. I can't do anything about that. You're stuck with what you get on the day.'

203

'In view of what you say, if we want to be at Drumgoole by noon we'll need an early start,' Curry said.

'I'd say seven to seven-thirty in the morning to be on the safe side,' Carson said.

'Fine.' Curry nodded. 'We'll be here.'

'And the return?' Carson asked.

'Let's say we'll be back with you by two o'clock,' Curry told him.

'That's good. I don't want to hang about.'

Grace said, 'Could we see the plane?'

'Sure. This way.'

It had started to rain as they crossed to the hangars. She said, 'It's a strange place, this.'

'RAF feeder station during the Second World War. Everything's falling apart now.'

He rolled back one of the hangar doors and led the way in. There were two planes in there, one single-engined, the other a twin.

'The single is an Archer, the twin is a Cessna Conquest. That's what we'll be using.'

'Fine,' Grace said.

They turned and went out and he closed the door. When they reached their car Tom Curry said, 'We'll be here at the crack of dawn on Sunday. Let's hope we have a good day.'

'I don't care what kind of day you have,' Carson told him. 'I'm getting more than well paid so I mind my own business. I'm an in-and-out man, that's all I'm interested in.'

'We'll be seeing you, then,' Grace said.

He frowned slightly. 'Do I know you from somewhere? You seem familiar.'

'I don't think so,' she said and got into the car.

Curry opened the door. 'The two suitcases aren't locked, so you don't need to break into them. Look after them until Sunday.'

He got behind the wheel and drove away. Carson watched

them go and then went back into the Nissen hut. He lit a cigarette and stood looking down at the suitcases. Finally he shrugged and put them on the desk. When he opened the first one he found a priest's cassock and clerical collar. The second one contained a nun's habit. Underneath there was an AK47 and a Beretta automatic.

He shivered and closed the cases quickly. None of his business, any of it. He didn't want to know, much better that way, and he put the cases on the floor against the wall.

In the study at Downing Street the Prime Minister sat grim-faced as he listened to what Ferguson had to say.

'So there it is, Prime Minister, I'm sorry. That's all I can say.'

'You were right, of course, to advise me to keep quiet about Sunday's meeting at Ardmore House,' the Prime Minister said. 'If there is any truth in what you say, if Rupert Lang is connected with January 30, the consequences could have been grave.'

'I must point out, Prime Minister, that even if January 30 knew of the meeting it doesn't necessarily mean they would have made an attempt on Senator Keogh's life. Their general motive has been obscure to say the least.'

'True, but you've made a more than circumstantial case against Lang and the others as far as I am concerned.'

'I'm afraid the word circumstantial is apt, Prime Minister. They can tough it out, the Browning woman and Professor Curry.'

'And Lang?'

'Well, there is a point there. The Beretta. Once in our hands we can prove that it is the weapon that killed so many people. He has no way of avoiding that.'

'Then let us confront him,' the Prime Minister said. 'Bear with me, Brigadier.' He lifted the phone. 'Find out where Mr

Rupert Lang, Under-Secretary of State for Northern Ireland, is at the present time.'

He put the phone down. Ferguson said, 'Are you sure you want to do it this way, Prime Minister?'

'Absolutely. He has not only betrayed his country and colleagues, he has betrayed me as his party leader.' The phone rang and he lifted it and listened. 'Thank you.' He replaced the phone and stood up. 'He's at the House, Brigadier. I intend to see him there and I'd like you to accompany me.'

Some people consider the House of Commons to be the best club in London with its numerous restaurants and bars. Most people's favourite is the terrace and it was to this the Prime Minister led the way, passing through the Central Lobby, acknowledging many people on the way.

The terrace itself was quite busy, plenty of people around, mostly with a glass in one hand. They leaned on the parapet, looking at Westminster Bridge on the left, and the Albert Embankment on the other side of the river. The Prime Minister waved a waiter away.

'A rotten business, Brigadier. I don't understand. Why? Why would he do it?'

Ferguson found a cigarette and lit it. 'You could say the same thing about Philby, Maclean, Blunt.' He shrugged. 'I can't give you an answer, sir.'

'It certainly won't do the Conservative Party any good.' John Major smiled. 'Sorry, Brigadier, politics is not your consideration in this matter.'

'No, but I sympathize, sir. Not your fault, but you get the flak.'

'One of the privileges of rank, Brigadier.'

At that moment, Rupert Lang appeared on the terrace, paused, then saw them. He hurried across smiling. 'Prime Minister. I got your message.' He nodded to Ferguson.

'Brigadier.' He turned back to the Prime Minister. 'You said it was urgent.'

John Major turned to Ferguson. 'Brigadier?'

Ferguson said, 'Mr Lang, as a Minister of the Crown you have a permit to carry a handgun when visiting Northern Ireland. The weapon, I understand, is a Beretta 9-millimetre Parabellum.'

Lang knew, knew at once what this meant, but he smiled. 'That's right.'

'I'd like to examine it, sir.'

'May I ask why?'

'To see if it is the weapon which has been responsible for the deaths of at least ten people, assassinations claimed by a terrorist group known as January 30.'

There was a long pause and then Lang said, 'This is nonsense.'

'Rupert,' the Prime Minister said. 'For God's sake. It's over.'

Rupert Lang stood there, staring at him, and then suddenly he smiled and turned to Ferguson. 'What is it you want, Brigadier?'

'The Beretta, Mr Lang.'

'Yes, of course, I'll get it. It's in my office desk.'

At that moment a crowd of Japanese tourists came on to the terrace. Lang turned and plunged into them, disappearing through the entrance on the far side before Ferguson or the Prime Minister could do a thing.

There are dozens of exits to the Houses of Parliament and Rupert Lang, an expert in all of them, was in his car in one of the underground car parks and driving away within five minutes of leaving Ferguson and the Prime Minister.

THIRTEEN

Belov was in his mews cottage off the Bayswater Road when he got Lang's call.

'My dear Rupert, how are you?'

'Not good, Yuri, I've been rumbled.'

'Calm yourself, Rupert and explain,' Belov said.

Lang went through exactly what had happened on the terrace with Ferguson and the Prime Minister. When he was finished he said, 'There was no mention of you or Tom or Grace, just the Beretta.' He laughed. 'I licensed it because I was entitled to, you know that, Yuri, but once they've tested it, fired a couple of rounds, I've had it.'

'Where is it?'

'I gave it to Grace. She wanted it for Sunday.'

'I see.'

'I've been thinking, Yuri. Perhaps Ferguson has made something of my connection with the Prime Minister's special security committee, but there's one thing they don't know. That we know that the IRA meeting at Ardmore is to take place on Sunday afternoon.'

'You're right,' Belov said. 'Let's make sure that stays that way. You see, my friend, if the Prime Minister and Ferguson think you don't know, the whole thing will go ahead as normal. No need to give Keogh any anxieties.'

'Of course, but that doesn't help me. I've got to get out of it.'

'Where will you go, Rupert?'

'I don't know. Perhaps to Devon. To Lang Place.'

'They'll catch up eventually.'

'Yes, it's the end of something, you don't need to tell me that. It's so bloody frustrating not knowing what Ferguson is up to. Is it just me and the damn Beretta or is more going on? Have other connections been made? If so they'll work their way round to all of us, I suppose.'

'Don't worry, Rupert, take care of yourself and good luck. They can't touch me if I go to the Embassy.'

Belov put the phone down, went to his bedroom and packed a bag with a few essentials. He left the cottage, went to his car parked at the kerb and got in. Ten minutes later he drove into the diplomatic safety of the Russian Embassy in Kensington Palace Gardens.

Lang stopped at a phone box and rang his house in Dean Close. The dialling tone seemed to go on for ever before Tom Curry answered.

'Thank God,' Rupert Lang said.

He told Curry what had happened. When he was finished his friend said, 'What will you do?'

'I'll go to Lang Place and think things out. I'll use the usual air-taxi people. I'll be there tonight. It's you I'm worried about, old sport. They didn't mention Yuri or you or Grace, but Ferguson's a downy old bird. It'll only be a matter of time.'

'Don't worry, old lad,' Curry said. 'We'll manage.' Suddenly he was choking with emotion. 'Take care, Rupert,' and then he said the words that were always so difficult for one man to another. 'I love you.'

He put down the phone, then picked it up again and dialled Grace Browning. When she answered he said, 'Just listen.'

She didn't feel afraid, more excited than anything else. When he was finished she said, 'So what now?'

'It could be a while before they make connections, and as regards the Ardmore House meeting, as far as they're concerned, Rupert doesn't know when it's to happen.'

'Sit tight, is that it?'

'I honestly think so. They can't touch Yuri if he stays in the Embassy. Diplomatic immunity. They don't have, can't have, any reason to move against you or me. I'll be around tonight as usual at the King's Head and take you to supper.'

'Look forward to it.'

She put down the phone and turned to the window and her head spun for a moment. She saw the shadow of a man, gun raised, but when she took a deep breath it went away.

It was late in the afternoon when Rupert Lang arrived at the small air-taxi firm in Surrey he habitually used for flights to Devon. His usual pilot, a young man called Alan Smith, greeted him as he got out of the car.

'All ready to go, Mr Lang.'

'Good,' Rupert said. 'Let's get moving.'

Ten minutes later the Navajo Chieftain lifted off the runway. He opened the bar box and poured a double Scotch into a plastic cup.

'Here's to you, old sport.' He toasted himself. 'I think Bloody Sunday has finally caught up with you.'

At the Ministry of Defence, Ferguson was at his desk at six o'clock that evening when Hannah Bernstein came in with Dillon.

'Our enquiries finally showed that he frequently flies down to his house in Devon, sir, Lang Place.'

'He uses an air-taxi firm in Surrey. We've checked and he flew down there during the late afternoon in a Navajo Chieftain. The pilot has not yet returned.'

'I see.' Ferguson looked out at the gathering gloom. 'Too late to do anything now. We'll fly down in the morning.

Use the same firm. He won't be going anywhere and he knows it. Make the booking, Chief Inspector.'

'Do you want the Okehampton police involved, sir?'

'No. Just tell the air-taxi people to arrange to have a car waiting to take us to Lang Place. Tell them we're expected.'

'And the Browning woman, sir?' Hannah asked. 'And Curry?'

'Oh, he'll have tipped them off and Belov. Unless I'm mistaken our Russian friend will have headed straight for sanctuary at the Russian Embassy, but to a certain extent they're in the dark. All they know for certain is that I asked for Lang's Beretta to see if it had any connection with the January 30 killings. He knew it damn well had which is why he did a runner, but there was no mention of any connection with the others. They may even be banking on the fact that there *is* no connection.'

'Well, all I can say is that if it was me, I'd smell a very large rat,' Dillon said.

'Yes, very probably.'

'Shall I have Curry and the Browning woman put under surveillance, then?' Hannah Bernstein asked.

'From the facts you've put before me of this young woman's life and background I've formed certain opinions about her,' Ferguson said. 'Something went very obviously wrong in her head a long time ago; possibly the trauma of her parents being murdered in Washington. A hell of a thing for a child to see. Though I suspect there may be more to it than that. We'll probably never know the whole truth.'

'But what if they decide to run, sir?' Hannah asked.

'Why should they? Lang and Curry lived together. What does that prove? They were friendly with Grace Browning. So what? Yuri Belov exchanged pleasantries with them at a drinks party. He also probably spoke to at least fifty people. Now, your fine police mind knows that everything about this case is circumstantial.'

'Except for Lang's Beretta. Once that's tested it's curtains for him and he knows it,' she said.

'And if he disposes of it, where's your evidence then?' Dillon asked. 'Another thing. Even under interrogation would he be likely to shop his friends? He doesn't seem the sort to me.'

'I agree,' Ferguson said. 'The blunt truth is we know what these people are and what they have done. Proving it will be another matter. In my opinion they'll sit tight for the moment and await developments.'

'So no surveillance?' Hannah said.

'She won't be going anywhere and neither will Curry. She's got a show to give. Last performance tomorrow night. She wouldn't walk out on that, would she, Dillon?' He smiled. 'Why not see if you can get us some tickets, Chief Inspector?'

Hannah offered Dillon a lift home and it was six-thirty as they drove out of the Ministry of Defence car park.

Dillon checked his watch. 'She'll be leaving for the theatre soon. Let's drive past her house.'

'Have you something in mind?'

'Not really, just idle curiosity.'

It was raining slightly as they turned into Cheyne Walk and slowed as they approached the house. 'Shall I stop?' Hannah asked.

'Just for a minute.'

At that moment she emerged from the side entrance on her BMW motorcycle. She wore black leathers and a dark helmet. She paused, pushed up the dark vizor and checked the traffic. In the light of the streetlamp they saw her face clearly. She pulled the vizor down and rode away.

'My God!' Hannah breathed. 'The final proof.'

'So it would seem,' Dillon said. 'So it would seem.'

★

Rupert Lang was sitting by the fire in the drawing room at Lang Place, with Danger lying in front of him, when the phone went. It was the Navajo pilot, Alan Smith, calling from Surrey.

'That you, Mr Lang? Alan Smith here. About the flight in the morning.'

'Which flight would that be?' Lang asked.

'A Brigadier Ferguson, a Miss Bernstein who made the booking and a man called Dillon. She said you were expecting them.'

'Ah, yes,' Lang said. 'What time will you drop in?'

'Nine-thirty start. A little wind forecast, but we should do it in an hour. They asked for a taxi.'

'No need. I'll have George Farne pick them up in the Range Rover. Thanks, Alan, and good night.'

He sat there thinking about it, then went and poured a Scotch. Finally he picked up the phone and called Dean Close. Curry answered at once.

'I've just heard they're flying in tomorrow,' Rupert told him. 'Ferguson, Bernstein and Dillon.'

'How did you find out?'

'The pilot rang me. Said he'd been told I was expecting them.'

'Strange, that. Ferguson must have known the pilot might do that.'

'Of course he did. Maybe he wants to give me a chance to do the decent thing and put a bullet through my head. Honour of the regiment and all that.'

'For God's sake, Rupert.' There was panic in Curry's voice.

'Don't worry, old sport, I've no intention of doing any such thing. I'll hear what he has to say. I want to know how close they are to the rest of you, if at all.'

'And the Beretta? What will you say when he asks for it?'

'That I found it had been stolen from my desk. I panicked,

213

shocked by the appalling suggestions made at that meeting with the PM, so I cleared off down here to think.'

'Rather weak, old lad.'

'Of course it is.' Lang laughed out loud. 'You know that and so does Ferguson, but let's see what he comes up with. You'd better phone Yuri at the Embassy and bring him up to date.'

'I'll do that.'

'Good night, old sport.'

Lang put the phone down, reached for his glass and sat staring into the fire while he stroked the wolfhound's head.

The weather was wretched the following morning when the Daimler turned into the entrance of the small airfield in Surrey and pulled up on the concrete apron. The doors of one of the hangars stood open and they saw the Navajo standing inside, the pilot beside it talking to an engineer in overalls. Ferguson, Dillon and Hannah got out and ran through the rain.

'Brigadier Ferguson? Alan Smith,' the pilot said. He nodded out at the curtain of rain. 'Not too good.'

'Are you saying we can't go?'

'It's up to you. Could be rough.'

'My friend here is a pilot.' Ferguson turned to Dillon. 'What's your opinion?'

'I wouldn't dream of interfering.' Dillon smiled and gave Smith his hand. 'Sean Dillon. I've got a commercial licence so it will comfort you to know that if you have a heart attack I can take over.'

Smith laughed. 'All right, then, if you folks are game so am I. Let's climb aboard and get on with it.'

It was raining steadily in Devon as Rupert Lang rode one of the Montesa dirt bikes along the track above the forest, Danger running alongside. Lang wore riding breeches and boots and an old paratrooper's camouflaged smock. Instead of a helmet he wore a tweed cap.

He paused beside a low wall. There were sheep over there, crowding around Sam Lee the shepherd, and Danger went over the wall and ran to them, barking. Sam Lee struck out at him with his shepherd's crook.

'Damn your eyes, Lee, I've told you before,' Lang called. 'Do that again and I'll break that thing over your head.'

'It's the sheep, Mr Lang, he won't leave them alone.'

'Damn the sheep!' Lang paused, looking up into the rain, aware of the sound of an aircraft in the distance. He whistled to the dog. 'Come on, boy!' He started the Montesa and rode off.

When the Range Rover entered the courtyard at Lang Place he was standing at the front door, still wearing the old cap and the paratrooper's smock, a curiously debonair figure.

'Ah, there you are, Ferguson, right on time.'

'Chief Inspector Hannah Bernstein, my personal assistant, and Sean Dillon.'

'Your personal hit man.' Lang smiled at Dillon. 'We probably traded shots back there in Derry in the old days.'

'And isn't that a fact?' Dillon told him.

Lang turned to Hannah. 'And what have they brought you along for, Chief Inspector? To read me my rights, make an arrest?'

'If necessary, sir.'

'Well, it isn't, I assure you. Stupid mistake, the whole thing, but come in out of the rain and I'll explain.'

He led the way into the drawing room where Danger, lying in front of the fire, got up. 'Down, boy.' Lang stroked him cheerfully. 'Not a bit of harm in him, believe me. Soft as a brush. I've got a bottle of Bollinger on ice and Mrs Farne will serve a light lunch in the conservatory before you go back.'

'Don't you mean we, sir?' Hannah said.

'A trifle premature, I would have said. Would you mind doing the honours, Dillon? It's stuffy in here.' He went and opened the French windows to the terrace. 'That's better.'

Dillon uncorked the champagne and poured.

'Not for me,' Hannah said.

'On duty, Chief Inspector?' Lang smiled, looking immensely attractive, and held a glass out to her. In spite of herself, she took it. 'Now, what shall we drink to?'

'Why not January 30?' Ferguson said.

'Oh dear, there you go again, Brigadier. I honestly don't know what you're talking about. As for the Beretta, well, unfortunately it's been stolen from my desk at the House . . .'

Ferguson held up a hand and took one of the chairs by the fire. 'I'd sit down if I were you.' He turned to Hannah. 'Chief Inspector, in the matter of Mr Rupert Lang's involvement in the terrorist group we know as January 30, make your case.'

Lang sprawled in a chair listening, a slight smile on his face, one hand stroking Danger's head, the other holding his glass of champagne. When she was finished, he stood up and went and recharged his glass.

'Anyone else?' he asked, holding up the bottle. 'No?'

'A convincing case, you must agree, Lang,' Ferguson said.

'Total fantasy, the lot of it. Tom Curry and I have lived together for years and quite openly, that's the connection there. Colonel Yuri Belov is someone I've met casually on the Embassy party circuit, as I'm sure many Members of Parliament have. Grace Browning is a dear friend to both Tom Curry and myself. To attempt to tie us all in together as members of this January 30 group, quite frankly beggars belief.'

'High melodrama, the whole thing, I grant you that,' Ferguson told him.

'And totally circumstantial. I mean, come on, Ferguson. I'm in Belfast on Government business, Tom has a few days at Queen's and Grace Browning happens to be performing at the Lyric Theatre, and when a couple of IRA louts end up dead in an alley, you accuse the three of us.'

'I accuse January 30,' Ferguson said, 'who claimed those killings. After all, there's the business of Dillon and the Sons of Ulster. Only Dillon himself, Chief Inspector Bernstein, Simon Carter, myself, the Prime Minister and you knew about that and the same circumstance applied in the unfortunate killing of Liam Bell.' He shook his head. 'Simple process of elimination, Lang. In both cases you had to be the leak.'

Lang stood there, the slight fixed smile on his face. 'Any good barrister could demolish that argument at an Old Bailey trial in five minutes flat. You see, Ferguson, the only link to the January 30 killings is the Beretta. Now, you say it's my Beretta, but as that has unfortunately been stolen we'll never know, will we? Of course I'm sorry I panicked and cleared off after finding the gun was missing. Naturally I'll offer the PM my resignation.'

It was Dillon who broke the log jam. 'Jesus, me ould son, but you've got a tongue on you.' He went to the table and took the bottle of Bollinger from the bucket. 'Is it all right if I help myself?'

'Be my guest, old sport.'

Dillon filled his glass. 'Why did you do it, that's what interests me. I mean, Belov I understand. He's a pro working for his own side and Curry is obviously your typical British middle-class wealthy liberal nutcase who wants to make the world safe for Communism. Have I left anything out?'

'He's Irish, actually,' Lang said.

'As for the girl, I've formed the opinion she's touched in the head,' Dillon told him, 'but that's another story.' He looked up at the portrait of the Earl of Drury over the fireplace. 'Ancestor of yours from the look of his face. A grand arrogant bastard who walked over everybody. He probably laid his riding crop over the shoulders of his servants and made all the maids have sex with him.'

Lang's face was pale. 'Take care, Dillon.'

'You'd rather be him, is that it? Modern life too boring? All the money in the world and all you could find to do was play at politics and then January 30 came along. I don't know how, but it came along.' There was a wolfish look on Lang's face now. Dillon continued, 'I'd like to know one thing. Did Grace Browning make all the hits or did you share?'

'You go to hell,' Lang told him.

Ferguson stood up. 'I believe there is enough evidence to take you into custody, Lang. You'll come back to London with us.' He turned to Hannah. 'Read him his rights and, for the moment, charge him with treason.'

'Nobody's taking me anywhere,' Lang said and snapped his fingers. 'Stand, boy.' Danger was on his feet instantly, a rumble like distant thunder deep in his throat. 'He'll tear your arm off, Ferguson, if I tell him to.'

'Is that a fact?' Dillon said and whistled, a strange eerie sound that seemed to come from another place. 'Now then, Danger boy.' He held out a hand. The wolfhound wriggled close, reached up and licked the hand.

'Good God!' Lang said.

'A man who was once my friend taught me that trick,' Dillon said.

'Ah, well, it just goes to show you can't rely on anything in this wicked old world,' Rupert Lang said and took a Browning from inside the pocket of his smock. 'Except one of these, of course. Sorry, Ferguson, but I'm not going anywhere.'

He backed out of the windows and was gone, the dog running after him. Dillon took out his Walther and ran on to the terrace, pausing to get his bearings. There was no sign of Lang. Then Dillon heard the roaring of an engine and Lang rode out of the barn on the Montesa, skidded out through the main gate and took the track up to the moor.

Dillon ran across to the Range Rover and in the same moment saw the other Montesa on its stand inside the barn.

He turned and called to Ferguson and Hannah, who had emerged on to the terrace. 'There's another bike. I'm going after him. I'll call you on my Cellnet phone, Hannah.'

A moment later, he roared out of the barn, turned through the gates and went after Lang, who was high up on the track now, the wolfhound chasing him.

Dillon's tweed suit was soaked within minutes, water spraying everywhere from the rough track, and the rain dashed in his face half blinding him. For some reason he seemed to be gaining and when he went over a rise after coming up through the trees he saw Lang no more than a hundred yards in front, Danger running alongside, keeping pace with him with apparent ease.

And yet it was the wolfhound in the end that was Lang's undoing for as they reached the crest of the track, high above the forest, three sheep came over the dry-stone wall. Danger, ahead of the motorcycle at that point, crossed in front to snap at the sheep. Lang swerved to avoid him.

At that point there was a wooden five-bar gate. He smashed through it, careered down a grass slope and plunged over a ledge of rock, still astride the Montesa, and amazingly, the dog leapt after him.

Dillon left his bike by the smashed gate, slithered down the slope and looked over. Lang lay there with the Montesa on top of him and the wolfhound was crawling towards him, dragging its hind legs. Dillon moved to one side where the grass sloped again and went down.

He got both his hands to the Montesa, lifted it up and

tossed it to one side. There was blood on one side of Lang's face. Dillon leaned down to lift him and Lang cried out in agony.

'My bloody back's broken, Dillon. Christ, I can feel the bone sticking out.'

'I'll get help, I have a phone.' Dillon got his Cellnet out and dialled Hannah's number.

She was with him in seconds. 'Are you okay, Dillon?'

'There's been a bad accident. Lang's crashed and broken his back. You'd better get on to the police at Okehampton. We'll need an ambulance or a helicopter if there is one. I'm high on the track above the forest.'

'I'll get straight on to it.'

Dillon turned to Lang, and Danger whimpered in pain, trying to drag himself to his master. Lang turned his head. 'There's a good boy.' He tried to reach the dog with a hand and groaned. 'My God, his rear legs, Dillon, the bones are jutting out.' He closed his eyes and took a deep breath. 'Finish him for me, Dillon, do the decent thing. Can't bear to see him suffer.'

Dillon took out his silenced Walther. Danger looked up at him, eyes filled with pain. 'There's a boy,' Dillon said, stroking his head, and shot him.

Dillon crouched beside Lang, lit a cigarette and put it to his lips. Lang coughed and said weakly, 'What a way to go. What a stupid bloody way to go.'

'Someone will be here soon,' Dillon said. 'One of the advantages of the Cellnet phone system. Instant communication.'

'Not instant enough. I'm dying, Dillon.'

'Maybe not. Just hang in there.'

'What for? A show trial.' He closed his eyes. 'I've always been so bored, Dillon, had everything and had nothing, if you follow. Ireland disgusted me so I left the Army for silly political games and then things happened, all by chance, wonderful, exciting things. Nothing was ever so exciting.'

His breathing was laboured. 'Take it easy,' Dillon told him.

'No, something I want you to understand, want to tell you because it doesn't seem to matter now. The first January 30 was a mistake. Tom was a delivery boy for Belov, but the Arab he met was supposed to kill Belov for the KGB. Tom shot him in a struggle for the gun – the Beretta. That's why we invented January 30. To explain the killing. But Tom was shot and I couldn't have that so I knocked off Ashimov, the KGB bastard behind everything. I killed people in Ireland, Dillon, so why couldn't I kill a piece of slime like that?'

Blood was trickling out of his mouth. 'Easy,' Dillon said.

'So it started and after a while came Grace.' His words were distorted now. 'Tom and I went to see her at the Lyric. On the way back, those two scum jumped her, heroes of the glorious revolution. Took her up an alley to rape her. Tom and I intervened. I was carrying, you see. I'd made the Beretta my licensed handgun for visits to the Province.'

'And you killed them.'

'They were armed. I shot one, there was a struggle and Grace picked up the Beretta and took out the other bastard.'

'And that was the start of it for her?'

'Got a taste for it. Another kind of performance. I put her through a weapons course here. Very apt pupil!'

He closed his eyes, his breathing shallow. Dillon said, 'The Beretta, has Grace got it?'

'Oh, yes, needs it.'

Dillon frowned. 'Why?'

'Poor Ferguson. Another Bloody Sunday. Like to see his face,' Lang said and coughed, turning his head to one side, blood erupting from his mouth. His body shook violently, then went very still.

A moment later Dillon heard his Cellnet phone. He took it

221

out and switched on and Ferguson said, 'Dillon, there's an RAF base only twelve miles away. They're sending a helicopter.'

'Too late,' Dillon said. 'He just died. I'll see you in a little while, Brigadier.'

He switched off and turned as stones cascaded down the slope, and Sam Lee arrived. 'What happened, then?'

'He crashed through the gate off the track and came down the slope.'

'Dead, is he?' There was a certain satisfaction on Lee's coarse face. 'Ah, well, that's the way of the world. Even the high and mighty come down to this.'

'Who the hell are you?' Dillon asked.

'The estate shepherd and that damn dog lying there like that is the best news I've had in years.'

He stirred Danger with his foot and Dillon, anger flooding through him like lava, put a knee in Lee's crutch and raised it again into the descending face, sending the shepherd back down the slope a good forty feet.

It was mid-afternoon when Alan Smith took the Navajo up over the trees at the end of the old RAF landing strip and climbed through the rain.

'One bright spot from the Prime Minister's point of view,' Hannah Bernstein said. 'With Rupert Lang's timely death, a rather large scandal is averted for the Conservative Party.'

'But it still leaves us with the Browning woman, Curry and Belov. Thanks to Rupert Lang's rather emotional leave-taking we now have our suspicions confirmed.'

'I'd like to point out, Brigadier,' Hannah said, 'that Dillon's account of Lang's dying confession carries no weight in a court of law. If it was put forward by the prosecution the judge would have no option but to throw it out.'

'Yes, I am aware of that sad fact, Chief Inspector.' Ferguson sighed. 'But I'm deeply disturbed by Dillon's other piece of information. He said that the Browning woman had the Beretta?'

'Yes,' Dillon told him. 'He said she needed it. I asked what he meant and he said: "Poor Ferguson, another Bloody Sunday. I'd like to see his face." Then he died.'

'How very inconvenient of him,' Ferguson said.

'Isn't that rather hard, sir?' Hannah protested.

'Not at all. There's only one Sunday that's important in my book – tomorrow – and any kind of involvement in that affair by Grace Browning fills me with horror.'

'But she's here in London, sir,' Hannah said. 'She's performing at the King's Head tonight.'

'So are we, my dear, but flying out to Shannon in the morning. She could do the same.'

'Shall I have her lifted, sir?'

'You got the tickets for the show?'

'Yes.'

'We'll allow her the final performance. Pick her up afterwards. My guess is Curry will be there.' He turned to Dillon. 'Are you looking forward to it?'

'I wouldn't miss it for all the tea in China,' Sean Dillon told him.

FOURTEEN

THE UNTIMELY DEATH of Rupert Lang, Under-Secretary of State at the Northern Ireland Office, was featured on television news as early as one o'clock. Tom Curry, preparing a sandwich in the kitchen at Dean Close, had the television on and could not believe what he had heard. He felt himself start to shake with emotion, stumbled across to the dresser and got a bottle of Scotch open and spilled about three fingers into a glass. He swallowed it down, then went into the drawing room and sat on the couch, hugging himself.

'Rupert! Oh, God, Rupert! What happened?' He started to cry and then the phone went. He let it ring for a while, then picked it up reluctantly.

Grace said, 'Are you there, Tom?'

'Rupert,' he said brokenly. 'Rupert is dead.'

'Yes, I know. Now just hang on. I'm on my way,' and she put down the phone.

But he couldn't do as she asked because there was nothing to hang on to. He had never felt so totally desolate in his life. Rupert was gone and in that moment he realized that the most important reason for his existence had gone for ever. This time he poured an even larger whisky and swallowed it down quickly, then he went and got his raincoat and let himself out of the front door.

It was raining quite hard, not that it mattered. Nothing

mattered now. It was as if his whole life had been for nothing and he kept on going in the general direction of the Houses of Parliament.

Grace, driving along Millbank, was astonished to see him walking along the pavement. She tried to pull in, but the traffic was extremely heavy, and then he crossed the road to the other side and there was nothing she could do, stuck for a moment in a long jam of traffic.

He was some distance ahead now and she tapped the wheel nervously, and then the traffic started to move. At the same time a delivery van moved out of a parking space and she swerved into it. She locked the car hurriedly, ran along St Margaret Street and entered Parliament Square.

She paused, looking everywhere desperately, then saw him on the corner of Bridge Street. She ran even faster now and reached the corner to see him on the other side of the street approaching Westminster Underground Station. He entered with a number of other people and she dodged her way through traffic and crossed the road.

Curry didn't have a destination. He simply took a pound coin from his pocket, put it in the appropriate slot, took the ticket that came up and went through the barrier. He went down the elevator with a large queue of people, walked along the corridors below, just another face in the crowd until he came out on to the station platform. There was quite a crowd, people standing shoulder-to-shoulder, and he pushed his way through to the front and stood at the edge of the platform.

The whisky had done its work now. It was not that he was drunk, just totally numb, no feeling at all. There was the roar of a train approaching, a blast of air and then a voice calling.

'Tom! Wait for me!'

He half turned and saw Grace Browning trying to push

through the crowd towards him and then he turned back and, as the train emerged from the tunnel, stepped off the platform in front of it.

It was no more than forty minutes later that Hannah Bernstein's computer buzzed in her office at the Ministry of Defence. She got up from her desk, crossed to the printer and tore off the strip of paper and read it.

'My God!' she said and called, 'Dillon? Where are you?' Then she knocked on Ferguson's door and went in.

Ferguson, at his desk, looked up. 'What is it?'

At that moment Dillon joined them. 'It's the professor, Tom Curry,' Hannah said. 'I had a general call out to Central Records Office to update me if anything new turned up on him as I did with the others. It seems he just stepped in front of a train at Westminster Underground Station.'

'Dead, presumably?' Ferguson asked.

'Oh, yes. Immediate identification from the wallet in his jacket. The police officer in charge radioed it in to CRO. When it entered their computer, it referenced to my enquiry.'

'Sweet Mother of God.' Dillon lit a cigarette. 'And why would he do that?'

'Rupert Lang, perhaps,' Ferguson said. 'They lived together for years, Dillon. Perhaps Lang's death was a blow he simply couldn't take.'

'So where does it leave us, sir?' Hannah asked.

'Two down, one to go,' Dillon said.

'Two,' Ferguson told him. 'There's Belov at the Embassy, remember.'

'What will you do about him, sir?' Hannah asked.

'Leave him to stew for a while. Always difficult, this diplomatic immunity business.'

'And Grace Browning?'

226

'Whichever way you look at it she's on her own now,' Dillon put in.

'I'm afraid so,' Ferguson said. 'I almost feel sorry for her.'

'Jesus, you old sod,' Dillon said. 'You never felt sorry for anyone in your life.'

Ferguson ignored the remark. 'She won't have heard about Curry yet. Of course the media will catch on to the fact that he lived with Lang for years and draw their own conclusions.'

'Very convenient when you think of it,' Dillon said. 'Now if only Grace Browning would break her neck on that motorcycle everything would be wrapped up nice and quiet. You could invite Yuri Belov to come over instead of going home to bread queues in Moscow. Lots of juicy information to be obtained there.'

'You're a callous bastard, Dillon,' Hannah told him.

'He's right, of course,' Ferguson observed. 'In the circumstances, I think I'll turn the screw on her.' He picked up the phone.

Grace Browning, back at Cheyne Walk, was drinking a cup of hot and very sweet tea, sitting at the table, trying in the most cold-blooded way to assess the situation. The phone rang and she picked it up.

Ferguson said, 'Brigadier Ferguson here, my dear. I think you know who I am.'

'What do you want?' she said calmly.

'I'm sure you're aware as it has been prominently featured in all news bulletins that your good friend Rupert Lang died earlier today in a tragic accident.'

'Yes, I know about that.'

'What you won't yet know is that your other good friend, Professor Curry, died under the wheels of a train at Westminster Underground Station within the past hour.'

Grace took a deep breath. 'That's shocking news.'

'Yuri Belov is in effect locked up at the Russian Embassy, which only leaves you. The game's over, I'm afraid.'

'And what game would that be, Brigadier?'

'I always did say you were a brilliant actress. That's why I got my aide, Chief Inspector Bernstein, to get us tickets for the King's Head tonight. You will be appearing, I take it?'

'I've never missed a performance in my life, Brigadier.'

'I'm looking forward to it. I'll tell you what I think of it afterwards.'

Hannah said, 'She could decide to run.'

'I don't think so,' Ferguson said. 'But if you want to keep a discreet eye on her, do so. She knows Dillon, so you'll have to take care of it yourself.'

'I'm on my way,' Hannah said. She picked up her shoulder bag and went out.

'Full of enthusiasm,' Dillon said. 'That's what I like. God save us, but the women are taking over the world.'

No alcohol, she needed a clear head. She made another very hot cup of tea, went into the drawing room and looked out at Cheyne Walk: lots of traffic and plenty of parked cars. Somebody out there would be keeping an eye on her, she took that for granted now, so she would have to be very, very clever. The one important thing was her firm intention of still keeping her date with destiny at Drumgoole Abbey. She owed it to Tom and Rupert if for no other reason. She lit one of her rare cigarettes, pacing up and down, and then it came to her – the perfect solution and devastatingly simple.

Yuri Belov was in his office at the Russian Embassy when the phone went. Grace said, 'Yuri, it's me. You've heard about Rupert?'

'Unfortunately yes.'

'I've more bad news. Tom flung himself under a train at Westminster Underground Station this afternoon.'

'Dear God!' Belov said.

'And they're definitely on to me,' Grace said. 'I had a cryptic phone call from Ferguson. He's coming to my final performance at the King's Head tonight with Dillon and this Bernstein woman.'

'Get out, Grace, while you can,' he said urgently.

'No way. I'm sticking to the plan. You see, I'm taking a chance. I'm betting on the fact that they don't know anything about Sunday. Rupert could have told them, but I'm sure he wouldn't have, and Tom's dead. That means it's all still in place, Carson at the airfield at Coldwater, the flight to Kilbeg. Will your people definitely leave a car there?'

'All taken care of, but Grace, this is madness.'

'Not really, I've worked it out very carefully. There is one thing I need to know, though. There's no chance of Ferguson ringing you up to offer you a deal? I mean, some of your people *have* come over in the past. Lots of information in return for a comfortable asylum.'

'He'll offer, I'm sure of it, but not yet.'

'But if you're shipped back to Moscow as a failure, wouldn't that be rather unpleasant?'

'But I won't be a failure if you succeed in shooting Patrick Keogh.' Belov laughed. 'Of course, if you fail, I can always do a deal with Ferguson then.'

She laughed back at him. 'That's my Yuri.'

'But tell me,' he said. 'What's your plan?'

'It's really quite simple, I'm going to die.'

'Grace!' he said. 'Tell me.'

So she did.

She found a large plastic bag in the kitchen and put in it an old navy-blue tracksuit, a light raincoat, some trainers and a pair of black leather flat-heeled shoes. She went to her safe, opened it and took out two bundles of ten-pound notes, a thousand pounds in each. She placed a bundle in each of the black shoes, thought about things for a while, then rolled up a kitchen towel and added that also.

When she left the house fifteen minutes later she wore an old Burberry and carried an umbrella against the rain. She turned along the pavement to where she had parked her red Mini, opened it and got in.

Hannah, parked further along on the other side of the road, watched all this with interest. She followed as Grace Browning pulled out into the heavy traffic, driving towards Westminster, skirting the Tower of London until she reached Wapping High Street, finally parking close to a department store. There was room a couple of cars behind and Hannah pulled in and switched off her engine.

Grace got out the plastic bag, locked her car, then paused to put money into the parking meter. She turned and made for the main entrance of the department store. Hannah went after her, but when she went into the store, it was crowded with shoppers and there was no way of knowing which department her quarry had gone to. There was also the chance that if she went walkabout looking for her she might miss Grace leaving. She decided to take a chance and returned to her car.

Grace Browning at that moment was visiting the toilet and rest room at the bottom of a short flight of steps at the rear of the building. There was a door which said Staff Only. She'd used it once out of curiosity and had discovered that it led into an alley at the side of the store. She hurried along to the end and came out on to the waterfront.

She walked quickly to an area of decaying warehouses, St James's Stairs not too far away. She knew this place well, had once done an episode for a television thriller here. There was a narrow alley called Dock Street, nothing but boarded-up windows and several old dustbins. She was taking a chance but there was a risk in everything now. She pushed the plastic bag down behind the dustbins, pulled a dirty old sack over it, turned and hurried back.

She was entering the staff door at the department store five minutes after exiting from it. She went up the stairs, walked to an area displaying bedding and towels, chose a couple of towels at random, paid for them and waited while the assistant packed them into a white plastic bag similar to the one she had entered the store with.

Hannah saw her at once as she came out of the entrance and walked to her Mini. Grace opened the door, tossed the plastic bag in the rear and slid behind the wheel. If she was being followed, she'd fooled them nicely, she was certain of that. She pulled into the traffic, followed by Hannah.

A little while later she approached Wapping Underground Station and turned into the multi-storey car park that was close by. She drove into the basement and pulled up at the car-valeting service. Hannah followed, took a vacant parking spot and watched.

Grace smiled at the young black man in overalls who came out of the office. 'A wash and wax would be fine. Can you manage that?'

'No problem. When do you want it?'

'The fact is I'm doing a show tonight and I might be late. Ten o'clock, something like that.'

'We close at seven.'

'Couldn't you leave the keys under the mat for me?'

'Well, we aren't supposed to do that, lady.'

She opened her purse. 'How much will it be?'

'Twenty pounds.'

'That's fine.' She handed him a twenty-pound note and gave him her most dazzling smile as she also produced a five-pound note. 'Perhaps you'd make an exception. I'd really be very grateful.'

231

He smiled. 'I never could resist a beautiful woman. You'll find it over there on that yellow section.'

'Bless you.' She turned and walked down the ramp, passing Hannah, who watched her go, then pulled out and followed.

Grace walked along the pavement until she saw an approaching black cab. She hailed it and got inside. Hannah followed and fifteen minutes later found herself once again in Cheyne Walk, where Grace paid off her taxi driver and went inside.

Hannah called in to the office and spoke to Ferguson. 'She took a drive to Wapping High Street, did some shopping at a department store, then she left her car with a valeting service next to Wapping Underground Station and caught a taxi home.'

'As I told you, Chief Inspector, there was no need for surveillance. She'll be there tonight, I'm sure of it. However, if it gives you peace of mind to stay and keep watch, do so. Dillon and I will see you at the theatre. I must go now, I'm due at Downing Street.'

Simon Carter was already seated in the Prime Minister's study when Ferguson was shown in.

'Ah, there you are, Brigadier. We've just been discussing those two extraordinary deaths. Fill us in as much as you can.'

'Of course, Prime Minister.'

Ferguson described in detail the events in Devon which had led to Rupert Lang's death. He also told them as much as he knew about Tom Curry's suicide.

'Strange,' Carter said when he'd finished. 'That remark Rupert Lang made about another Bloody Sunday. What in hell was that supposed to mean? Is Keogh at risk? Is that the reference to a Sunday? Do you think there is a threat of some sort?'

'*Was* a threat,' Ferguson said. 'Certainly there is no threat now, with two dead and Belov trapped in the Russian Embassy.'

'And the woman?' Carter demanded.

'We'll pick her up after her show tonight. My Chief Inspector is on her tail. She isn't going anywhere.'

The Prime Minister nodded. 'I wish we could keep this whole damn thing under wraps. My God, a Minister of the Crown a traitor.' He smiled ruefully. 'And I'm not just thinking of the welfare of the Conservative Party, though there would be those who might think so.'

'We'll have to see, Prime Minister, but there is a legal difficulty. Many murders have been committed by January 30 and we know now that Grace Browning was responsible for a number of them. Rather difficult to get round that.'

'God help us all, then,' the Prime Minister said.

It was about six-forty-five when Grace Browning appeared from the side of the house in Cheyne Walk on the BMW. She sat astride it wearing her usual black leathers and adjusted her helmet so that anyone watching could be sure it was her, then she rode away and Hannah pulled out and followed her.

Twenty minutes later they arrived at the King's Head. Grace Browning parked the BMW and got off. Hannah pulled up and watched her take off her helmet and enter. When she was satisfied that Grace was safely in, she found a parking space herself.

She saw Ferguson's Daimler with his chauffeur at the wheel a few vehicles away, crossed the pavement and went into the King's Head, which was as crowded as usual just before a show started. Ferguson and Dillon were at the far end of the bar and Dillon called to her.

As she approached he said, 'Jesus, woman, a fine boring day you've given yourself.'

'Never mind, my dear,' Ferguson told her. 'Have a drink.'

'No, thank you, sir, I'm driving.'

233

'God save us, what a woman, but as it happens I'm not.' Dillon turned to the barman. 'Another Bushmills while the going's good.'

A moment later the five-minute warning sounded over the tannoy and everyone crowded in. They found their table and settled, the lights dimmed and a moment later Grace Browning came on stage to strong applause.

When the interval lights went up Ferguson said, 'She is really quite remarkable. All that talent. What a pity.'

Dillon stood up. 'I'm going to go round and speak to her.'

'No you're bloody well not. I mean, what for?' Ferguson demanded.

'Because I bloody well feel like it.'

Hannah stood up. 'Then, if you go, I do.'

'Suit yourself.'

Grace Browning's dressing room was cramped and untidy. She was drinking a glass of white wine when Dillon knocked and entered.

'Why, Dillon!' She looked genuinely pleased. 'Was I any good?'

'Bloody marvellous and you know it. This, by the way, is Detective Chief Inspector Hannah Bernstein, one of Scotland Yard's finest.'

'What a pleasure,' Grace said.

'We will be expecting you to accompany us after the finish of the play,' Hannah said. 'I hope you understand that.'

'Oh, I do.' Grace poured another glass of white wine. 'Sorry how things worked out, Dillon. I think you and I could have been friends.'

He smiled and gave her the time-honoured good wish from one actor to another. 'Break a leg, my love,' he said, pushed Hannah Bernstein out of the door and closed it.

★

At the play's end, the applause was tumultuous and when Grace Browning came on she received a standing ovation. She bowed, linked hands with other members of the cast, glanced towards Dillon and Ferguson and gave them an extra bow. When she went off she found Hannah in the corridor being jostled by members of the cast and stage crew.

'Ah, there you are, Chief Inspector. I must change.'

'Yes, you do that,' Hannah said. 'I'll wait for you here.'

In the dressing room Grace stripped, then pulled on her leathers. The one change from usual was that instead of wearing heavy leather boots she wore a pair of black dancer's pumps. She went out, gloves in one hand and helmet in the other.

'You won't need that,' Hannah said, nodding at the helmet.

'Oh, dear.' Grace Browning smiled. 'Aren't you supposed to read me my rights or something if you're going to charge me?' She smiled. 'Not that it matters. You'll have to excuse me. Call of nature.'

She had the door of the toilet on the right side of the corridor open and closed again in a second, the bolt rammed home. She'd checked the window earlier and now she stood on the toilet bowl as Hannah thundered on the door. Grace got the window open and dropped her gloves and helmet into the yard.

'Bye-bye, Chief Inspector,' she called and climbed through.

Outside in the corridor, Hannah turned and ran into the theatre, where she found Ferguson and Dillon at the bar entrance.

'She's done a runner,' Hannah called.

Dillon actually laughed. 'Jesus, girl, that was careless of you,' and he turned and hurled his way through the crowded bar.

He arrived on the pavement, Hannah close behind, and

there was a roaring in the night as Grace Browning exploded on the BMW. She skidded to a halt, caught for a moment by heavy traffic, and Hannah got the door of her car open and slid behind the wheel.

'In, Dillon, in!' she called and switched on her engine.

Ferguson shouted, 'I'll follow in the Daimler.'

Grace moved out into the traffic, turned to look at Hannah Bernstein's car and raised her arm in that inimitable salute to Dillon, then she was away. Hannah pulled a blue police reflecting light from under her seat, slammed it through the open window on to the roof and went after her.

Grace sped down Upper Street, turned left at the Angel and took the City Road, weaving in and out of heavy traffic, but Hannah, driving brilliantly and with the help of her police warning light, managed to stay on her tail.

Ferguson's voice came through on the police radio she had fitted in her car. 'What's the position, Chief Inspector? We're well behind.'

'Way down the City Road, sir,' she replied. 'I'd say making for the City now.'

Grace turned off the road, moving from one street to another. Hannah said into the radio, 'She seems to be aiming for the Tower of London.'

'All right, enough is enough,' Ferguson replied. 'Put out a general alarm. I want her stopped.'

As Grace Browning reached St Katharine's Way, a police car moved to block her. She swerved around it and carried on. Hannah mounted the pavement to pass the police car and went after her.

They were into Wapping High Street now and on the other side of the road, bearing down on her, Grace saw two police cars. One of them edged out to block her way and she put a foot down like a dirt rider, broadsided and disappeared into a narrow side road. Hannah turned after her and the two police cars followed.

They twisted from one narrow street to another, passing between tall, decaying warehouses, old-fashioned streetlamps on the corners, and finally turned into a slightly broader street, the lights of boats on the river beyond. She roared to the end of the street and stopped. Hannah braked to a halt, the two police cars behind her. The four uniformed men in them jumped out and ran forward.

'Detective Chief Inspector Bernstein,' Hannah told them.

'Is this important, ma'am?' a young sergeant asked.

'Very much so. The target is also highly dangerous. Are any of you armed?'

'Only me, ma'am,' the sergeant said and produced a Smith & Wesson.

At that moment the Daimler arrived. Ferguson got out and hurried forward. 'This is Brigadier Ferguson, my boss,' Hannah said.

'What the hell is going on?' Ferguson demanded. 'What's she playing at?'

Grace Browning sat astride the motorcycle, the engine turning over as she looked towards them, anonymous in the dark helmet.

'She, sir?' the sergeant asked.

'Yes,' Ferguson told him, 'but don't let that deter you.'

'He's right, son,' Dillon cut in. 'You've never faced a harder prospect.' At that moment Grace Browning raised her arm. 'She's coming!' Dillon cried.

She revved the engine and roared down the street towards them, putting a foot down at the last minute and sliding round, pointing the other way.

'What's she playing at?' the sergeant asked. 'No way out. A dead end. That's Samson's Wharf.'

Grace Browning increased her speed and at the last moment

237

raised the front wheel and lifted off high over the edge of the Wharf, pausing for a moment, then plunging down into the Thames.

They all ran along the street and stood at the edge of the wharf looking down at the swirling water, but nothing showed except white foam in the murky yellow light from the streetlamps and then the black helmet bobbed to the surface.

'Jesus!' the sergeant said. 'Why did she do that?'

'Because as you said, sergeant, it was a dead end, no way out,' Charles Ferguson told him. 'Better call in the River Police and all the usual services, we'll leave it in your hands.' He turned to Hannah and Dillon. 'One person who won't be too displeased at this outcome will be the Prime Minister,' he said as they walked to the cars. 'Lang, Curry, and now the woman, all dead. Easy to say none of it ever happened. Rupert Lang can have an honourable funeral as befits a Minister of the Crown.'

'And Belov, sir?' Hannah asked.

'No problem, Chief Inspector. Just leave him to me.'

Fog rolled across the river, rain drifting in, and something washed in through the shadows by St James's Stairs. Grace Browning surfaced and hauled herself up a ladder on to a wharf. Her leathers were wet and she unzipped the jacket and tossed it into the river then turned and ran along the deserted waterfront, a shadowy figure moving from one patch of light to the next.

She reached Dock Street within ten minutes, scrabbled behind the old dustbins and found her plastic bag under the sack. There was no one about and she stood under a streetlamp bracketed to the wall above and stripped off her pumps, the leather trousers and soaking tee-shirt. She stood there quite naked for a moment, towelling her hair and body, then pulled on the tracksuit and trainers. She put the raincoat on, took the two black shoes from the bag, each with a thousand pounds inside and put them in the raincoat pockets. Then she started to walk.

Fifteen minutes later, she reached the multi-storey car park next to Wapping Underground Station. When she went down into the basement it was a place of shadows, cold and damp, but her Mini was waiting in the yellow area. She opened the car, got inside, found the keys under the mat, then she took a towel from the bag on the rear seat and vigorously rubbed her hair dry. Finally, she found a comb, put her hair into some sort of order and tied it back. A few moments later she drove out of the car park, turned into the main road and was on her way.

In his office at the Ministry of Defence Ferguson spoke to the Prime Minister on the red phone, giving him an account of the night's proceedings.

When the Brigadier was finished, the Prime Minister said, 'I don't want to sound callous, but a rather satisfactory end to the whole saga. Lang, Curry, and now this Browning woman, all gone. Only Belov left and I'm sure you'll sort him. I presume you'll have no difficulty in treating her unfortunate death as accidental?'

'You may rely on it, Prime Minister.'

'Good. All good fortune in Ireland tomorrow.'

The Prime Minister put down the phone.

At that exact moment, Grace Browning was coming out of a motorway service restaurant on the outskirts of London, a bacon sandwich and two coffees inside her. She felt warm again, the chill of the River Thames long gone. She got behind the wheel of the Mini, pulled out on to the motorway and started on the next stage of her journey to Coldwater.

Kent
Drumgoole Abbey
Ardmore House
London

1994

FIFTEEN

I T WAS JUST AFTER one o'clock in the morning when Grace Browning reached Coldwater village, passed the George and Dragon and the village green and found the sign a quarter of a mile further on that pointed the way to the airfield. She turned down the narrow lane, then pulled in on the grass verge and switched off her lights.

She found a small torch in the glove compartment, got out and proceeded on foot, the final caution, but she had to be sure. She paused on the edge of the runway. There was a light on a bracket above the hangar door where she and Tom had inspected the Conquest and there was another in the Nissen hut.

She waited for a moment then, keeping to the shadows, crossed to the hangar and worked her way to the Nissen hut. When she peered through the window she saw Carson sitting at the table, an enamel mug in one hand, a chart spread in front of him. Satisfied, she turned back across the runway and returned to the car.

She switched on the lights, started the engine and set off across the runway. When she reached the Nissen hut, she turned off the engine and sat there, waiting. The door opened and Carson appeared.

'Who's there?'

'It's me.' She got out of the car and looked across at him.

'You're early. Where's your friend?'

'Change of plan. He won't be coming. I thought I'd get here early in case of weather problems.'

'You'd better come in, then.'

It was warm in the hut, so warm that she could smell the heat from the stove on which an old coffee pot stood.

'The coffee's fresh. Help yourself if you like.' He wasn't wearing the flying jacket, only the black overalls, and his beard seemed more tangled than ever. He sat down at the table and lit a cigarette. She found a spare mug, poured coffee into it and crossed to the table. The chart was the one covering Ireland to the Galway coast.

'Checking our route?'

'For about the fifth time. I never leave anything to chance. I've been flying a long time and that's why I'm still here.'

'I've been thinking,' she said. 'I'd definitely like to be at Kilbeg by eleven. I've spoken to Colonel Belov within the last few hours and the car will be in place.'

'We'll have to leave no later than seven, then.'

'Fine by me.' She sipped some coffee. 'Where are my cases?'

'On the bed in the next room.'

'Did you open them?'

'Of course not.' He tried to sound indignant. 'Not my business. I'm not interested in what you're up to. Like I said, I'm an in-and-out man. I'm getting paid well over the odds for this one and that's all that interests me.'

He was lying, she knew that, but she nodded calmly and sipped some more coffee. 'Good. I think I'll lie down for a while.'

'You do that.' As she went to open the door to the other room he said, 'You know, it's funny, but I seem to know you from somewhere.'

She turned and shook her head. 'Not possible, Mr Carson. You see, I'd have remembered you.'

She went into the bedroom and closed the door.

★

244

Curry's case with the priest's cassock was not needed now and she pushed it under the bed. She examined the other, placing the nun's habit on the bed, taking out the AK47 and Beretta, removing the clips, then reloading them. There were two spare clips for each and a capacious shoulder bag in soft black leather. She took the two thousand pounds from her raincoat pockets and put them in the bottom of the suitcase under the nun's habit, placed the AK47, its butt folded, in the shoulder bag, then dropped the bag back in the suitcase.

She put the suitcase against the wall, then took off the raincoat and lay on the bed in her tracksuit, her right hand on the Beretta beside her. The light was so dim that she left it on. In any case, she didn't want total darkness in case she saw him again, that shadowy figure with the arm raised and the gun. In spite of herself, her eyes closed and after a while she slept fitfully.

Across the Atlantic at Andrews Air Force Base, a black sedan drove across the tarmac and pulled up beside the waiting Gulfstream. It was three o'clock in the morning in England, but with a five-hour time difference, only ten at night in America. Patrick Keogh was quite alone except for an air force driver. The base commander got out and opened the door for him.

'Nice and private, this plane, Senator, as requested, but the crew are air force.' There were three of them, all wearing anonymous navy-blue airline uniforms. 'Captains Harris and Ford take care of the flying and Sergeant Black takes care of you.'

Keogh shook hands with all three and turned to the base commander. 'Many thanks.'

'Your luggage is on board and you're cleared for immediate take-off, Senator.' The base commander saluted. 'Good luck, sir.'

Keogh went up the steps into the luxurious interior of the Gulfstream, found himself a seat and strapped in.

Sergeant Black checked him out. 'I've got full meal facilities, Senator. I believe your wife suggested the menu. Anytime you like once we're airborne, just say the word.'

'Sounds good to me,' Keogh said.

The engines had already fired and Black went and strapped in himself. A few moments later, the Gulfstream roared down the runway, lifted off and started to climb.

Grace came awake with a start and stared at the window. A grey light filtered in and rain pattered against the pane. She realized she could smell cooking, got up and sat on the edge of the bed for a moment. She put the Beretta in one of her tracksuit pockets, moved to the door and opened it.

Carson had a frying pan on the stove and he turned and smiled. 'Eggs and bacon. Best I can do, but you'll need something inside you.'

She was surprised to find that she felt hungry and checked her watch. It was six-fifteen. She opened the door and looked outside at the relentless rain.

'It looks rough. Will there be a problem?'

'Not really,' he told her and dished out the bacon and eggs on two metal plates. 'A bit bumpy to start, but we'll soon climb above it. There's bread and butter there and tea in the pot. Help yourself.'

At about the same time, Dillon and Hannah Bernstein arrived in Cavendish Square and were admitted to Ferguson's flat by Kim, who vanished at once into the kitchen. Ferguson appeared from his bedroom fastening a Guards tie.

'Ah, there you are. Have you had breakfast?'

Hannah glanced at Dillon. 'Hardly, sir, we knew you were anxious for an early start.'

'Very conscientious of you, Chief Inspector. We'll beat the

traffic to Gatwick. Time enough to have breakfast at one of the airport cafés.'

'Jesus, but you're a thoughtful man, Brigadier,' Dillon said.

'Aren't I? Which is why I told Kim to make us a nice pot of tea.' At that moment the Ghurka came in with a tray. 'There you are,' Ferguson said. 'Help yourselves while I finish dressing.'

The Cessna Conquest roared along the runway at Coldwater and lifted into the rain. Carson was sitting in the pilot's seat, a chart spread on the right-hand seat. Grace sat at the rear of the cabin, her suitcase wedged between two seats on the other side.

She looked out of the window and saw only rain and heavy cloud. The plane rocked from side to side and was buffeted by a crosswind as they turned and climbed. After a while they broke out through the cloud, but there was no sunshine, only a great vault of grey.

The buffeting had stopped now and they seemed to have levelled out. 'Curtain up,' she said softly. 'First act.' She leaned back and closed her eyes.

At precisely nine o'clock the Lear jet lifted off at Gatwick and started to climb. Ferguson sat on the right of the gangway, Hannah Bernstein on his left, and Dillon sat opposite, facing them.

The phone rang and Hannah answered it. She listened, then said, 'Thank you,' and put it down.

'What was that?' Ferguson asked.

'The Yard. The River Police have recovered Grace Browning's BMW but not her.'

'Oh, she'll come up eventually,' Ferguson said. 'And we'll have a lovely funeral, with half of show business crying into their hankies.'

'If you don't mind me saying so, sir, that *is* rather callous,' Hannah told him.

'That's as may be.'

'As for me, I'd be happier if I'd seen her laid out on the slab,' Dillon said. 'It's my superstitious nature.'

'Now that *is* being melodramatic,' Ferguson told him. 'Go and do something useful. From what the pilot tells me the weather at Shannon isn't marvellous. Go and check with him. You're the flyer.'

Dillon unbuckled his seat belt and Ferguson took a *Times* from the pile of newspapers he'd purchased at Gatwick and opened it.

After a while he said, 'Here we go. Coroner's inquest on Rupert Lang today.'

'Shouldn't Dillon have been there, sir?'

'I got an exclusion order from the Home Office. Defence of the Realm and all that, so the Coroner has agreed to accept Dillon's written statement. I wrote it myself. Rather good, actually: Dillon was acting as a security guard, Lang suggested they go for a ride on the motorcycles and it went tragically wrong.'

'What about the shepherd, Sam Lee?'

'All that lout can say is what he saw. They were riding along the track and Lang lost control and went through the gate. The funeral's tomorrow. St Margaret's, Westminster.'

'I should think that will be quite a turnout,' Hannah said.

'Good God, yes. They'll all be there. The PM and the Cabinet, Leader of the Opposition, not to mention officers from the Grenadiers and the Parachute Regiment. After all, he *was* a hero. MC and all that, brave officer. They'll see him out in style.'

'He must be laughing his head off,' she said.

'Yes, he always was a cynical bastard.'

Dillon came back and slid into his seat. 'Low cloud and turbulence at Shannon and heavy rain that's expected to last most of the day.'

'Any problems?' Ferguson asked.

248

'Not with the two lads up there in the cockpit flying this thing. They flew Tornadoes in the Gulf War. Twenty trips each to Baghdad.'

'That's all right, then.'

'Good,' Dillon said. 'We'll have some tea and just to stay politically correct and on the right side of Miss Wonderful here, I'll make it.'

The Conquest came out of cloud at approximately a thousand feet. The coast of Ireland lay ahead, County Waterford to be precise. Carson went lower, approaching the coastline at five hundred feet over a turbulent sea. And then, as Grace looked out, they were across, green fields, hedgerows and farmhouses. A few miles inland and he started to climb until they were enveloped in cloud. She unbuckled her belt, went forward and tapped him on the shoulder. He pulled down his earphones.

'Any problems?' she asked.

'None so far, but there are headwinds from now on.'

'Will it hinder us? My timing is of absolute importance.'

'I shouldn't think so, thanks to that early start. If it stays like this we'll have a tailwind most of the way back – a much quicker trip home.'

'Good,' she said.

'There's a black box back there by the luggage compartment and toilet. You'll find a thermos flask of boiling water and coffee and tea bags.'

'What's your preference?'

'Coffee, very black.'

'I'll see to it.'

She turned and went along the gangway.

The Lear jet came in to Shannon Airport sixteen miles west of Limerick at twenty minutes to eleven. The pilot made an excellent landing and proceeded to a dispersal point at the far end of the hangars as ordered, an area of little activity. The only other machine in sight was a helicopter, with two crew visible in the cockpit. There was also a black Rover parked there, a driver at the wheel. A large man wearing a navy-blue raincoat and carrying an umbrella came forward as one of the pilots opened the door of the Lear jet and the stairs came down. Ferguson went first, followed by Hannah Bernstein and Dillon, who carried a canvas holdall.

The big man had a Cork accent and a tough, hard face to him. 'Brigadier Ferguson? I'm Chief Superintendent Hare, Special Branch.'

Ferguson shook hands. 'This is my assistant, Chief Inspector Bernstein of Scotland Yard's Special Branch.'

'A great pleasure.' Hare shook her hand.

'And this rogue is one Sean Dillon, of whom you may have heard over the years.'

Hare's astonishment was plain. 'Holy Mother of God, I can't believe it.'

'In the flesh,' Dillon said. 'I remember back in the eighties I was on the run in the Republic and you were snapping at my heels. You were Chief Inspector then.'

Hare grinned reluctantly. 'So you've gone over?'

'Haven't we all these days?' Dillon offered his hand.

After a slight hesitation Hare took it and turned to Ferguson. 'There's an office in the hangar we can use. The Gulf-stream carrying Senator Keogh is twenty minutes out. As you can see, the helicopter is ready and waiting.'

'How much do you know?' Ferguson asked as they went into the hangar.

'Everything. I've been briefed by the Prime Minister himself, who stressed the need for total secrecy, which is why he's not here himself. It would obviously attract too much attention.'

'Of course,' Ferguson said as they went into the office.

There was a tray with cups, a thermos flask and milk on a desk. Hare said, 'Tea there if it takes your fancy.'

'How long to reach Drumgoole?' Ferguson asked as Hannah opened the thermos.

'Half an hour. I'll wait until you're ten minutes on your way and then I'll telephone the Mother Superior, Sister Mary Fitzgerald. A good, kind soul. I know her well. The father confessor to the Little Sisters of Pity at Drumgoole is Father Tim McGuire, a decent ould stick. Just the nuns and the school kids there, and they'll all go potty when they hear Keogh is coming.'

'But not for long. Ardmore House is what's important,' Ferguson said as Hannah handed tea round.

'Well, I wish him well there,' Hare said. 'I think he's going to need it.'

'How close?' Grace was at Carson's shoulder now.

'Not far. Fifteen miles.'

'And where is Drumgoole Abbey from here?'

'We fly over it.'

'Good, I'd like to take a look.'

She went back to her seat and peered out of the window. The Conquest came out of cloud at two thousand feet into heavy rain and there it was in a pleasant wooded valley below: the abbey, a schoolhouse and several cottages. Grace took in the lie of the land, the approach road leading up from the valley and disappearing into a vast forest area.

The Conquest continued for another ten miles. During that time, she opened the suitcase, took off her tracksuit trousers then dressed in the nun's habit, not easy in the restricted space of the cabin, but years of having to change in cramped dressing rooms had given her a certain expertise. She finished off by pulling on a pair of black knee socks and the black flat-heeled shoes. She took the shoulder bag out, pushed the case between two seats and sat waiting.

Kilbeg was a desolate sort of place, the grass runway plain. There was a windsock on a pole, a ruined cottage at the north end, and a shed beside it. As they landed she could see a dark green car parked inside the shed.

The plane rolled to a halt close to the cottage and Carson switched off. When he got out of the pilot's seat and saw her he looked truly shocked.

'God in heaven.'

'The door, Mr Carson.'

He got the Airstair door open and went down the steps, turning to give her a hand. She accepted, lifting the skirt of her cassock with the other, and they ran through the relentless rain to the shelter of the shed.

The car was a Toyota saloon. The door wasn't locked, but when she opened it there was no key in the ignition. She felt under the rubber mat and found it at once. She turned to Carson and held it up.

'Here we are.'

She got behind the wheel and put the shoulder bag on the passenger seat.

'How long will you be?' Carson asked.

'Two to two and a half hours if I'm lucky.'

'I've got to have a time. Can't wait for ever.'

She looked up at him calmly. 'Be here when I return, Mr Carson. I need hardly remind you that Colonel Belov has a very long arm. There would be nowhere you could go that he couldn't find you.'

He shrugged. 'Don't get me wrong. It's just that I don't want to hang around too long.'

'You won't have to.' She switched on the engine and drove off.

The Gulfstream landed and taxied towards the hangars, taking up position beside the Lear jet.

Patrick Hare said, 'I'll go and get him.'

He walked out towards the Gulfstream under the shelter of his umbrella. The door opened and the stairs came down

252

followed by Sergeant Black. A moment later Captains Harris and Ford appeared. They lined up at the bottom of the stairs and Keogh joined them, shaking hands with each in turn. As Ferguson watched, Hare engaged the Senator in a brief conversation, then they walked towards the hangar.

'Brigadier, great to see you again,' Keogh said. 'And you, Dillon.'

'Allow me to introduce my aide, Detective Chief Inspector Hannah Bernstein,' Ferguson said.

Keogh gave her his best smile. 'A real pleasure, ma'am,' and shook hands.

Dillon said, 'We have a present for you, Senator.' He opened the holdall he had been carrying. 'Kevlar jacket, latest model.'

'Oh, no,' Keogh groaned. 'Must I? Those things make you look like you've put on twenty pounds!'

'They also stop most bullets from most modern rifles stone dead,' Dillon said. 'Unless they're armour-piercing.'

'Am I supposed to feel happy with that thought?'

Keogh took off the jacket and waistcoat he was wearing and Hare and Dillon helped him into the Kevlar jacket. 'We'll get Armani to make this stuff into suits next season,' Dillon said. 'It'll save everyone a lot of trouble.'

They fastened the velcro tabs and helped him back into his waistcoat and suit jacket. There was a small mirror on the wall and Keogh stood back and examined himself.

'Yes,' he said, 'I can see now that I'll definitely have to cut out the potatoes.' He grinned. 'Can we go now?'

Grace Browning followed the road through the forest and halted while still in its cover to look at the abbey. To her left there was a track leading into a further spread of trees. She drove along it, then paused while still screened from view, reversed and parked the Toyota pointing back the way she had come. She could see down into the abbey gardens.

Various paths led down to the abbey itself, although there was no one about in the heavy rain.

She turned to get her shoulder bag and noticed that there was a black folding umbrella on the back seat. Whether by accident or design, it didn't matter. She pulled out the telescope handle, put the umbrella up against the rain and went down through the gardens.

At that moment Patrick Hare telephoned Drumgoole Abbey and asked for Sister Mary Fitzgerald. There was a slight delay before she came on.

'Yes, who is it?'

'Sister Mary, it's Chief Superintendent Pat Hare. I've got a shock for you. In approximately fifteen minutes a helicopter will be landing on your front lawn.'

'And why would it be doing that?'

'Because it has Senator Patrick Keogh on board. He wants to visit the Keogh Chapel and see the stained-glass window.'

'Holy Mother of God, I can't believe it.'

'You'd better, Sister, because he'll be dropping into your lap minutes from now.'

She slammed down the phone and ran into the main office, where three sisters were working at their desks.

'Drop everything, Sisters,' she cried. 'I've just heard that a helicopter is arriving with Senator Patrick Keogh on board. We've fifteen minutes at the most. Sister Margaret – you and Sister Josephine get over to the school and have all the children taken to the abbey church. Sister Amy, you will see that the acolytes are properly dressed for whatever service Father Tim wants to give. I'll warn Father Tim. Now hurry.'

She chased them to the door and was about to leave herself when she remembered and went to the internal phone. 'Sister Clara? We're going to need you to play the organ, so get over to the church. Senator Keogh is coming.'

254

She slammed the phone down, went out and ran along the corridor, holding up the skirts of her habit. She went out of the main door and ran through the rain to the great door of the abbey, pushed it open and hurried inside.

When she opened the vestry door, Father Tim was sitting at his desk, very frail with snow white hair and steel-rimmed glasses. He turned in shocked surprise.

'Sister Mary, what on earth is it?'

She collapsed in the other chair, quite breathless, and told him.

Grace Browning moved down through a walled kitchen garden, her umbrella sheltering her from the rain. As she got closer to the abbey she saw considerable activity: nuns running backwards and forwards through the rain and then a crocodile of young girls in white blouses, navy-blue school skirts and white socks moving from the school to the abbey, a number of nuns hurrying alongside and trying rather ineffectually to protect them with umbrellas.

Grace stood watching and a nun turned and on catching sight of her, called, 'Come, Sister, we need you. Senator Keogh is coming.'

At that distance, and with the umbrella over her head, she was just another nun, but she seized the opportunity, hurried down and joined on the end of the tail of children as they went in through the great door of the abbey.

Inside, they moved up the centre aisle towards the high altar. Grace Browning put down her umbrella, paused just inside, glancing around her, then saw a stone spiral staircase through an archway, with a gallery above it. She moved forward without hesitation and went up.

As the helicopter approached Drumgoole Senator Keogh said, 'What is it with the Kevlar jacket and so on, Brigadier? Do we really have a problem?'

'Let me put it this way, Senator. If there was a problem, it no longer exists. We're just taking full precaution.'

'Well, one thing's for sure,' Keogh said, looking out as they approached the abbey. 'The visit down there should be the least of my problems. It's what I'm going to say at Ardmore that concerns me. We're so close, Brigadier, so damn close to getting the IRA to make a peace initiative. We've got to make it work, we've just got to.'

'I couldn't agree more, Senator,' Ferguson told him as the helicopter settled on the lawn.

The second pilot came back and opened the door. Sister Mary Fitzgerald and Father Tim, wearing an alb over his cassock and a stole around his neck, stood waiting.

Dillon handed Keogh an umbrella. 'You'll need this, Senator. This is Ireland, remember.'

'And how could I forget that?' Keogh grinned.

He went down the steps and crossed to the abbey, and Ferguson, Hannah Bernstein and Dillon went after him.

From the gallery Grace Browning had had a perfect view of events below – the young schoolgirls so excited, half-a-dozen boys, acolytes, bright in their scarlet cassocks and white cottas. Although she did not know who Sister Mary Fitzgerald was, she realized she was in charge from the way she marshalled people, and she'd also noticed Father Tim arranging things in the side chapel – that must be the Keogh memorial.

There was a sudden excited murmur from the nuns grouped at the door which spread to the children, and then Patrick Keogh walked in, followed by Ferguson, Dillon and Hannah Bernstein.

'Well, well,' Grace said softly. 'Old Home week.'

She moved to a position behind a pillar from which she could see across into the Keogh Chapel, put the shoulder bag on the floor, took out the AK47 and unfolded the butt.

★

'Such an honour, Senator,' Sister Mary Fitzgerald told him.

'The honour is mine,' he replied.

'If we could show you the window, Senator,' Father Tim said. 'A fitting memorial to your great ancestor.'

'I'm sure it is,' Keogh said and followed him.

There was a small altar in front of the stained-glass window and three young girls, neat in their school uniforms, stood in front of it holding tiny bouquets of flowers. Patrick Keogh smiled and stepped towards them.

'What's this?'

In the gallery, Grace leaned against the pillar, took aim and her finger eased on the trigger. At the same moment, a young girl ran forward towards Keogh, holding out a bunch of flowers, and Grace pulled the weapon up. There was the inimitable muted crack of a silenced AK47 and a large vase on the altar disintegrated.

Dillon called out, 'Down, Senator, down! That's rifle fire!'

The girls at the altar turned and Patrick Keogh, presenting his back, flung his arms around the three nearest, pulling them close, and Grace Browning shot him twice.

SIXTEEN

Dillon DREW HIS WALTHER, looking up, saw a movement and raised his gun to fire. It was Hannah who called out to stop him.

'No, Dillon, no!'

And then he saw the figure in the gallery and realized it was a nun. He turned and ran to Keogh. Ferguson was already bending over the Senator. He was gasping for breath as they pulled him up.

'Bring him into the vestry,' Father Tim said. 'He needs to sit down.'

As Grace Browning stepped back, she heard a sound, turned and saw a small boy dressed in a scarlet cassock and white cotta. She stood there looking at him, holding the AK47 across her front. He gazed at her round-eyed as she folded the butt and replaced it in the shoulder bag. She put a finger to her lips.

'Be a good boy, now,' she said in an Irish accent, 'and be off with you.'

He turned and ran the other way and she went down the spiral staircase.

In the vestry they got Keogh's jacket and waistcoat off and removed the Kevlar jacket.

'God help me,' the Senator said, 'but I feel like I've been kicked in the back twice by a mule.'

Dillon showed him the two rounds embedded in the Kevlar jacket. 'You could have been dead.'

'Except that you made me wear that damn thing,' Keogh said.

Ferguson shook his head. 'Not good enough, Senator. I was responsible and I got it wrong. In some way I got it wrong.'

Sister Mary Fitzgerald, standing listening, opened the door and went out. There were children at the main door, nuns trying to control them in the porch, and Father Tim was doing his best to help. Sister Mary took him to one side.

'It's incredible. Someone tried to shoot Senator Keogh.'

'The IRA?' Father Tim asked.

'And why would they do that to one of their own? Praise be to God he was wearing a bullet-proof jacket. He's all right.'

At that moment, the young acolyte from the gallery ran up, sobbing. 'What is it, Liam?' Father Tim asked.

'I'm frightened, Father. I was in the gallery and there was a nun there, someone I didn't know.'

'And what was so special about her?'

'She had a rifle, Father.'

On the other side of the pillar where she had overheard everything, Grace Browning eased away and slipped out of the church through a side door. Putting up her umbrella, she started up through the gardens. She reached the woods and her car within five minutes, got behind the wheel and drove away. She felt quite calm. She had tried and she had failed. That was how the script had turned out and there was nothing to be done about it.

'She was here,' Dillon said, 'instead of at the bottom of the Thames. The whole thing was a trick, can't you see? Lang and Curry were dead, so she had to die, too, to fool us.'

'My God!' Ferguson said. 'What a woman.'

'But how?' Hannah Bernstein demanded. 'That charade in Wapping. That was only a few hours ago. How did she get here?'

'How did we get here?' Dillon said. 'I suspect she did it the same way.'

Ferguson said, 'There's only one important thing at the end of the day. She failed.' He turned and went to Keogh, who sat there on a chair breathing deeply. 'Are you all right, Senator?'

'I'm here, aren't I?'

'And do you feel up to Ardmore House?'

Keogh laughed and yet there was a hard edge to the sound. 'I sure as hell do. I've come this far, so let's do it, Brigadier.'

Grace Browning drove very fast most of the way through the forest, and was at Kilbeg within twenty minutes of leaving Drumgoole. There was nothing to keep her here now, no way of interfering with what was to take place at Ardmore House. The best thing to do was to get out.

She parked inside the shed beside the ruined cottage and killed the engine, then she got out of the Toyota, her shoulder bag in one hand, and walked towards the Conquest, holding the umbrella over her head.

Carson got out to meet her. 'Everything okay?'

She smiled calmly. 'Couldn't be better. Coldwater next stop, so let's get moving.'

She went up the steps in front of him.

In the helicopter Ferguson sat apart from the others, the telephone to his ear. Finally he put it down and moved to join them.

'I've spoken to Chief Superintendent Hare. He'll do what he can, but I don't think it will be much. I mean, what do we have? An eight-year-old boy says he saw a nun in the gallery with a rifle.'

'Not much of a description, a nun in Ireland,' Dillon said.

'Exactly.'

Keogh was drinking black coffee supplied by Hannah from a thermos. 'It seems to me there's more here than meets the eye, Brigadier. Do I get to know?'

'Of course, Senator. If anyone has a right to know it's you.' Ferguson turned to Dillon. 'You're the Irishman, the storyteller, so let's see what you can do.'

When Dillon was finished, Keogh said, 'Let's stick with the basics. This woman, this Grace Browning, is what's left of January 30?'

'That's right,' Dillon said.

'You last saw her apparently going into the River Thames yesterday. You assume it was she who tried to shoot me. Now, how could she have been there and turn up here?'

'We were there, sir,' Hannah Bernstein said, 'and we turned up here. A few hours' flying, that's all.'

'And I suspect she did the same,' Ferguson added.

'But where is she now?' Keogh asked. 'Adrift in Ireland?'

Ferguson shook his head. 'I doubt it, sir. If she flew in, she'll already be flying back.'

'Leaving us with one God Almighty mess,' Keogh said. 'The whole Drumgoole thing could hit front pages all over the world.'

'I don't think so, sir. Most of the children, virtually all of them, have no idea what happened back there. There was one hell of a scrummage. As for the little boy in the gallery – he can be handled. Mother Mary and Father Tim will do whatever Chief Superintendent Hare suggests, I'm certain of that. It's a remote place and the damage limitation will keep the lid on things in the immediate future. By the time any kind of story leaks out it can be dismissed as fantasy.' He smiled. 'This is, after all, Ireland, Senator.'

'My God!' Patrick Keogh said. 'After this, events on Capitol Hill will seem like an everyday story of country folk.'

The Conquest was heading east fast. Grace Browning changed out of the nun's habit, carefully folded everything and replaced it in the suitcase. She had failed. All that effort and she had failed. Strange, because that wasn't the finale the script had intended at all. She opened the thermos, had some coffee and sat back thinking of Rupert and Tom. She closed her eyes. The man wasn't there, only the darkness, and after a-while she slept.

The helicopter dropped in at the lawn in front of Ardmore House. Two men were posted in the porch on either side of the door, both carrying Armalites, and two men stood on the lawn itself, holding umbrellas against the rain – Gerry Adams and Martin McGuinness.

The helicopter settled and the pilot killed the engine. Patrick Keogh turned to Ferguson. 'This is it, then.'

'We'll wait for you, Senator.'

'Like hell you will. After what we've been through I want you to hear what I have to say.'

The second pilot opened the door, Keogh clambered out, and Dillon grabbed an umbrella and followed. Gerry Adams came forward. 'A pleasure to see you again, Senator.' He shook hands. 'This is Martin McGuinness.'

Ferguson and Hannah emerged and joined the group. Keogh said, 'Brigadier Charles Ferguson, his aide Chief Inspector Hannah Bernstein and Sean Dillon.'

'We know only too well who Brigadier Ferguson is,' Gerry Adams said.

'Good,' Keogh told him. 'I'd like the Brigadier and his people to hear what I have to say.'

Gerry Adams looked at McGuinness, who nodded. 'Fine,

262

Senator, whatever you want. They're all waiting for you. They've just been told.'

They walked towards the house, Keogh leading, with Ferguson and Hannah behind. Adams and McGuinness took up the rear on either side of Dillon.

'A long time, Sean,' Adams said.

'Belfast, seventy-eight,' Dillon told him. 'I remember it well. We got out of the Falls Road one night using the same sewer.' He turned to McGuinness. 'And you, Martin. The old days in Derry were like a bad movie.'

'Incredible,' Adams told him. 'You nearly got John Major and the whole British Cabinet in Downing Street in ninety-one and here you are with Ferguson.'

'Turncoat is it, Sean?' McGuinness asked.

'And aren't we all that now in the cause of peace?' Dillon shot back.

Gerry Adams exploded into laughter. 'God help us, but he's got you there, Martin,' he said as they followed the others up the steps to the entrance.

The entrance hall of Ardmore House was very large and there were at least fifty men crammed in there and a handful of women. Ferguson, Hannah Bernstein and Dillon stood against the wall at the back, and Keogh was halfway up the huge staircase, flanked by Adams and McGuinness.

Gerry Adams said, 'One of our own, Senator Patrick Keogh. Listen to what he has to say, that's all I ask.'

There was a murmur that stilled as Keogh started to speak.

'When my great-grandfather left Ireland all those years ago for East Boston, it was to find a new life, to be an American; but like so many other families in the same tradition, we were Irish-Americans – good Catholics with warm memories of home and nationalist ideals. Ireland must be free, that was our creed, but I think we perhaps forgot one thing and it's

263

this. There are just as many Irish-Americans with Protestant roots as Catholic.' There was a murmur from the crowd and he raised his hand. 'Bear with me, friends, I beg you. I'm a Catholic by birth – perhaps not a good one, but I'll always remain one – yet isn't there room for all of us? When I was a youngster and involved with Irish history, I was much influenced by Wolfe Tone, who founded the United Irishmen. He said that Ireland had a right to assert its independence. I agreed with everything he wrote and was amazed to discover that he was a Protestant.'

Someone laughed and there was scattered clapping. He carried on, 'The other day someone quoted an ancient Protestant toast to me: "Our country, too".' He paused and there was total silence. 'We should seize that toast, my friends. Ireland belongs to every decent Irish man and woman, irrespective of creed. If you can go forward and declare that as *your* belief, make peace after twenty-five bloody years, reach out your hand and say to the other side, let's go forward together, then I think that would be the most significant step ever taken in the history of this country.'

There was total stillness and then someone started to clap and the clapping spread and suddenly there was cheering and the applause mounted.

Ferguson turned to Hannah Bernstein and Dillon. 'That's it. Back to the helicopter.'

Walking through the rain beneath the single umbrella Dillon had, Hannah said, 'What did you think, sir?'

'Very impressive.'

'And you, Dillon?' She turned to him.

'I've lived my life day-by-day for the past twenty-five years,' he said. 'I've a habit of expecting the worst.'

'Bastard!' she said.

At the bottom of the steps leading up to the Gulfstream, Keogh turned to Ferguson and shook hands. 'An interesting experience, Brigadier. If I can ever do you a favour . . .'

'Thank you, sir.'

Keogh took Hannah's hand. 'Chief Inspector.' He turned to Dillon. 'You know, you haven't said much since Drumgoole. Come on, Dillon, one Irishman to another.'

'I was thinking what a terrible pity it was that there wasn't a press photographer present when she fired at you and you turned your back and protected those little girls. God, they'd have elected you President.' Dillon sighed. 'And nobody will ever know.'

'I'll know.' Patrick Keogh grinned. 'Goodbye, my friend.'

He went up the steps.

They stood in the shelter of the hangar and watched the Gulfstream lift into the grey sky. Hare turned to Ferguson. 'What about this Grace Browning?'

'I don't think you need to worry about her,' Ferguson said. 'Instinct tells me she'll be on her way back to my patch.'

'And what then?'

'An interesting point,' Ferguson said. 'She's dead, remember, drowned in the River Thames after an unfortunate accident.'

'But she isn't,' Hare said. 'What happens when she surfaces?'

'She won't. Not in the way you mean. You see, she's not quite on her own yet, Chief Superintendent. I do have a source I can go to. Don't worry about it. I'll handle it, believe me.' He shook hands. 'Thanks for your help.'

'Just do me one favour,' Hare said. 'Don't come back for a while. I don't think I could stand the excitement.'

Ferguson laughed, then turned to Dillon and Hannah. 'Come on, you two.' He put up his umbrella and walked towards the Lear jet.

★

265

The Conquest landed at Coldwater just before darkness fell. Inside the hangar Carson killed the engines, got out of the pilot's seat, dropped the Airstair door and went down. Grace Browning slung her bag over her shoulder, picked up the suitcase and followed.

He was lighting a cigarette and paused in the entrance to look out at the desolate landscape and the rain. When he turned there was a different look on his face, hard, calculating.

'I said I thought I knew you and now I remember. I saw you in a film on television.'

'Really?' she said. 'So what?'

'I don't know what you've been up to, but whatever it is it's worth more than I've been paid. I had a look in your suitcase while you were away. I found that two thousand pounds. I've taken it.'

'You shouldn't have done that,' she said calmly.

'You can suit yourself.'

'Oh, I will.'

She reached into her shoulder bag, took out the Beretta and shot him twice in the heart. Carson fell back against the tail of the Conquest, bounced off and fell on his back. He was already dead when she leaned down, felt inside his flying jacket and found the two bundles of ten-pound notes. *Her mad money.* She frowned at the thought. Is that what I am? She put the money in her shoulder bag, picked up the suitcase, went out and rolled the hangar door shut. Then she walked to her Mini, got in and drove away.

The Lear jet had already landed at Gatwick, and as the Daimler drove up into London, Ferguson spoke to the Prime Minister on the phone. Dillon and Hannah Bernstein sat there listening and finally Ferguson put the phone down.

'And what did the great man have to say?' Dillon asked.

'Damn glad things worked out for Keogh as they did, but

he's horrified that the Browning woman is out there like a loose cannon. Wants to make sure we do something about her.'

'But what can we do, sir?' Hannah asked.

Ferguson smiled. 'I think it's time I spoke to Yuri Belov.'

Grace Browning drove into a motorway service area just before reaching the outskirts of London. She sat there in the car in the rain for a while feeling very tired, drained of all emotion. Finally she got out and made her way through the parked cars to the café.

There was a news-stand by the shop just inside the entrance, stacked with copies of the latest edition of the *Evening Standard*. Rupert Lang's face stared out at her. She bought a copy, went into the café and got a coffee, then went and sat at a corner table and looked at the paper.

It was all there: his career in the Army, his presence at Bloody Sunday, his subsequent years in politics and then the tragic accident. There was a smaller photo of Tom Curry, a discreet mention of the fact they had lived together for many years. The circumstances of Curry's unfortunate death were treated fully and the inference was plain.

She turned the page automatically and saw a standard theatrical photo of herself. The article was brief and to the point. On her way home from the King's Head on her motorcycle the police had attempted to stop her from speeding. For some reason she had refused to stop and after a furious chase had gone over the edge of a wharf in Wapping. River Police were still looking for her body.

'Very clever, Ferguson,' she said softly, drank some of the coffee and turned back to the front page.

Rupert was in uniform in the photo and wore the red beret of the Parachute Regiment and two medals – one for the Irish campaign, and the Military Cross. He was standing outside Buckingham Palace and the photo had obviously been taken after being decorated by the Queen. He looked handsome and devil-may-care.

'Dear Rupert,' she said. 'I never really understood why you did it. Not any of it.'

The article said that his body would be on view for friends who wished to pay their last respects at an undertaker's named Seaton and Sons in Great George Street by the Treasury. The burial service would be at St Margaret's, Westminster, at three in the afternoon. She thought about it and smiled to herself. She had to say goodbye to Rupert, that was obvious, but first there was one last thing to do. She went and got some change at the counter and found a telephone.

Belov, in his office at the Embassy, picked up the phone and recognized her voice instantly. He was excited and nervous.

'Where are you?'

'Motorway service station just outside London.'

'What happened? There's been nothing on the news. Did you get him?'

'Oh, I got him all right, Yuri, twice in the back, only he was wearing a Kevlar jacket.'

'My God!'

'They were all there – Ferguson, Dillon, Bernstein – but I got away with no trouble.'

'And flew back with Carson.'

'Yes, but there was a slight problem there. He recognized me, then stole a couple of thousand pounds I had in my case.'

Belov's heart sank. 'And you killed him?'

'He didn't leave me much choice, did he? I left him on his back beside his plane in the hangar.'

'You kill everybody, Grace, and so easily,' Belov told her.

'You helped create me, Yuri. An Angel of Death was what you wanted and that's what you got. Anyway, what will you do now?'

'I don't know.'

'Personally I don't see that you have a choice,' she said. 'If you go back to Moscow they'll shoot you in some cellar – isn't that the usual reward for failure handed out by your people? I'd make my peace with Ferguson if I were you. He'll look after you, Yuri. You're too valuable to waste.'

'And you?' he asked. 'What about you?'

'Oh, I'll go and see Rupert. His body is on display at an undertaker's in Westminster. The funeral is tomorrow.'

'But what happens then? Ferguson and Dillon now know you're not at the bottom of the river. They'll hunt you down. You've no place to go.'

'I know, Yuri, but I don't care any more. Take care of yourself.'

She hung up the phone, left the café and walked to her car. A few moments later she was driving to London.

Yuri Belov sat at his desk, racked by conflicting emotions. She was right, of course. There was nothing back there in Moscow but a bullet, and the trouble was he actually preferred London now. He opened a deep drawer and took out a bottle of vodka and a glass. He filled it and poured the vodka down. At that moment his phone went again.

'Colonel Yuri Belov? Charles Ferguson here. Don't you think it's time you stopped playing silly buggers? Senator Keogh is alive and well; Grace Browning is on the run.'

'Yes, I know all this,' Belov said. 'She's just spoken to me.'

'Really?' Ferguson said. 'Now, that is interesting.'

'An extraordinary woman, but I now believe her to be truly mad,' Belov said.

'We can discuss that later. The point is, are you going to let your people ship you back to Moscow in disgrace? Not a very agreeable proposition. The crime rate there is worse than in New York now, bread queues, winter coming on and they'd very probably shoot you.'

269

'And what's your alternative?'

'Come over to us. My dear chap, it would be the intelligence coup of my career to get my hands on someone like you. You'll be well taken care of financially. We'll find you a decent apartment, new identity.'

'Very tempting,' Belov said.

'And all you have to do is put on your coat and leave the Embassy now. Just walk out. You know the pub on the opposite side of Kensington Palace Gardens?'

'Of course.'

'I'll be there in twenty minutes. I'll expect you.'

Belov put down the phone and poured himself another vodka. He raised his glass in a toast. 'To ideals,' he said softly. 'But then one must have a practical approach to life.'

He swallowed the vodka, then went to get his coat, switched off his office light and went out.

In the booth at the pub opposite Kensington Palace Gardens, Ferguson, Dillon and Hannah Bernstein listened to Yuri Belov.

'There it is,' the Russian eventually concluded.

Ferguson nodded. 'So she said she was going to see Rupert? Well, we know where that is. He's lying in his coffin at Seaton and Sons, Undertakers, in Great George Street.'

'You actually think she'll turn up, sir?' Hannah Bernstein asked.

'She's nowhere else to go, Chief Inspector,' Ferguson told her. 'By the way, you'd better get on to the Kent Constabulary. Tell them to check out this airfield at Coldwater.' He sighed. 'Poor devils. They're going to have another unsolved murder case on their patch.' He stood up and checked his watch. 'Seven-thirty on a nice, dark, rainy London night with a touch of fog at the end of the street. It would take Dickens to do justice to it.'

Dillon said, 'Are we going where I think we are?'

'Seaton and Sons, Great George Street,' Ferguson said. 'I've always been fascinated by funeral parlours.'

Grace Browning pulled into another motorway service area as she reached London. She parked, took her suitcase and went into the ladies. There was no one about and she went into a vacant stall, closed the door and opened the suitcase. When she emerged five minutes later she was dressed as a nun again. She walked back to the car, put the case on the rear seat and drove back on to the motorway, heading for Central London.

It was just after nine-thirty when she arrived at Great George Street in Westminster and found herself a vacant parking place at the side of the street. She sat there for a while, then reached for the black shoulder bag and opened it. She removed the AK47 and put it in the suitcase, then she got out, the bag over her shoulder, and walked along the street, her umbrella up.

There was a uniformed policeman walking towards her and she paused and said in a soft Irish accent, 'Excuse me, officer, but I'm looking for an undertaker's. Seaton and Sons. I believe it's somewhere about here.'

His raincoat was wet, sparkling in the light from a street-lamp. 'Indeed it is, Sister. Just over the road on the right. You can see the light over the door.'

'Thank you,' she said, and crossed the road. He watched her go, then turned and carried on.

She found the door, the name Seaton and Sons etched in acid on the glass, paused, then tried the handle and went in.

There was the all-pervading smell of flowers peculiar to funeral parlours. She walked forward and found a small glass office, where an old white-haired man in a dark blue uniform sat dozing in a chair. She put her umbrella down and tapped on the window and he sat up with a start.

He got to his feet and opened the door. 'I'm sorry, Sister, how can I help you?'

'Mr Rupert Lang,' she said.

'Ah, yes, we put Mr Lang in the main parlour. We've had visitors most of the afternoon. Let me show you.'

He led the way along a dark corridor with doors opening off it and inside she could see coffins banked with flowers.

'These are our normal chapels of rest,' he said. 'But Mr Lang being a special case, he was put in the main parlour. As I said, we've had a lot of visitors to see him. There were three gentlemen and a lady a little while ago, but they must have gone.'

He opened the door and led her into a large room. It was a place of shadows, with just a little subdued lighting. Flowers were banked everywhere and the coffin stood at the far end on a plinth.

'I'll leave you now, Sister.' He closed the door and went away.

She stood beside the coffin and looked down. Only his head and shoulders showed. He wore a navy-blue suit and a Guards tie. His face was very calm, not Rupert at all, more like a wax mask.

'My poor Rupert,' she said aloud. 'I let you down, I'm afraid. It all went wrong.' She leaned over the coffin and kissed the cold mouth.

There was a movement at the other end of the room, and as she turned, Ferguson, Dillon, Hannah Bernstein and Yuri Belov moved out of the shadows.

'We've been waiting for you, Miss Browning,' Charles Ferguson said.

She looked at them and smiled. 'So you made your choice, Yuri?'

'No option, Grace,' he told her.

'And now what?' She smiled again, at Hannah Bernstein this time. 'Now you really do get a chance to read me my rights, Chief Inspector.'

'I'm afraid so,' Hannah said.

Grace Browning reached into her shoulder bag and took out the Beretta. She worked the slider and Hannah pulled a Walther from her bag and did the same.

'Please, Miss Browning, be sensible.'

It was Sean Dillon who took two paces towards her. 'This isn't Stage Six at MGM, Grace, it's for real. It's not a script any longer.'

'Oh, yes it is – it's my script.'

Her hand came up and she took deliberate aim at him. Hannah Bernstein fired twice very fast and Grace Browning was thrown back against the plinth on which the coffin stood, before sliding to the floor.

'Oh, my God!' Belov said and Dillon knelt beside her.

Hannah Bernstein stood there holding the gun at her side, stunned. 'Is she dead?'

'With two in the heart she would be,' Dillon told her and picked up the Beretta. Suddenly there was a frown on his face. He examined the gun and worked the slider, then he held it up. 'Empty.'

'It can't be,' Hannah said.

'Her way out, my dear,' Ferguson told her. 'She spoke to Colonel Belov, told him she intended to be here and knew he'd tell us. She'd nowhere else to go, you see.'

'Damn her!' Hannah Bernstein said. 'Damn her! Damn her! Damn her for making me do that.'

Dillon went and took the Walther from her. He put an arm round her. 'Hush, girl dear, it isn't on you, this thing,' and he held her close.

Behind them Ferguson was using his Cellnet phone. He punched out the number and a calm, detached voice said, 'Yes?'

273

'Ferguson. I have a disposal. Total priority and utmost discretion. Seaton and Sons, Great George Street. I'll wait.'

'Twenty minutes, Brigadier.'

Ferguson put his phone away and turned. 'All for the best. She'll be picked up in twenty minutes. A few hours and she'll be five or six pounds of grey ash.'

'But you can't do that,' Hannah Bernstein said.

'Oh, yes I can,' Charles Ferguson said calmly. 'As far as the papers and the media are concerned, her body was discovered downriver. There will be no problem with the inquest, I'll see to that. She had no relatives, remember?'

'Terrible,' Hannah Bernstein said. 'Terrible.'

'It's the business we're in,' Ferguson said and nodded to Dillon. 'Take her home. Colonel Belov and I will wait here.'

It was Friday of that week that the cortege wound its way through Highgate Cemetery. It stopped at the designated place and two members of the funeral firm involved carried the cask containing her ashes to the grave. It was raining heavily.

'Jesus,' Dillon said. 'I've never seen so many umbrellas.'

'An impressive turnout,' Ferguson said. 'Sir John Gielgud over there, Kenneth Branagh and Emma Thompson, Ian Richardson. The great and the good.'

They were standing well away from the throng, Ferguson, Hannah Bernstein and Dillon. Hannah said, 'Isn't it extraordinary – all those people and not one of them knows the truth.'

The priest's voice was faint through the rain. Dillon said, 'Right to the end she always played to a full house, you have to give her that.' He put an arm around Hannah's shoulders. 'Come on, girl dear, let's go,' and they walked away, Ferguson following.